This

Th
a

Wendy Jones was the first person to do an MA in Life Writing at UEA and is currently completing a PhD in Creative Writing at Goldsmiths, where she teaches. Wendy hosts *Interesting Conversations*, a literary programme on Resonancefm. She lives in London.

THE THOUGHTS AND HAPPENINGS OF WILFRED PRICE, PURVEYOR OF SUPERIOR FUNERALS

In 1924, in the Welsh village of Narberth, undertaker Wilfred Price proposes to a girl he barely knows at a picnic. Almost instantly he knows he has made a mistake — he does not love her. He thinks it will be easy to extricate himself — but a chance meeting at a funeral and the revelation of a long-held secret complicate his world beyond recognition . . .

WENDY JONES

THE THOUGHTS AND HAPPENINGS OF WILFRED PRICE, PURVEYOR OF SUPERIOR FUNERALS

Complete and Unabridged

CHARNWOOD
Leicester

First published in Great Britain in 2011 by
Corsair
an imprint of Constable & Robinson
London

First Charnwood Edition
published 2013
by arrangement with
Constable & Robinson Ltd
London

British Library CIP Data

Jones, Wendy, *1967 –*
    The thoughts and happenings of Wilfred Price,
    purveyor of superior funerals.
    1. Wales- -History- -20th century- -Fiction.
    2. Love stories.
    3. Large type books.
    I. Title
    823.9′2–dc23

    ISBN 978–1–4448–1479–8

Published by
F. A. Thorpe (Publishing)
Anstey, Leicestershire

Set by Words & Graphics Ltd.
Anstey, Leicestershire
Printed and bound in Great Britain by
T. J. International Ltd., Padstow, Cornwall

This book is printed on acid-free paper

For Solly, whose enthusiasm for watching *Thunderbirds* DVDs made this book entirely possible.

And he saw a tall tree by the side of the river, one half of which was on fire, from the root to the top, and the other half was green and in full leaf.

> The Mabinogion,
> eleventh-century Welsh epic

1

The Yellow Dress

Spring, 1924

It was because of a yellow dress. She was
wearing a yellow dress and her arms were bare.
It was slightly tart, the colour of lemon curd.
He couldn't remember seeing a dress in that
shade before. It was pleated silk and sleeveless,
with a low waistband and a square neck that
was slightly too low, perhaps only by half an
inch.

Wilfred wondered how she got the dress on.
Maybe there were hooks and eyes hidden on the
side, under her arm. Ladies' dresses sometimes
had those. Women hooked and encased themselves in their dresses but there was always a way
out.

'And there's trifle,' Grace said triumphantly,
'with cream from the Clunderwen Dairy.' Wilfred
noticed the trifle was sealed with thick whipped
cream, and the cream was scattered with flaked
almonds. She laid the white bowl on the Welsh
wool picnic blanket.

'There are grass cuttings everywhere; my
brother Madoc mowed the lawn this morning,'
she said, brushing splices of grass from her dress.
'I asked him not to, but he would insist.' She
waved an inquisitive honeybee away from the

bowl. 'I do hope you like trifle, Wilfred. I made it earlier so there would be time for the jelly to set before the cream spoiled.'

She leaned forward to serve the dessert. The neckline of her dress was cut slightly too low, he noticed again. And he wanted to glance but knew better of it, knew how women always noticed those glances from men, no matter how subtle men tried to be. Men's eyes were too slow. It was not only how she got into the dress that Wilfred wondered. He wondered, too, how Grace got out of it.

She laughed lightly and brushed her fair hair from her face.

'Wilfred, are you listening to me? Would you like the trifle, or there's some Bara brith in the house?'

'Grace, will you marry me?'

Wilfred saw an animal panic flash over her but then she very quickly reined herself in. The bee buzzed while Grace served the dessert in the small bowls slightly sloppily, almost as if she was over-focusing on what she was doing, as if the trifle was something safe to think about. With a clink, she had put a silver dessert spoon into a trifle bowl. She gave him the trifle with both hands.

'Here you are, Wilfred, darling — and yes, it would be delightful.'

He wasn't able to meet her eyes — he'd been gazing at her waistband when he'd inadvertently proposed in a shame-faced way. It wasn't that he had intended to get down on one knee — he hadn't intended anything at all. What he had

2

meant, if only he could have said it, was, '*How do you get out of your dress?*'

★ ★ ★

After the picnic, Grace went to her bedroom. She drew the curtains so the room was dusky. Wilfred had asked her to marry him! In the moments before he proposed, she had been bending forward, scooping some trifle into the gold-rimmed bowls. Then he asked, and she waited one shocked moment before replying.

'I would be delighted,' she had answered. Or perhaps she had said, 'That would be delightful.'

Earlier in the day, her brother Madoc said to her as she was laying out the crockery, 'You look splendid, Grace. Really quite dolled up. I should think that Wilfred Price will like your dress, too.' But before the picnic Grace had had her trepidations. Would Wilfred like it? What did Wilfred like? She didn't know. In fact, she didn't really know him that well. She knew him vaguely from her childhood and recently they had met at a dance, taken tea and then gone for that walk last Sunday. Then Wilfred had suggested an afternoon picnic and she said perhaps they could eat in her garden, to save carrying the food.

But Wilfred had seemed distant during the picnic. She had been anxious — was it perhaps that he didn't like her in her new dress? She had bought it especially from Mrs Russell's Haberdasher's & Draper's. Mrs Russell said yellow was all the rage with Flapper girls in London, though surely a yellow dress was too fussy for a picnic in a garden in Pembrokeshire?

Grace lifted her arm, looking for the first hook and eye in the bound seams at the side of the dress and undid each of the fastenings. She pulled the delicate garment over her head then shook it out. Grace looked for an empty clothes hanger in her wardrobe, one with a knitted cover because the silk was fragile.

Wilfred had arrived on time for the picnic and greeted her politely but had not complimented her on her appearance and was so distracted that even when Grace offered him sandwiches, she had to ask him twice.

'They're egg and beetroot, Wilfred,' she had encouraged. Grace had read in her *Miss Modern* magazine that the way to a man's heart was through his stomach. But Wilfred had seemed almost saturnine until she'd suggested the trifle. Fancy being proposed to because she had offered a man trifle!

Grace opened the wardrobe, hung the dress on the brass rail then looked at her reflection in the tainted mirror on the inside of the walnut door, thinking, Imagine! I'm going to be married. A married woman.

★　★　★

Wilfred drove swiftly along the coastal road. He was shocked. What on God's earth had he done? He'd left the picnic — said his goodbyes — gone to the garage, jumped in the hearse and started driving somewhere, anywhere, far away from that garden and Grace, but he couldn't stop thinking about what had happened, couldn't focus on the road, barely even saw it. How had he come to ask her? He hadn't meant to, hadn't even wanted to. Yet he had: 'Grace, will you marry me?' He saw her in his mind's eye sitting on the blanket, in a yellow dress, her feet to one side. He realized he hadn't looked her in the eyes when he proposed.

Wilfred rammed his foot down hard on the accelerator and the engine roared. He yanked the visor down; he was driving into the sun. He shoved the gear into third with a crank and saw the quivering needle of the speedometer leap to the right.

He thought he would stop here, before Saundersfoot, get out, walk, think. Saundersfoot would be jam-packed with day-trippers taking the sea air. But this cove was quiet. He threw on the brake and jolted to an abrupt stop.

Once he was on the sand and had removed his shoes and socks, Wilfred, deaf to the screaming gulls, blind to the shifting clouds and light, strode briskly. He must clear his head. He must pull himself together. His apprentice-master, Mr Auden, had instructed him to get married, saying, 'The moment you have a profitable funeral parlour you will need a wife. Don't wait. No life without a wife, Wilfred.' But Wilfred had made a mistake. But people made mistakes — made them all the time. He wiped the sweat from his temples. He must do something about it. Rectify it. Yes, just because a chap blundered once he shouldn't have to pay for it for the rest of his life — good God, no! He'd act, tell the girl, say he didn't want to get married, after all. By damn — he hardly knew her! She was nice, but then what girl wasn't? He'd spoken out of turn. There we are then, it could happen to any man, but it didn't need to *mean* anything. He wiped his forehead with the back of his hand.

Wilfred stepped over a rock pool, hardly noticing it. At work he saw time and time again how each person had to take every opportunity, to make the absolute most of things. And he certainly wouldn't want to waste his life because he'd once made a mistake.

The solid ripples of wet sand were uneven under the soles of his feet and slightly unbalanced him as he walked. He ran his hands through his hair. He had desired Grace but, well . . . a man could want all manner of women; it didn't follow he had to marry them, he thought, thrusting his hands deep into his pockets. Wilfred felt himself strong in his decision, felt the solidity and the power in the muscles of his legs, felt his capacity to punch and hit out. He kicked a pebble. He would seize the day. He'd explain it to Grace straight away, that he'd made a mistake. She would understand; he felt certain. Yes, she would understand.

★   ★   ★

Wilfred stood on the imposing doorstep and tapped the brass door-knocker. He had lost all sense of time while pacing along the cove perturbed by his predicament, and it was now early evening. Grace's mother, Mrs Reece, a bony woman with a sharp nose, unlatched the front door.

'You must come in,' she said formally. 'You'll be wanting to speak to Doctor Reece.' Mrs Reece directed Wilfred into the hallway. Grace appeared at the top of the staircase, covered her mouth then rushed along the landing corridor and back into her bedroom. She was no longer wearing her yellow dress, Wilfred noticed.

'Doctor Reece is sitting in his surgery.' Mrs Reece said. She rapped on the door. 'Doctor Reece, Wilfred Price is here. He is requesting an audience with you,' she called shrilly through the closed door. Grace's father appeared and held out an arm, indicating that Wilfred was to enter the front room where his patients visited him. It was a dark room with peacock-blue wallpaper and a couch to one side.

'Wilfred? Have a seat. Take this chair.'

Wilfred waited as Grace's tall father walked behind his desk and settled down heavily in a high-backed chair, Wilfred sitting down a second or two afterwards as good manners dictated. Dr Reece slowly moved his stethoscope off his blotting pad and placed it next to the table telephone.

'Now, Wilfred,' he began austerely, 'you have come about Grace.'

'Yes, sir,' said Wilfred, quickly pulling down the cuffs of his shirt.

'To ask for her hand in marriage,' Dr Reece stated. 'She has informed us of your proposal today.'

There were several mute moments. Dr Reece

picked up the blue glass paperweight on his desk and turned it in his large hands. Wilfred watched. This was his opportunity. He would say what he'd practised saying on the beach earlier. He waited a moment longer. The grandfather clock ticked and marked time. He would just wait until Dr Reece finished knocking the papers on the desk to straighten them. And replace the paperweight. And then he'd tell him. Wilfred knew that in these moments, many things were held in the balance. Dr Reece patted the paperweight. What Wilfred earnestly felt, and thought would be simple to say, was proving more complex. He still didn't want to marry Grace, but the execution of his sentiments was more formidable than he had imagined.

Eventually Dr Reece looked up. 'There are', he boomed confidently, 'one or two matters on which you will understand I require clarity. It is your own funeral business, is it not?'

'Yes, sir.'

'May I be so bold as to ask the state of the business's affairs?'

'I get by, sir.'

'You don't go without? You earn sufficient living from the funeral trade?'

'I do, sir.' Then added, 'Just about.'

'No debts in the company? We wouldn't want that, would we now, Wilfred? Perhaps from the purchase of the hearse?'

'No, sir.'

'It isn't something one imagines one's daughter marrying into, mind. But you say that it's a solid business, which is important what

8

with all this unemployment. And there will always be custom for an undertaker, mercifully less so now than during the Great War.'

'Yes, sir.'

'Is it what you would call a family business?'

Wilfred nodded. He looked down at his shoes, scuffed by the sand, and took a deep breath, ready to speak.

'So any children,' Dr Reece continued, running his hand across his beard, 'well . . . that's getting ahead of ourselves. And you intend to do well by Grace?'

Wilfred hesitated. 'Sir . . . ' He would speak out. 'Sir, I . . . ' He moved forward in his chair and the waxed floorboards underneath him squeaked.

There was a knock at the door. Grace's brother Madoc poked his head round. 'I'm popping off to the picture palace in Tenby with Sidney to watch *The Thief of Baghdad*. See you later, Father. Evening, Wilfred. Oh, and I've mended the lock on the suitcase.'

'All right, Madoc,' replied Dr Reece, smiling leniently. 'Forgive me, Wilfred,' he continued, stroking his thick grey beard, 'these are most personal inquiries and are liable to stir one to great feeling. Because Grace is delicate, Wilfred, and she will need your solicitousness and patience, now and in the years to come. We need not dwell on it, only to say you must give Mrs Reece and I your absolute word of honour that you will be an upright husband to our daughter, Grace.'

'Yes,' Wilfred said quietly.

★ ★ ★

Grace lifted the roof of the hive then broke the honey seal. Her hands moved clumsily as she pulled out the first frame. She was wearing her brother's white apiary suit, and the gloves, certainly, were too large for her but Mother thought it highly imprudent to purchase a suit especially for Grace when Madoc's just about did. Nurse bees were crawling over the honeycomb busy caring for the larvae, feeding them nectar and pollen. Grace cautiously turned the cedar frame over — there was more honey than she expected. She stroked the bees away before uncapping the wax-topped hexagons and watched a golden line of honey as thin as a silk thread, flow lethargically into the waiting bowl.

Grace liked how beekeeping required dexterity, holding the frame in one hand, scraping the honey off with a knife with the other. Slowness was needed, so as not to alarm the bees and make them swarm, as was patience. Slowness and patience were lovely qualities though she struggled to have them herself. She felt not much could go wrong in a world that was slow and patient.

She liked being in the garden and spent many spring mornings tending to the white peonies, irises and foxgloves and lightly trimming the old, woody lavender. The lavender was the most important plant: bees flocked to it. Tomorrow she would filter the pale spring honey through muslin then pour it into sterilised jam-jars, labelling them: *Lavender honey, Narberth,*

Spring 1924. She wasn't sure why Mother told her to date the jars, as honey didn't spoil: it would last an eternity, as far as anyone knew. The honey that was buried with Tutankhamun and had been unearthed two years ago was still fresh and edible. Later she would take the honey to Mrs Annie Evans at the Conduit Stores where it would be sold. She liked to keep herself busy, she didn't want time to think.

The hum of the hive made a soft sound. The bees were calm and drowsy now: that was the effect of the smoke. They hovered lazily or flew slowly. She wondered, when they were married, if Wilfred would like to do beekeeping with her. It was now almost a week since she had last seen him, six days since he proposed to her. She wondered what he was doing and what he was thinking; whether everything was all right. The relief she had felt at his proposal was beginning to fray. She had expected him to send a postcard or even use his telephone asking her to meet, but there had been nothing. She could use her father's surgery telephone to call him, however. She knew his number, had memorized it from his weekly advertisement in the *Narberth & Whitland Observer*:

Telephone number for all inquiries:
Narberth 103.

But her mother would be appalled at the thought of Grace approaching Wilfred. 'Too modern,' she would admonish. Mrs Reece would consider telephoning a gentleman, even if he were one's fiancé, extremely forward. And perhaps it was, thought Grace.

★   ★   ★

Nine days later, Grace still hadn't heard from Wilfred. She stood on Mrs Prout's doorstep, rang the brass doorbell and heard it trill sharply. Waiting on Mrs Prout's doorstep, Grace realized there was nothing obviously strange about the house: it was like many houses in Narberth — symmetrical with lime-washed walls a foot thick — but it had an eeriness to it that she could feel even when walking past. And the vicar would dislike her coming here, she was certain, because he had preached against it at the end of October, the Sunday before Hallowe'en; the Revd Waldo Williams MA knew his congregation.

'Necromancy is very wrong — evil. It is the work of the Devil, of Lucifer himself,' he announced, and he had read a lengthy passage — twenty-two verses — from the Book of Deuteronomy. He laid his gnarled hand on the open page of the Bible and intoned magisterially the words of Moses to his flock, *"There shall not be found among you any one that maketh his son or his daughter to pass through the fire or that useth divination, or an observer of time, or an enchanter or a witch. Or a charmer or a consulter with familiar spirits, or a wizard or a necromancer'.'* Then the Revd Waldo Williams MA, his voice rising to so great a pitch that his throat was strained, proclaimed, *"FOR ALL*

THAT DO THESE ARE AN A-BOM-IN-ATION TO THE LORD'. Deuteronomy. Deuteronomy.' Then, just before Handel Evans struck up on the organ, the Reverend added in a breathy whisper, 'We should be like the fowls of the air or the lilies of the valley: they don't worry. No, no.' But the Revd Waldo Williams's words wouldn't stop Grace: she was fond of the Reverend but this was far more important than chapel. Grace *had* to know.

Mrs Hilda Prout threw open the door, looked Grace up and down and stated, 'You'll have come with a question.'

'Yes,' Grace said, taken aback by Mrs Prout's abruptness. 'There is something I'd like to ask, if you don't mind.'

'Well,' said Mrs Hilda Prout, 'every question has an answer. And you must cross my palm with money.'

There must have been a Mr Prout once, Grace thought, as she followed Mrs Prout up the wide staircase and past the mahogany grandmother clock. Mrs Prout entered a small parlour that was crowded with two glossy mahogany sideboards, a tweed-covered settee with white antimacassars, a glass cabinet and several gold-framed paintings on the wall. There were ornaments too, of china, silver and glass. The old woman went to the window where she opened a carved bible box, unwrapped a huge Welsh bible from a cream linen cloth then set it down on the occasional table in the centre of the room. The table tipped slightly under the weight of the book.

'Is it the key you'll be wanting?' she asked.

'Yes, Mrs Prout.'

'Then run to the back door and fetch it from the lock.'

Grace turned swiftly, weaved her way around the furniture and ran down the stairs, coming back with a rusted iron key that was as large as her hands.

'This will be a question about birth?'

'No, Mrs Prout.'

'Death?'

'No, Mrs Prout.'

'Then it must be about love. So we will ask a prophet.' She split open the pages of the family Bible and tucked the key deep into the Book of Jeremiah.

'Why Jeremiah?' Grace dared to ask, still standing.

'Because the prophets were wild and love is wild, isn't it, Grace?'

Grace knew enough to agree.

'If you had come to ask me the day on which you'll die, I would have put the key in the Revelations of Saint John the Divine. Do you want to know the date of your death, Grace?'

'No. No, thank you, Mrs Prout,' Grace replied modestly, pulling the sleeve of her cardigan over her hand. 'I have a question about love, only love.'

Mrs Hilda Prout clamped the Bible shut with a flat thud.

'Step back,' she snapped. 'Ask the key your question.' Grace did as she was told. She spoke faintly but felt bold. She waited. Then slowly, almost achingly so, the key began to move,

14

twisting itself over. Grace was transfixed. She chilled. It wasn't right, keys weren't supposed to turn on their own, not when no one was touching them. How could a key twist in a Bible by itself? It was unnatural. Now the key lay stock-still. It was over. But then it turned again.

'Yes,' Mrs Prout said, unsurprised as if she had known the answer all along. 'You'll marry him.'

'Yes?' Grace exclaimed. 'Yes, I knew it would be yes! Oh, thank you, Mrs Prout.' Her anxiety melted within her.

'Don't thank me; thank Jeremiah,' Mrs Prout stated flatly. 'And how is your brother Madoc? He had a bad war, didn't he?'

'He's well, thank you.'

'But he wanted to stay in the Army?'

'Yes.'

'Has he gone back yet?'

'Not yet. Before long. I'll go now, Mrs Prout.' Grace opened her purse and handed over a neatly folded shilling note. 'I can see myself out.'

'Aye, aye,' murmured Mrs Hilda Prout, 'and take this key. Lock the back door with it before you leave.'

Grace felt confident now she had spoken to Mrs Prout, now she knew what would happen.

⋆   ⋆   ⋆

Wilfred had to do something about Grace. He scratched the remains of a couple of dead flies from the window screen, lifted up the wipers and sloshed the glass with water before wiping it dry. The Super Ford hearse needed to be clean and

15

ready for the chap he was burying soon: Mr James L. Davies of Dourigan House, Templeton. The newspaper was right; twenty-four was an early age. No wonder there was quite a gloom over Templeton. *Deep sympathy is evinced with the bereaved at their loss* it said in the obituary.

He knew he would be expected to call on Grace. Wilfred began cleaning the top of the car, leaning over to reach the middle. He had proposed to her. He put the chamois in the bucket of cold water, swirled it about, wrung it out and went back to wiping under the wheel hub, where there was a lot of grit. Wilfred then wiped the mud from the numberplate. How was he going to break it off? He put some more wax on the chamois and gave the headlights a rub.

It was no good being this worried about the predicament with Grace; he couldn't go around worrying about it all the time — and now he had a rash on his forearms that itched at night. And his stomach was in knots. Wilfred opened the car door and stroked the dashboard — it was varnished burlwood — then wiped away some fingerprints. His Super Ford hearse was six years old so needed very careful handling. Wilfred tried to imagine what his apprentice-master, Mr Ogmore Auden, would have advised him to do about Grace. Certainly, when Wilfred was an apprentice, Mr Auden absolutely forbade what he called 'fancy business with the ladies', and consequently, Wilfred had had none during his apprenticeship. He had been very shy around girls; he knew next to nothing about them and now he was an undertaker, he still didn't know

16

very much about ladies.

He put some more wax on the chamois and gave the headlights a rub. It was a beautiful motorcar, sleek as a cat, and age and careful polishing had given it even more grace than when it was completely new. The car was solid, square, dependable. It didn't break down, didn't get lost but took his passengers inevitably and elegantly to the place they least wanted to go: the freshly dug grave of a loved one.

At any rate, Wilfred decided, standing back and admiring the car, it was clean enough for a superior funeral. He was the proud owner — *very* proud owner — of a Super Ford hearse. With a motorized hearse, despite the cost, all that polishing and the occasional temperamental behaviour from the engine, Wilfred was on to a winner. He was fond of his motorcar. Could he say that he loved his Super Ford hearse? He wouldn't go so far as to say that. Could a man love a car? He put the silver key in the ignition. Did he love his car in the way he had thought, in that disastrous moment, that he loved Grace? *Did* he love Grace? he asked himself. No.

He looked up through the skylight in the garage roof and thought how the sky went on for ever. There *must* be an answer to every question out there, somewhere. Questions must have answers. His father found answers in the graves and in the stars, by digging into the dark earth and by looking up into the lights in the heavens. And then Wilfred realized, looking at the gleaming metal and glass, that his father might have an answer.

★　★　★

'Da?' Wilfred called, putting his head around the kitchen door. His father often sat peacefully at the small kitchen table, drinking tea from his blue teacup, but now the cup was standing empty on the table. It was really Wilfred's cup but his father had appropriated it. The cup had been a present from Auntie Blodwen to Wilfred: she'd gone to Tenby for the day on her honeymoon and brought it back for him. Printed on it in red ink was a rhyme that Wilfred knew by heart:

> *However far we wander*
> *Wherever we may roam,*
> *Our thoughts are always turning*
> *To those we love at home!*

TENBY

If his father wasn't in the kitchen having his Typhoo tea and browsing through the *Narberth & Whitland Observer* then Wilfred knew exactly where to find him. He marched out of the back gate, turned left and made the short walk along Church Street, past James Williams's bottling factory to St Andrew's Church. As he walked along he thought about his father — a good man who lived a simple life — and thought how a life well lived resonated peacefully. His da dug graves when he was required to, then in the day walked the countryside around Narberth picking mushrooms, fat hen, parsley and berries, or came here

18

. . . Wilfred was right. There, sitting on the earth, his knees apart, was his father close by his mam's gravestone.

As Wilfred trudged over the lumpy grass with its coffin-shaped hummocks and the indents where other centuries-old boxes had collapsed, he could see that his father was talking — he knew — to his mam. His father came here almost every day and the grass where he sat was constantly flattened. When he was younger Wilfred had thought his father was foolish for talking to someone who was dead, that it was a waste of time spending an afternoon in the graveyard of St Andrew's, especially when it was sunny. But then, what was that verse in the Scriptures? *For love is stronger than death.*

Wilfred saw his father reach out and put his arm around his mam's humble gravestone and lean his head briefly against it. Is it foolish, Wilfred thought to himself, to cuddle a cold slab of white marble and pretend it is a person? He waved at his father and his father began to slowly, almost arthritically, get up to greet him.

'What are you doing up here then, boy?'

'I could ask the same of you, Da!' Wilfred joined his father and they sat and rested peacefully, the three of them: Wilfred, his father and his mother.

The awkwardness of unsaid words settled between them. Wilfred wanted to tell his father all about Grace; say: 'I asked Doctor Reece's daughter to marry me. I proposed. But I didn't fall in love, I don't love her and I don't want to marry her. What shall I do? I don't know what to do.' He yearned to admit his vulnerability and uncertainty to his da, but he and his da didn't talk about private matters so Wilfred said nothing. But it was as if his father had heard him.

'There we are then, Wilfred, my son,' he said. 'There we are then.' And with that he placed his weathered hand on the soft earth in which his wife was laid, and Wilfred understood.

★   ★   ★

Ten days later, Wilfred was walking home when he jolted involuntarily. There was Grace, right in front of him, plain as day, a real, solid person, standing on the pavement in the High Street by the Angel public house. She was holding a wicker basket with jars of honey in it. For a split second he didn't know what to do. Then he froze his face — put on his 'funeral face' as he called it, very serious, very formal — 'as if you've never laughed or used the WC in your life,' was how Mr Auden described it. Occasionally Wilfred used his funeral face when he wasn't at a funeral. He straightened his necktie and began buttoning up his waistcoat.

'Wilfred? Where have you been?' Grace asked plaintively.

Wilfred was at a loss. Grace . . . the proposal. His stomach turned. He felt a sense of dread. Suddenly it was easy to look serious.

'I've . . . I've been busy, Grace, with a funeral. Young man over Loveston way, died of flu.'

Grace was watching him intently. Grace

always seemed to be watching intently. She had been watching like that at the picnic when he asked her to . . . He didn't like how Grace looked at him, didn't like the way she asked where he'd been. He didn't like it at all; and then with a flush of realization — he didn't like *her* at all!

'Grace, I don't want to marry you.' There! He'd said it. He'd said he didn't want to marry her. It was said. It was over now. He would never have to see her again.

Grace was speechless.

'Pardon, Wilfred?' she said weakly.

Wilfred knew he meant it. He would say it again with resolution — properly and slowly.

'Grace, it is not,' — how shall I put this, he thought — 'I don't, I think it's best, I think, if we are no longer engaged.'

'Pardon?' The basket was hanging limply in her hand. A couple in tennis whites holding racquets strolled up to them; they wanted to go into the Angel Inn but Grace and Wilfred were standing in front of the doorway.

'Sorry,' said Wilfred, and he stepped aside, aware the couple were waiting.

'Thank you,' said the woman pleasantly.

'Better get in before it starts to rain,' the man added cheerfully, swinging his racquet and looking up at the gathering clouds, adding, 'I expect Wimbledon's been rained off.'

'Yes,' said Wilfred, trying to sound perky. Grace was still blocking the entrance, dumbstruck and unaware of the tennis players waiting for her to move.

'Excuse me, miss,' the man said.

'But, Wilfred, we are supposed to get married.'

Wilfred noticed the couple looking on with interest, especially the chap: the moment they'd ordered their drinks they'd be talking about the to-do outside the Angel.

'Please could you move so these people can get in?' he said to Grace, but she stood there, stock-still. He took her arm and tried to move her to one side of the pub's door as the first fat drops of rain began to splatter. She looked hurt, Wilfred could see.

'Grace, come to one side,' he said more gently, guiding her. Grace's eyes had welled up and her face whitened.

'But Wilfred . . . ' she said, blinking, two tears falling out of her eyes. 'But Wilfred . . . '

She was looking up at him with her watery blue eyes and had said his name as if it was an answer. She didn't seem to realize she was crying. Wilfred knew he had to be brutal — swift and savage — in the way one had to be when one breaks an injured bird's neck, smacking its small head down hard on a stone wall. He would say it again, here in the High Street, in front of the couple who wanted to go into the Angel, as it was beginning to rain. He spoke clearly and confidently.

'Grace, I am not going to marry you.' Somewhere inside himself Wilfred heard a snap, like the fine neck of a small bird being broken.

* ★ ★

Grace stood facing the counter, her back to a wall of shelves lined with tins and with sweet jars.

'Next time ring the bell — I didn't know you were here!' exclaimed Mrs Annie Evans. 'Quiet as a mouse, you are. And you're wet.'

'Oh, yes,' said Grace, noticing the raindrops on her bare, goose-pimpled arms.

'There's rain we've been having now just. I was on the horse and trap this morning, delivering grocery to the farms in Lampeter Velfrey and got drenched. Oh, it never stops.'

Grace smiled automatically.

'Have you brought the honey? Your mother told me you would.' Mrs Annie Evans shuffled behind the high counter in the middle of her small grocery shop.

'Yes,' replied Grace, though her voice sounded feeble to her, almost faint. She lifted the heavy basket on to the counter.

'Well, I can't keep myself from saying it. Your mother called three days ago — she bought Glitto polish and Nippy scouring powder — and told me *all* about you and Wilfred Price. Heck, you must be tickled pink.'

Grace smiled. She placed the glass jars one by one on to the wooden counter.

'It'll be the summer wedding, won't it? Nothing nicer than a summer wedding.'

'Well . . . ' mumbled Grace. The air in the shop was cloying and she was aware of the slightly nauseous smell of camphor and sweetly ripe apples.

'It'll be the talk of the town. Will Madoc be

able to get leave from the Army — he'll be an usher, won't he?'

Grace looked down at her trembling hands.

'And only last week I saw a pattern for a *beauteous* veil in *Fancy Needlework Illustrated*. It would go nicely with your fair hair. It will be your mother embroidering the veil, won't it, now?'

'I should think so.'

'She's nifty with the needle, your mam.'

Grace noticed her fingers trembling.

'By damn, it will be difficult for Wilfred to concentrate on funerals with a wedding on his mind.'

'Yes,' Grace murmured. She coloured.

'Oh, you're the image of the blushing bride!' said Mrs Evans, unscrewing the lid on one of the jars and dipping her little finger in it. 'Delicious. That's three jars at a shilling each; I'll be owing you three shillings now. And I'll take it off your ma's grocery bill as usual, shall I, Grace?'

'Yes, Mrs Evans.'

'Well, mind you keep providing Conduit Stores with honey, marriage or no marriage. There's a thing now: Grace Reece, Doctor Reece's only daughter, getting married.'

Grace felt a surge of anxiety.

★   ★   ★

Later that afternoon, back in his workshop, Wilfred's relief was palpable. It was as if his body had shrunk with the reprieve; even his neck seemed smaller and his shirt collar looser now all

24

the tension had left him. It was easy again, since he had refused Grace, to smooth a plank; he was more able to hold the tote and the handle to plane the plank along the grain. He used his strong nail to clean some sawdust stuck to the blade. When he was engaged to Grace, he couldn't plane the wood well; he stuttered with the weighty cast-iron tool and sometimes nicked the plank. During the engagement, he couldn't go with the grain in his carpentry and he couldn't go with the grain in his life. Wilfred thought how these sayings — metaphors, he thought they might be called, he would check that in his red dictionary — were often true. But Grace was gone now. And he wouldn't need to see her ever again.

He cleared the sawdust from the beech he was shaping into a casket lid. He felt remorse. She was hurt. He, Wilfred, had hurt her feelings; she'd cried, and he regretted that. He hadn't wanted to upset her in the same way that he hadn't wanted to marry her. Now there was her father to contend with. Her father might be cross. Or he might not make it his business. And there would be gossip, though he wasn't sure whom Grace had told; Wilfred had told no one. But there would still be gossip. He would be teased at the Rugby Club and talked about in the tearooms. To be born in Narberth was to be gossiped about. He would feel ashamed but he would survive it.

He looked up at the glass roof of the workshop: the sawdust was shimmying in the spring sunlight that had come after the rain shower, and he breathed in the aroma of glue and freshly sawn wood. He had made a misjudgement, he knew, in asking Grace to marry him. But the bigger mistake, he told himself, would have been to marry her. They both would have been unhappy then. For ever.

Wilfred dusted the plane with a piece of lint, which he took from his dungaree pocket, and looked for some fine sandpaper because the edges of the coffin lid needed smoothing. Imagine being unhappily married for eternity. He shuddered at the thought. It must be like . . . well, what would it be like? He remembered the sense of dismay he'd had when he was a schoolboy at Narberth Church School and was given hours of homework. He began sanding the bevelled edges of the lid. Being unhappily married might feel a lot like the dread of doing hours of prep — mathematics prep — algebra and logarithms, inescapable problems with no obvious answer, no solution he could ever find, every day for the rest of his life.

He folded the sandpaper in half and brushed the dust from his hands. He'd been impulsive before, there was that time he punched boss-eyed Sidney Thomas during a game of hidihop on the castle field and given him a bloody nose because he'd been chanting, 'Wilfred Price got no mam! Wilfred Price got no mam!' His impetuousness, he thought, was something to do with being an undertaker and spending so much time around death, because death was absolutely certain and being a bit rash in life balanced that certainty a little.

26

He remembered too, though, how womanly Grace had looked in the yellow dress she had worn to that picnic. It was a lovely dress. She was an attractive woman. And he truly hadn't wanted to hurt her. But if Wilfred had learned anything through all this, it was not to be impulsive. Beautiful women and lovely dresses: it wasn't enough.

★ ★ ★

Grace yanked the head off a lavender flower and rubbed it between her fingers, crushing the small, lilac petals to release their scent. She held her fingertips to her nose, inhaling the soothing aroma of lavender oil. Lavender oil healed burned skin. But it wasn't Grace's fair skin that was burning — the spring sun was too weak for that. It was inside her that a fire was beginning to rage, threatening to scour her out and leave sooty ashes.

Grace shifted in the deckchair — why were these things so uncomfortable to sit in? She was slumped, her spine curved and her back aching. Splices of the conversation with Wilfred kept flashing into her mind.

'*Wilfred? Where have you been?*' It had come out all wrong, Grace had realized a split second after she had said it. Then Wilfred's consoling of her, '*Please could you move so these people can get in?*' and the sure strength of his touch on her arm. The memories were so full of heat and they caused her to blush violently with shame. That couple had overheard! She twisted in the deckchair and turned the other way, wiping her eyes: her new Elizabeth Arden mascara that was supposed to be waterproof rubbed off on to her hand. And she'd cried! Wilfred had seen her actually cry; cry because she'd cared, because she liked him, had all her hopes pinned on him. And she didn't want to care. So she imagined herself once again, standing outside the Angel, this time answering back. 'Really, Wilfred? It is *such* a relief you said it. Actually, I was going to say the same to you. It would have been disastrous!' and laughing elegantly, reaching up to her hair and smoothing it behind her ears. Then she imagined commenting on the weather before dashing into the Star Supply Stores with Wilfred looking after her wistfully, Wilfred the hurt one.

Grace tried to reconfigure the memory so she had some dignity, so Wilfred would see her as the light, carefree woman she wished to seem: casual, informal, unburdened. She wanted to care for the marriage as little as he cared for it.

A bee landed on the frame of the deckchair; it appeared unsure which way the flowers and the nectar were so it hovered lazily, as lost and lacking in direction as she was. The deckchair irritated Grace — the ticking was scratchy — and the lackadaisical bee irritated her. Perhaps she could take the bee, grab it in the palm of her hand, encase it and squash it while it buzzed frantically and abruptly stung her. It would be easy to crush. She, Grace, could also crush, kill and cause death. Perhaps the violence of the bee's panic would ignite the fire of feelings

28

she knew she was holding deep inside her.

Grace twisted, edging her hand near the resting bee. She could just cup her hand over it . . . but the bee would sting her and she might jump and yelp and cry and rage, might ultimately erupt with everything pent up within her. She would issue such an almighty scream that she — and Narberth — would explode ferociously into an ever-expanding nothingness. She doubted that Narberth, even the world itself, could contain the rage and pain and the shame that she felt sitting here in the deckchair in the back garden. The honeybee, still resting on the beech frame, buzzed obliviously. She watched it do a quiet two-step on the wood.

But perhaps, Grace thought, Wilfred loved her really. And it was all a mistake. At that thought, her heart soared and it seemed as if the sun suddenly burst out from behind the clouds and illuminated the day. But Wilfred had meant it. He had *repeated* it. He said he didn't want to marry her not once, but twice, maybe three times when hearing it just once made her feel hope itself was lost. She closed her eyes while her shame attacked her and humiliation seeped out of her skin. Why didn't Wilfred want to marry her? She needed to know. Although the why was no longer as burning a question as the one that now preoccupied her: was her monthly period late?

2

Mister Wilfred Price,
Purveyor of Superior Funerals

The following morning Flora Myffanwy Edwards was in her bedroom bending down tucking in her bedsheet when she heard an ominous thud downstairs; there was a moment of silence before her mother's voice rose up.

'Decimus? Decimus!' Then, 'Flora! Come quick. *Decimus!*'

Alarmed by the anxiety in her mother's voice, Flora stood up straight. She ran swiftly down both flights of stairs, one hand on the banister, the other on the wall to balance herself. In the hallway her mother was leaning over her father, who was slumped on the red hall rug, lying on his stomach.

'He fell. He was talking, then he fell. He was right as rain, telling me about a carthorse he'd seen with a lame leg,' her mother gabbled by way of explanation, 'then he collapsed, just like that. *Dihuna! Bryn. Dihuna!* Wake up!'

Flora looked at her father lying prostrate. Her mind was suddenly extremely clear.

'I'll get a doctor.' She stepped carefully around her father. She must sprint to the post office. No, she would cycle; it was quicker. She dashed round the back to the outhouse, jumped on her bicycle and set off. The rubber pedals were heavy

30

at first, resisting her weight, but once she cycled up the incline it would be downhill, and then she would go much faster.

At the post office, she flung open the garden gate, crying out, 'Mr Lewis — I need to use the telephone!'

The post-office master appeared from round the side of his house holding a cluster of India rubber bands. 'What is it, Flora?'

'It's Father, he's fallen.'

Mr Lewis, sensing Flora's panic, immediately opened the red front door of the Stepaside post office, which was a one-roomed building tacked on the side of his cottage, and rushed to the wall telephone. He dialled *one, nought, nought*.

The telephone rang sonorously. Eventually a voice answered, 'Operator speaking.'

'Operator, it's Bryn Lewis.'

'Morning, Bryn, how are you then? I've heard they've put central heating in the post — '

'Doctor Hedley. Immediately, please.'

'Doctor Hedley's not here, he's gone to the British Empire Exhibition in London. There's no doctor in Stepaside, you'll have to get the doctor from Narberth.'

'*Narberth?* But that's almost seven miles away!' exclaimed Flora, overhearing.

'I'm connecting you right now.' Flora heard a telephone bell reverberate feebly in the distance. She waited long seconds for someone on the other end to lift the receiver.

'This is Narberth 102.'

'We need a doctor. A doctor straight away,'

stated Mr Lewis. 'At White Hook. On Cliff Road.'

Mrs Reece knew to write the address exactly. 'Is that Kilgetty?' she enquired.

'No — further. Stepaside.'

A portentous voice came down the line. 'This is Doctor Reece speaking.' The doctor had taken the receiver from his wife. 'What seems to be the matter?'

'It's Decimus Edwards of White Hook, Cliff Road, Doctor. Tell him, Flora.'

'He's fallen,' said Flora urgently into the receiver.

'Is he breathing?'

'I think so.'

'I will drive over promptly in my motorcar. Cliff Road, you say? White Hook. Stepaside. Wait outside the gate for me.'

★   ★   ★

When Flora reached White Hook, she pitched her bicycle against the gatepost, pinned back a curl of her brown hair and turned to the direction of Narberth. The exertion of cycling had tired her, her back was damp with sweat so that her cotton blouse was sticking to her skin and her hair was loose and dishevelled. She listened for the sound of a motorcar. *Come on, Doctor, come on.* She listened, but she couldn't hear a car.

It began raining hard so Flora moved to stand under the branches of the cedar tree. What if her father was really sick? What if something had happened to him? No, he was fine. He had fallen, that's all, she told herself. Probably he had banged his head and was unconscious. She would stay calm. He must have tripped on the stair carpet — she did it often herself, catching her foot on the corner. Of course her mam would have been frightened but, by now, he would have come round, her mam would have helped him into his armchair in the parlour, made a cold compress from a flannel and put it on his forehead, perhaps holding it to his temples as well.

Soon she would be able to have some lunch, warm soup and a leek pasty, then perhaps go to the cove and find some shells to photograph. Father would be mortified that she had called the doctor. '*Dim byd oedd e, yr holl ffws am ddim,*' he would say. 'All that fuss for nothing.' He'd have a quiet rest of the day and a nasty bump, then no doubt be up and about tomorrow, back in the forge, levelling horses' hooves and nailing on shoes.

Suddenly she saw a dark green Austin Seven approaching. Flora started waving desperately. 'Doctor! Here!' The car slowed and Flora pointed the way up the drive, towards her family home. At the top of the drive, Dr Reece stopped the car by the kitchen window and stepped out. Flora was startled by how tall and severe he looked.

'This way, Doctor. You came quickly,' she added gratefully. 'I'm sure it's nothing, but thank you for coming anyway.'

Dr Reece nodded, unsmiling. At the porch he

stopped, wiped his feet on the mat and said, 'After you,' so Flora entered her home first, walking hurriedly through the kitchen and into the hall. Her father was still there on the red rug in exactly the same position but her mother was no longer with him.

'Mam?' she called. 'The doctor is here. Mam?'

Mrs Edwards emerged from the parlour, eyes rimmed red; she was tucking a handkerchief into her cuff and there was the sharp smell of ammonia in the air. She must have been inhaling her smelling salts.

'Good morning, Doctor Reece.' Mrs Edwards spoke formally to the doctor who was already down on one knee by her husband's head. The doctor was searching for a pulse in his patient's wrist and simultaneously studying his pocket watch. He then opened his doctor's bag and brought out a stethoscope.

'Would you mind helping?' he asked. Flora moved forward, her mother hesitated. 'I need to turn him on to his back.'

Flora, Dr Reece and her mother carefully rolled her father over, Flora holding his head in both hands, and he sighed loudly as they laid him supine. Flora's heart skipped at the sound of his breath, though his face was almost mauve.

The doctor leaned over, swiftly unknotting her father's tie and undoing his shirt, accidentally ripping free a button. The button fell on the tiles and bounced a few times before coming to a standstill. Dr Reece pressed the stethoscope to her father's chest and listened intently. The room was hushed while he concentrated, his eyes shut.

As he got up from his knees, he picked up the small bone button, offered it to Flora and said, 'I'm sorry.'

She rushed forward, taking the button from the doctor's hand. 'I can easily sew it on later,' she said.

'I beg your pardon?'

'I can easily sew on the shirt-button later, it won't take a moment.'

'No, I'm sorry, your father has passed away.'

★   ★   ★

'Could it not wait until tomorrow night, Da?' Wilfred asked, putting down a half-eaten pie on the *Daily Express* crossword and finally taking his mind away from Grace and his guilt over hurting her. He sat back in the chair and watched his da ready himself to leave. It was dark outside and rain was drumming heavily on the windowpane. His da would get soaked — absolutely drenched — within a few minutes of going out of the back door despite his felt hat, fustian coat and the heavy leather gloves sticking out of the pockets. At least it wasn't cold.

'You could always dig tomorrow night,' Wilfred suggested, stretching his arm along the back of the chair.

'No,' his da replied, tying some twine around his coat for a belt. 'If it rains again the ground will be waterlogged.' He was right: it rained frequently in South Wales. 'No point putting it off. Got to be done. Should be home by around four in the morning,' his da said, adjusting his hat.

The grave was for a chap from right out Stepaside way. He'd keeled over yesterday, just like that. Wasn't ill. Been nothing wrong with him at all, as far as his wife could see. Out of the blue, she'd told Wilfred when he'd gone to collect the body on Sunday evening. Must have been a stroke.

'The deceased was five foot seven, or thereabouts,' Wilfred stated, taking a bite of steak and kidney pie, 'and portly around the middle.'

'I'll dig a standard size grave, then,' his da replied, while looking around for his muffler, 'maybe slightly larger girth. The Reverend Waldo Williams said to dig next to the fenced plot belonging to the Nicholas family.'

'Nice spot. Crowded part of the graveyard, mind,' Wilfred remarked, brushing crumbs off the newspaper.

'You're right. I'll take the oilcloth and put it over Edward Thomas and his son's headstone to stop it getting splattered with mud.'

'But Da, you'll be digging up to your knees in water once you're a few feet down.'

'Aye, aye,' his da replied, pulling the end of his muffler out from under a tin of Smith's potato crisps.

Wilfred sometimes wished his father didn't dig graves for a living. Funerals, like this one on Thursday for a man in his late fifties, the same age as his da — and surely someone's father — brought it home to Wilfred. His father might catch something on his chest digging in hinderable rain like this. Wilfred knew from his work that you could never be too careful with a cough. On a night like this he would have liked to see his da inside by the fire. But his da wouldn't be hearing of it.

'They need me,' he would say. 'And I need them.'

*   *   *

It was the day of the funeral. Flora looked at her shoes — they were polished to what her father would have called 'within an inch of their life', and were reflecting tangents of light. Her father had always expected gleaming shoes, probably because of his days in the Royal Welch Fusiliers. Her silk stockings were new, her hair was finger-waved and she was wearing an ebony-coloured blouse that was stiff with starch. They were her silk crêpe mourning clothes which she'd last worn for her fiancé's funeral, that unbearable, soul-destroying day six years ago.

Flora was waiting in the kitchen with her mother for the funeral director to come from Narberth at half past two. It would make sense to wait for the undertaker in the hall but since Daddy had passed away — so abruptly and unexpectedly — in the hallway, neither she nor her mam wanted to linger there so instead they were huddled by the gas stove.

'Have you got everything?' her mother asked, warming her hands. 'You won't be taking your camera with you?'

'No, of course not,' Flora replied, though she

felt almost naked without her Kodak Brownie.

Flora clicked open her handbag. She had two linen handkerchiefs with her. At the funeral service for her fiancé, Albert, she had only taken one hanky — her best one, naturally, the one edged with her grandmother's handmade lace — and by the end of the service it was sodden and useless. That was when she'd realized lace handkerchiefs weren't only genteel accessories for ladies but necessary and hardworking objects that helped to keep one respectful and one's grief discreet. All her handkerchiefs had a small, cursive *F* embroidered in sea-green on them — her grandmother's work again. It was as if the tears dabbed into her handkerchiefs were named and labelled.

'A stiff upper lip for Daddy's sake,' her mam encouraged.

'Yes, Mam,' Flora said, moving closer to her mother. Flora felt it was more a case of a numb upper lip, numb face, numb — everything. She had been so utterly shocked to see her daddy there, dead, in the hall on Sunday morning, lying on the red rug and the geometric tiles, that she hadn't been able to feel anything else since. She'd gone through the motions of getting up, washing herself, dressing, eating — at her mam's insistence — small amounts at each meal but really she could barely swallow water, never mind eat food. Somehow she'd done what she needed to do for five, dazed days.

'Daddy would appreciate the effort you've made with your shoes,' her mam commented, her voice quavering.

Flora checked the time on the kitchen clock. People spoke about funerals honouring the dead. Flora, though, only wanted the funeral service to be over with because the day felt so intolerable. She knew there would be a service, a burial, and high tea afterwards but she felt benumbed and was expecting nothing from the day.

'He'll be here in a minute. He knows the way,' her mam said anxiously.

The undertaker had come immediately to collect the body, so soon it was almost unseemly. Flora had been unable to go downstairs to meet him — she was too upset and had told her mam to say she was resting in her room. A few days later the funeral hymns had been chosen: 'When I Survey the Wondrous Cross' and — Daddy's favourite — 'Bydd Myrdd o Rhyfeddodau', then the order of service had been printed on thick white card with a black rim. She imagined the grave had also been dug. Finally, she had hand-washed her best blouse which she had last worn, utterly heartbroken, in 1918, and now again.

'I thought we would grow old together,' her mother confided plaintively to the quiet room.

'Don't fret, Mam.'

'I didn't think it would come to this.'

The mantelpiece clock chimed half past the hour. At the sound of the car's tyres approaching the house, Flora and her mother went through the porch. A moment before she left the house Flora pulled her veil from her hat and placed it across her face. All I have to do, she thought to herself, is get through this day.

Wilfred opened the back doors of the car for the two women who were waiting on the doorstep.

'Good afternoon, mam. Good afternoon, miss,' he intoned, doffing his top hat. His apprentice-master, Mr Auden, had taught him that, drummed into him the importance of good manners. 'A funeral director is always polite,' he'd state. 'No effing and blinding around a corpse, Wilfred.' Mr Auden would say it like an aphorism every time he settled into the driving seat and revved the hearse engine, the coffin in the back, before they pulled out of the garage and drove to another funeral. 'No damn and bloody blasting around the dead, Wilfred.'

He waited, standing to his full height while the two ladies quietly came forward. Mrs Edwards and a younger woman — that must be her daughter — stepped into the motorcar. His eyes were drawn towards her. Wilfred noticed the younger woman's well-shaped ankles in delicate stockings. Her head was slightly lowered and Wilfred couldn't see her face clearly because she was wearing a black veil and, besides, he could only glance as it would be unkind to look closely into the face of someone who was so newly bereaved. Nevertheless, Wilfred noticed beneath the fine netting of her veil the elegant lines of her profile: her graceful brow and her delicate neck. Her hand was to her throat, touching her jet beads, and he saw her slender golden arm. The young woman had the straitened air of someone in great shock, and beneath her veil her face glistened with the wet of recent tears. Wilfred was used to this, but it never failed to move him.

At Mrs Edwards's request, Wilfred was to drive the chief mourners to the funeral and, as Wilfred didn't have a car — apart from the motorized hearse — Mrs Edwards had offered the use of her late husband's motorcar. Though unfamiliar with the car, Wilfred deftly swung the vehicle in a wide arc so it was facing the opposite direction then he peered in his driving mirror to check that the two ladies were settled before embarking on the slow drive to the funeral. The younger woman was beautiful, arrestingly so — and looked familiar to him. He felt as if he had seen the softness of her face before, but couldn't think where. That abundant pile of brown hair, her quietude . . . was he acquainted with her? He tried to think. Surely he would have remembered. He could not ask her now, of course, that would be the greatest impropriety, but he felt he knew her.

Wilfred glanced in the mirror again. He saw that the young woman looked pink and hot from the heat and an inner anguish. These people, he thought as he drove, this endless parade of people journeying to the newly dug grave of the person they loved. Sometimes Wilfred wanted to stop the car and turn around and reach out to his passengers, to this young woman here, and touch them very lightly on the wrist, that place above the wrist where a person's forearm tapers and which Wilfred thought seemed a vulnerable part on a human body. Wilfred imagined stretching out his hand and gently touching the

41

narrowness in the forearm and looking into his passengers' eyes. Usually they had red, swollen eyes. He imagined saying something. What would he say, though? It would be a difficult moment for the speaker and the listener. He could say, 'It will be all right.' But that would be audacious. If Wilfred spoke, the person might be offended, might not believe what Wilfred said. But it would be all right in a way, Wilfred knew.

He had, of course, never reached out to any of his broken passengers.

★   ★   ★

Flora was feverish beneath her lace veil. She knew her cheeks were red and she needed to blow her nose. She removed her gloves to look in her beaded handbag for a handkerchief. Her mam was bearing up well, sitting upright and looking straight ahead. Her mam was older though, forty-seven. Middle-aged people, Flora had learned, knew death happened, were calmer around it, less shocked, unlike the young who didn't believe in its existence until they experienced it for themselves.

They drove majestically past Saundersfoot railway station. Flora felt impatient to get to St Andrew's Church. I want to go and I don't want to go, all at the same time, she realized. This restlessness was grief. She couldn't keep her hands still, kept reaching for the beads of her French jet glass necklace. Really, there was nowhere in the world she wanted to be, if it was a world without her father. And Albert.

The car turned regally around the corner and the Pembrokeshire coast came swinging into view. She had often photographed this vista. And there was the cove. Flora had come here with her father many times when she was a small girl. He had shown her how to build a dam and block the stream. Together they would place flattish pebbles one on top of the other, making several rows until a small pond grew. They watched and waited until the pebbles were eventually dislodged and the wall broken by the force of the water. For a long time, building a dam in the stream had been Flora's favourite game. On Sundays after St Issell's Chapel and before Sunday dinner she would ask her father to take her to the cove and, if the weather was clement and he thought the stream wouldn't be too icy, they would walk down the hill together and spend an hour or so splashing in the water. That innocence felt a long time ago to Flora now. It was painful to remember.

Flora turned her gaze away from the window. The undertaker, she noticed, was looking at her in the driving mirror. Perhaps it was her grief — she was crying — perhaps he was discomforted by that. But he was an undertaker, he must be used to grief. She adjusted her veil. He glanced at her again. Their eyes met. He had blue eyes — dark blue, watchful eyes — the eyes of a man who observed life and saw death. And he was looking at her. Flora stared down at the palms of her hands. This was unexpected. A man was giving her the glad eye on the way to her father's funeral. And what was even more shocking to Flora was that she didn't altogether mind.

★　★　★

'Excuse me, Miss Edwards, if you wouldn't mind coming this way, down the nave,' Wilfred said in a confident voice, once the service was over. He put a guiding hand a few inches from the young woman's back. She followed him towards the west doors at the end of the church, her skirt rustling and her heels clicking on the mosaic of tiles. He noticed a perceptible vitality in her step, and there was something intangible about her that inspired him, as if her beauty gleamed from her. She had beautiful, enchanting posture. That's what he liked about women, their grace, the poise with which they moved. It wasn't true of all women but it was true of most; they moved in a way that men couldn't. Except perhaps male ballet dancers, like that Russian chap Nijinsky in the newspaper.

The church was dim and musty. Other mourners collected their service sheets, neatened their ties and adjusted their hats, but Wilfred was less aware of them than he would usually be as he walked beside Flora to the end of the aisle. He glanced at her. It would be ridiculous, he thought, to say a woman moved like a deer: that would mean she skipped on all fours, but Wilfred could understand, looking at Flora's slender figure, what people meant when they said a woman had a deer-like grace.

At the last pew she stopped for a moment and

44

rested, as if to gather her strength. She lifted her eyes up to him as if she sensed he was thinking about her. He looked at her gentle, sad eyes and warm mouth, and smiled consolingly. The young lady had deep-set brown eyes and a startled look, as if she had been hurt, like the shocked eyes of an animal caught in a trap. But perhaps that was because she was grieving now. Then he did something he never expected to do as an undertaker; he put his hand on her bare forearm for a moment, looking down at her golden skin.

As they were walking along the uneven gravel path in St Andrew's churchyard, Wilfred said in a low, earnest voice, 'It would be best if you stand close to the grave and then it will be that bit easier for you to drop your handful of earth in.'

Wilfred wanted the funeral to go well. No hitches was his constant aim. A hitch was never a good thing at a funeral. His job was to oversee the small details so that the family, lost in the enormity of their grief, would be free to mourn their loved one.

'It's a windy day,' the undertaker continued. 'If you move forward you will be better able to hear the Reverend Williams speaking.' Wilfred liked to give advice to his mourners, to 'help them', as Mr Ogmore Auden used to say, 'get the most from the day'. That was true, Wilfred knew. A guiding word here or there, even the most obvious advice, was often needed — people at funerals sometimes looked so lost they appreciated being shown the way.

They reached the newly dug grave with its

neat corners and pile of displaced, raw earth lying beside it.

'Just by here, now,' Wilfred said to Flora. 'There we are then,' he added, placing his hand gently and close — very close — to the curve of her back.

★ ★ ★

'Thank you again, Mr Price, it's been an exemplary service.' Mrs Edwards shook Wilfred's hand. Once the funeral was over, he had driven Mrs Edwards and her daughter home as carefully and surely as he had driven them to the funeral earlier in the day. They were all standing on the gravel outside the front door of White Hook.

'Not at all, Mrs Edwards,' Wilfred replied, bowing slightly and feeling obsequious.

'And a bright day too! My husband would have appreciated that. He always liked a sunny day — it helped if the horse's hooves were dry, made it that much easier for him than the rain.' Wilfred knew that Mrs Edwards's jollity was forced. He was used to the bereaved trying too hard.

'Yes, Mrs Edwards, we were most fortunate with the weather. Most fortunate,' he added self-consciously. Wilfred knew there weren't many things more desolate than a funeral in the freezing cold and pouring rain. Actually it had been a surprisingly blowy day — bright but blustery — though it was always best to agree with the recently bereaved. Mr Ogmore Auden had made a rule of it: 'Agree with them, Wilfred, or there'll be a to-do about the bill.' Wilfred understood why. People who were grieving were in so much pain they could easily be argumentative.

Flora Myffanwy dallied with the button on the wrist of her glove, listening to the exchange. Inside the silk-lined gloves her hands were dirty because the earth she had scattered over the grave while the Reverend was intoning, *'Ashes to ashes, dust to dust,'* had been sodden — almost mud. The sludge had seeped under her nails, forming brown half-moons, and her fingers would hold the scent of the earth. She imagined when she was an old lady being constantly stained with earth because she probably would spend all her days gardening and her hands would get dirty. That's what many old ladies did, tended to the earth and covered it with flowers, before eventually being laid down in it. Suddenly Flora felt spent; it had been a long day.

She turned to look at the undertaker: his black hair shone brightly with hair oil, his side parting was exact. He is a man, she thought, who visits the barber often. In her mind's eye she framed him. He would make an interesting — and handsome — subject for a portrait photograph. He was broad, and taller than her, but the same age, she would suppose — a little older perhaps. Twenty-seven? Perhaps twenty-eight. He was wearing a crisp white shirt, and his sideburns were precisely trimmed and he was carefully and closely shaved, and she imagined that gave an unnatural smoothness to his cheeks. It was a long time since she had touched a man's face. There were Albert's stubbly cheeks, scratchy like the corn stubble they had laid in that last August of his life, but Albert was blond, sandy-coloured. This man — the undertaker — would have dark stubble.

The undertaker was looking at her again, offering his outstretched hand. They shook hands. His hand was warm and strong, not cold and flaccid like that of a corpse, which was what her father's fingers had been when she kissed them before the lid had been placed — presumably later on nailed down — on the coffin.

'It has been a pleasure,' Wilfred said to her. Flora noticed her mam's slight surprise at his choice of words, but Flora knew what Wilfred meant.

★　★　★

Wilfred sat down heavily on the wooden seat, his thick woollen trousers settling around his ankles. It was always a relief to use the lavatory after a funeral. He put his feet wide apart and opened up the *Narberth & Whitland Observer*. He tried reading: *PATIENT NOT ADMITTED TO HOSPITAL. WAS THE PROCEDURE CORRECT? The unusual occurrence of a patient who was sent to the County Hospital for an operation and then was sent back home* — but he couldn't concentrate on the story. His mind was on that young lady — he had heard her mother call her Flora. That was a nice name. He couldn't imagine anyone called Flora being horrible.

48

He would like to see her again. But how? He turned the front page of the newspaper absentmindedly. If he was truthful with himself he hadn't been able to stop looking at her, although he was certain that she hadn't noticed. He had needed to be attentive to the funeral proceedings; indeed, he had kept his eye on the ball, but it was also true that, while the Revd Waldo Williams had delivered his eulogy and when Flora — he liked saying her name in his head — and when *Flora* had been seated in the pew in front of him with the other chief mourners, Wilfred had had what Mr Ogmore Auden once referred to as 'lustful thoughts'.

'Young men,' Mr Ogmore Auden had announced confidently as Wilfred was cleaning some gummy sawdust off the saw-blade, 'are prone to lustful thoughts. Wilfred, do not be prone to lustful thoughts.'

Wilfred had looked up. 'No, Mr Auden.'

'Refrain from dwelling on thoughts of a lewd nature while in the presence of the deceased. Especially when using a sharp tool.'

'Yes, Mr Auden.' Wilfred had been using the new motorized saw when Mr Ogmore Auden had made his wholly unexpected pronouncement. He was seventeen at the time.

Wilfred shook the newspaper to flatten the creases and rested his elbows on his knees. Maybe Flora went to the tea dances or fancy-dress parties in the Queen's Hall; perhaps he could meet her again accidentally — well, accidentally on purpose — at a dance. Lord knew it would look better than meeting her at a

49

funeral. But she wouldn't go dancing, Wilfred realized, because she was in mourning. Weeks, months of misery, drawn blinds, draped mirrors and plain dark clothes in lifeless crêpe. It would probably be autumn, he thought sadly, before Flora would be in her glad rags and doing the Foxtrot or the Twinkle. He liked the thought of Flora dancing, and lingered on it. Then he wondered what she would be like when she laughed.

He glanced at the *Notes of the Week* column. *Opening the Narberth Nurses Fête last week Miss Lewis of Trefilan paid quite a neat little compliment to our town, which she described as 'a wonderful place'. Her eulogy was inspired by the remarkable fact that in connection with nursing services the town raises between £400 and £500 yearly, which we should imagine stands unique in Pembrokeshire.*

Then it occurred to Wilfred: he could call at White Hook with the invoice for the funeral. He decided to do it as soon as possible, but not too soon or it might look as if he was being greedy or avaricious. Though it might be better to appear avaricious than lustful. But he was a man too, not just an undertaker! And at that thought, Wilfred stood up.

There were no newspaper squares again on the nail in the wall. By damn, that was awkward. It was difficult to remember to rip up old newspaper when there was a funeral to organize. Both he and his da always forgot to tear up old copies of the *Radio Times* or the *Narberth & Whitland Observer.* Wilfred would have to use a

50

piece of today's *Observer*, so that when his da sat down by the fire this evening to read the paper and found the centre pages missing, he would be under no illusions as to what Wilfred had done with it.

3

The Red Dictionary

The bar of Narberth Rugby Club was straining with the mountainous bodies of the rugby team. The walls were lined with ancient team photographs and there were silver trophies proudly and confidently displayed in glass cabinets. Wilfred had come for a swift half before lunch.

'Price is here!' someone roared.

'The handsome bugger's come to bury us!'

'Well done, lads,' Wilfred called back, raising his hand in greeting and referring to the morning's win against St Clears.

'They didn't stand a chance,' the tighthead prop replied. 'You should have seen them — like gnomes they were!'

Jeffrey, Wilfred's old schoolfriend, came up to him with a pint of pale ale.

'Wilfred Price — you bugger!' enjoined Jeffrey, patting him on the back and handing him his drink. 'I've heard the latest — congratulations! You never even mentioned you were seeing Grace Reece.'

'No,' said Wilfred cautiously.

'All right, you two?' said a man, shoving past and spilling beer.

'All right, Sidney? You back to the Army soon?' asked Jeffrey.

'That's right,' Sidney replied curtly, walking by and getting lost in the throng.

'Never liked that Sidney,' Jeffrey confided to Wilfred, 'too fly for me. So,' he continued, supping ale, 'I heard the news you're marrying her.'

'No, no.'

'But Mrs Evans at the Conduit Stores said.'

'*Wilfred Price!*' hailed Norman Collins from a nearby table. 'Have a pint before you get to the altar.'

'*No,* Collins,' Wilfred rejoined, waving his hand.

'So, then you's not marrying her?' Jeffrey queried, looking up at Wilfred.

'No . . . '

'But you *asked* her?'

'Yes,' said Wilfred guiltily. There was a sudden round of applause from the players at the bar.

'Nice legs on her,' Jeffrey commented, adding somewhat doubtfully, 'Nice legs isn't everything, mind.'

'No, that's exactly what I thought myself.'

'Was she upset?'

'Yes. I feel dreadful about it.'

'Nothing is simple,' said Jeffrey, stroking the red whiskers of his droopy moustache. 'Mind, you would have had Doctor Reece as your father-in-law.' Jeffrey nudged him. 'That would have been a barrel of laughs. Would have been like living with Moses.' After a pause, he asked, 'You all right, Wilf?'

'Aye.'

'That's what happens, you see,' Jeffrey said,

sipping his pint, 'when you spend all your time locked up with corpses in a workshop making coffins; you's like a child in a sweetshop the moment you sees the fairer sex.'

Wilfred wiped the froth from his mouth with the back of his hand; the beer was warm, familiar and comforting.

'True enough.'

'Now you'll have to tell the whole of Narberth.'

'No, I won't — now that I've told you,' retorted Wilfred.

'Come to the Young Farmers' dance with me next Friday,' Jeffrey offered. 'There's a charabanc of girls coming from Llawhaden.'

'They'll be straight back in the charabanc when they sees you.'

'Well, you'd be lucky if they let you bury them!'

'You still seeing Elizabeth?' asked Wilfred.

'No, seeing Clementine.'

'Clementine?'

'Everything changes,' said Jeffrey.

'Come again?' mouthed Wilfred, nodding towards the rugby players in the corner who were freshly showered, rosy-faced and shiny, all proudly wearing their blue Narberth Otter ties. It was like a room full of bellowing, huffing prize bulls, Wilfred thought as the men erupted, for no apparent reason, into a body-shaking, heart-bursting rendition of '*Hen Wlad fy Nhadau*'.

★ ★ ★

Back in the workshop, Wilfred removed the lid of an empty coffin. There, stowed under a bundle of linen winding sheets, was a hessian bag. Wilfred guessed correctly that no one, not even a thief, would have the courage to open the lid of a closed coffin in a chapel of rest. Barclays Bank was in the High Street but Wilfred didn't believe in interest, debt and security. Instead, their money was kept in two coarse hessian bags — one here, the other one hidden under the floorboards beneath his bed.

In the scully he took his da's spade from the kitchen chair and sat down. Mr Auden had taught him about money: 'We've buried some rich old buggers. Spend it while you can. But save some too — life is very unexpected.' So each time Wilfred was paid for a funeral he strove to put aside a third, and discreetly, slowly and steadily, his savings had grown. Mr Auden had also advised him that, when he had completed his apprenticeship — was solvent — he must take a wife.

Wilfred cleared a space on the table, upended the bag and let the money topple out. Coins clattered down and notes fluttered around. He piled the money together, brushing his bare arm along the table to gather it when, unexpectedly, an image of Flora came into his mind's eye. He paused for a moment, struck by an unexpected sense of her nearness.

A few coins had fallen on to the flagstones so he got down on all fours under the table to pick them up, and he was there when his da walked in.

'Hang on — another ha'penny's fallen next to those dumbbells, Wilf. And one by that snail in the corner.'

'Thanks, Da.'

'There's a hell of a mess on this table,' his da commented, taking off his cap. 'What's wrong with using the Barclays Bank? You usually like to be modern.'

'No, Da, I's not putting our hard-earned savings in the bank. Goodness knows what they do with it. Safer under the bed. Or in a coffin.'

'But the bank manager is a God-fearing Calvinist. He goes to church three times on a Sunday.'

'No doubt about it, Da. But I'm not trusting our money to a bank. Mark my words. I's read the newspaper every day, Da. And the Bible.'

'Wilfred! You don't read the Bible from one year to the next.'

'Well, I's remember what it says: *Neither a borrower nor a lender be.*

'Where's that in the Bible, then?'

'Don't know. Sermon on the Mount?' Wilfred speculated, rummaging for guineas and piling them up in groups of five.

Wilfred's da fished a sixpence out of the remains of a bowl of soup.

'I can always dig at St Issell's graveyard,' he said. 'They have a lot of deaths that way from the coalmine at Bonville Court — when they're not on strike.'

'No, Da. You dig for Narberth, that's plenty for you. I'll look after you.' Wilfred collected the half-crowns together. 'I could put up my charges,' he said, running his hand through his hair, 'but I don't like to, what with times being hard and getting harder . . . I's need a new pair of trousers, my other ones are worn through. And a pair of socks. I could buy them from Mrs Russell's Haberdasher's and Draper's this month. Or I might be able to wait for another month or two.'

'Ask Auntie Blodwen to mend them for you.'

'I have. But she's already darned them five times. She said she wouldn't do it again and that I should buy a brand new pair. Anyone would think we were made of money.'

'I thinks she was cross because you don't wash them properly. Said they were stiff with dirt, like cardboard, and she didn't want to touch them.'

'Well, there's fussy! I have a clean pair every day — it must be the floor that's dirty. And no one ever died of stink.'

The higgledy-piggledy pile of money was being turned into exact piles of coins and notes.

'You not going out today?' his da asked.

'No, thought I'd stay in.' Wilfred was waiting for the talk of him and Grace to die down a little and for some other choicer gossip to replace it before going out and about too much.

He jotted down some numbers on the back cover of the *Undertaker's Journal* and totted them up.

'*Five, ten, fifteen, twenty,*' he counted to himself. 'We'll be all right now, Da, don't worry, even if no one pops their clogs for two or three months — and someone surely will.'

'Mustn't be thinking too much about money,

Wilfred. It's not the be-all and end-all.'

'But it is important. And we have this now — this is for us. And it means we can look after ourselves, and not worry.'

But Wilfred did worry. Wilfred who, as a child, was always starving hungry; everyone said he had worms and hollow legs because he ate so much. He remembered the way his father had eked out his paltry wage so Wilfred might have more food. When money was very short, his da made kettle broth with hot water poured over broken bread, and when there was no work as a gravedigger, he would spend his days walking the hills and valleys around Narberth foraging for food with an instinctive sharpness born of hunger and the imperative to feed his child. He would find mushrooms and wild garlic, occasionally potatoes, and in the late summer there were hazelnuts, walnuts, many blackberries and sometimes strawberries. Then in their small yard his da grew vegetables, willing himself to be green-fingered while tending the peas, turnips, cauliflowers and the parsnips, and feeling dismayed if there were caterpillars on the cabbages.

Hunger made Wilfred eat every morsel in his bowl, even the tasteless kettle broth, scraping the enamel until there was nothing left. Then his da would turn from the table and stand at the sink tidying so Wilfred could lick his bowl clean while his da pretended not to see, because he knew that his son was hungry and needed all the food he could get. And they shared their meals with great generosity because they had both lost so

58

deeply and dearly when Wilfred's mam had died that neither of them could bear the thought of life without the other — and so their consideration for each other overrode their own hunger.

'No, Da, I'm not hungry — you have the last slice of bread,' Wilfred would insist when he got older. 'I found an apple on the way home.' From necessity, he had become an adept scrumper of the many pears and apples in Narberth's orchards.

'You eat it, boy,' his da would urge. 'I've had more than enough, an ample sufficiency.' Both of them knew the other was fibbing.

But there were many nights when Wilfred, despite his da's very best efforts, went to bed hungry, his stomach taut over his hipbones, and he would lie, listening to his da snoring and harrumphing in the next room, unable to think of anything but Mrs Annie Evans's magnificent Conduit Stores with its breathtaking array of sweet jars crammed with pastel-coloured sugar almonds, sticky liquorice allsorts and toffee, precious as gold. Then there was the counter lined with fresh, hot, wondrous loaves. In those famished bedtimes of his childhood, Wilfred imagined eating huge mouthfuls of bread spread munificently with butter and piled high with jam before falling asleep while saying his prayers: 'Our Father, Who Art in Heaven, eating jam.'

★　★　★

Wilfred settled into the driving seat of the hearse and adjusted the mirror. He found a barley sugar

59

in his trouser pocket, brushed the lint off it then popped the sweet in his mouth. He still felt guilty about Grace, very worried that he had hurt and humiliated her in the High Street, but he must try and put thoughts of Grace out of his mind and focus on the matter at hand today: young chap from Templeton. Flu.

At Templeton Church the pallbearers were waiting, bowler hats held tightly, looking out desolately to the empty road and the green valley beyond, waiting for Wilfred to arrive.

'Good afternoon, Mr Enoch Davies. And Mr James Davies and Mr David Davies,' said Wilfred, nodding at the father and brothers of the deceased. 'My sincerest condolences to you all.' He had already offered his condolences to the next of kin but one could never say enough comforting words to the anguished souls of the bereaved. The men collected sombrely and silently around the sleek hearse to help slide the casket out.

'At the count of three: one, two, three.' Wilfred took his usual position of back right and checked the pallbearers were ready to process. Today the chief pallbearer was the deceased's father. Sons, sons-in-law, sometimes brothers and the occasional husband carried the casket, but fathers were unusual now the Great War was over. This father would be weakened by his grief, perhaps struggling to stand upright under the burden of intolerable feelings. Wilfred would have to ensure the other pallbearer at the front was strong and could carry the weight on his shoulders alone should the father falter, as fathers were wont to

60

do on these occasions.

'Right we are then, in we go,' he instructed. At the tabernacle the four men stopped, adjusted their shoulders under the wooden box to calibrate the weight of it between them and began walking the long path through the graveyard into the sturdy church, past the congregation to the waiting vicar. The intensity of the mourners' grief increased the nearer to the altar they were sitting. In a funeral, unlike the theatre, no one wanted to be entitled to a front seat.

The Revd Waldo Williams preached the peroration on the verse *Blessed are the pure of heart for they shall see God.* Wilfred sat quietly in an empty pew behind a professional mourner and listened while the Reverend spoke earnestly about the brief life of the deceased.

'And Mr Davies, who was known for enjoying a flapjack . . . ' A muffled squeak emerged from a grieving lady in the next pew who quickly put her hanky to her mouth. Wilfred bowed his head.

'Mr Davies was a keen horticulturalist of root vegetables and celebrated throughout all of Templeton for his inventive carnival costumes,' the vicar declared.

Wilfred surreptitiously stretched his long legs, which were getting stiff, and lost himself in his thoughts. I did a good job on that coffin, he thought to himself. As the Revd Waldo Williams continued his — it had to be said — rather lengthy sermon, Wilfred noticed how the vicar spoke. The Reverend had come to Narberth from Birmingham: he spoke differently and it wasn't only his funny-peculiar accent. His family, Wilfred had heard, owned a locks-and hinges factory, and as a boy he'd been sent away to a school called Rugby where the game of rugby football was created, then on to the University of Oxford. Wilfred knew that because after the Reverend's name on the Tabernacle Chapel board it was painted: *Minister: The Reverend Waldo C. Williams, MA (Oxon.)*. MA meant Master of the Arts, which is what you were, Wilfred knew, if you had been to Oxford University. (Oxon.) had nothing to do with dairy farming.

Wilfred stood again for the New Testament reading, barely listening to the familiar words of the Gospel of St Mark nor to the second hymn, 'Nearer My God to Thee'. He wanted to improve himself, to keep on learning. Mr Ogmore Auden often said, 'As long as you're reading, you're learning.' Indeed, his father spent many evenings before going to the graveyard bent over the pictures of the celestial spheres in *The Constellations of the Stars for the Enthusiastic Amateur*. It was the only book in the house — apart from the family Bible, of course. Wilfred liked the names in his father's book: Cassiopeia, Virgo, Venus, Ursa Minor, Ursa Major — they sounded like lovely ladies rather than burning balls of gas in the heavens.

The thought of ladies reminded him of Grace. He had not been very clever towards Grace. It was not his finest hour. Quite undignified, really, if he thought about it. And hurtful. Caused him no end of worry. Perhaps if he had a bit more learning and a bit less stupidity — if he knew more things — then that could only be a help.

'Mr James L. Davies has ascended on angelic wings of burnished gold,' preached the Reverend, 'with seraphim and cherubim, into the immutably effulgent dominion of Heaven!'

They were big words, Wilfred thought, but a clever man such as the Reverend Waldo Williams, MA (Oxon.) used a great many difficult words — and furthermore knew what they meant. What was the word the Reverend had used in a sermon a while back? Necro-something. Wilfred had never heard of that word before. But a man of the world, a man of commerce, should know what long words meant, be able to use them in his sentences and in conversations, particularly with his elders and betters. Wilfred was proud of what he had achieved: coffin-making was a craft and there would always be a call for craftsmen. He did an honest day's work for an honest day's pay and there was honour in that, but he felt that if he wanted to be a man about town, a man about Narberth and a purveyor of superior funerals, then there was a call for him to have some learning.

Wilfred knew the words for undertaking, the unusual words: pall, formaldehyde, catafalque, moment of committal and veronica, he even knew columbarium, but he wanted a better vocabulary. Vocabulary — that was a big word. There were big words in the dictionary. The answer, Wilfred realized, with the suddenness of inspiration, was to buy a dictionary and read it.

* * *

First thing the next morning, Wilfred caught the train to St Clears and from there the number 29 bus to Laugharne and, in the damp cellar of Laugharne Books under the lopsided staircase amid a mountain of books, found, with no help at all from Mr Rudyard Sackville — miserable bugger — an old dictionary with red cloth covers and no dust jacket. Wilfred read the gilt lettering on the front cover: *The Concise English Dictionary: Literary, Scientific and Technical with Pronouncing List of Proper Names: Foreign Words & Phrases: Key to Names in Mythology & Fiction and Other Valuable Appendices. Also a Supplement of Words of Recent Occurrence. By Dr Charles Annund.* And he felt confident that, with such a title, the dictionary would surely include all the words he should ever need and all the words that could answer all the questions in the world. It might even help him be somewhat kinder and wiser with ladies. There were green mould spots all over the endpapers, it smelled as mildewy as Laugharne Books itself and the silk ribbon was broken, but no matter. Nor was it a new dictionary, but words were words. They never changed, did they? thought Wilfred.

'I'll take this dictionary, please,' he said to the very fat Mr Rudyard Sackville who was wearing a food-stained waist-jacket and slumbered behind a desk tottering with books. 'I came from Narberth specially to get it.'

'Three shillings,' Mr Rudyard Sackville stated,

and sighed hopelessly.

Wilfred counted out his shillings one by one, then said, 'Thank you.'

The bookseller nodded regretfully and slumped back in his chair with a deep fatigue.

'It's useful to have a dictionary,' enjoined Wilfred.

'Who's to say?' Mr Rudyard Sackville replied, then asked, sighing, 'What's it for?'

'Well, actually, to tell the truth, I thought I might read it.'

'What's it all for?' the man mumbled.

There are happier buggers in the graveyard, Wilfred thought to himself.

The inscription on the inside cover read *Presented to Caradoc Griffiths for Sunday School Attendance, in the Year of the Lord, 1892. PWLLGWAELOD Chapel.* Then underneath someone had written, presumably Caradoc Griffiths in a less Christian moment:

Black is the raven and black is the rook
But blackest is the person who stealeth this
*   book.*
Steal not this book for fear of life
For the owner carries a carving knife.

Wilfred — once he'd bought it, of course — went straight home and immediately put a bold line straight though *Caradoc* and *Griffiths* and wrote his own name in obsidian ink in his best cursive hand, *Wilfred Price*, then added, <u>undertaker</u> so that the red dictionary was officially his. He could start reading it from the

65

beginning at the letter *A* . . . well, he would think how he would do it, but for now he only knew that he would start.

★ ★ ★

Wilfred was full of purpose; he had some business he needed to attend to. The sun was on his broad neck and he was cycling powerfully. He could have pushed the bike up the hill instead of pedalling because the road was very steep — all the hills near the sea in Pembrokeshire were steep and it was many miles. But, well, Wilfred told himself, if Flora is wearing a dress, a flimsy summer dress that goes in at the waist and out at the . . . and her arms are bare and her wild brown hair loose, then it would be all to the best if he was physically *exhausted*. Even if Flora's clothes and dark hair were very becoming, he resolved that he would: Not. Be. Overcome. There were many very attractive ladies in Narberth — some real tomatoes! — but he couldn't be proposing to them all. He had learned that now, and felt another pang of remorse towards Grace. He dearly hoped she was well and no longer hurt.

Wilfred cycled arduously upwards, past clusters of bluebells by the hedgerow, a profusion of them in a clear, strong lilac colour. '*Come on, Wilfred, come on!*' he said to himself. Heck, he thought, it'd be nice to live in Norfolk: it was as flat as a pancake apparently. That would be marvellous for any cyclist. Mind, if he lived in Norfolk and didn't wear himself ragged cycling strenuously up almighty hills he might be proposing willy-nilly to all the peachy girls, and that would never do. He didn't want to hurt anyone else. No, hills were God's gift to the unmarried man. And he must be careful not to suffer from aboulia again, he thought, using a word he had acquired from his dictionary. Aboulia had already caused him — and Grace — enough anguish.

He hunched his shoulders and leaned forward on the handlebars. Wilfred wanted a wife — that much he knew. It was a big decision for any man to make, no doubt about it, especially one such as himself who had already been none too clever in these difficult matters of matrimony. And he also knew that from now on, he would approach these things differently, more considerately for starters. He knew he wanted a good woman but beyond that Wilfred wasn't at all sure what made a good wife. He would need to have what his apprentice-master Mr Ogmore Auden had once called 'lustful thoughts' about his betrothed — Wilfred was confident that he wouldn't find that difficult.

He stopped to wipe his brow with his handkerchief. He knew he couldn't feel towards his prospective wife as he had towards Elizabeth Thomas, who was a very pleasant person, no one could doubt it. But with her buck teeth and unfortunate frizz of hair, Elizabeth Thomas from Plain Dealings Road had been a relief to Wilfred when he was an apprentice because she was one of the very few young women in Narberth he *didn't* have lustful thoughts about. That was why they'd been friends; he could actually have a conversation with Miss Elizabeth Thomas without being distracted.

Wilfred fell into a rhythm with the pedalling and was making slow and steady progress up the incline. What did a man look for in a wife, he wondered. Was it cooking? Cleaning? Cleaning would be handy: neither he nor his da were very particular around the house and it could get a bit much sometimes. Perhaps a lady who liked wallpaper and who would be good as a shop assistant in a paint and wallpaper shop.

He arrived at the crest of the hill, dismounted from his bike and quenched his thirst with some water from his glass bottle while he surveyed the cove. The water was placid, the clouds fluffy. It was beautiful here, high up and close to the heavens. Wilfred didn't know what marriage involved. Because his father was widowed, Wilfred had had no insight into the day-to-day goings-on of marriage, hadn't grown up enveloped in one. He imagined the worst ones were like Punch and Judy's marriage. He'd seen the puppet show once on the annual Bethesda Chapel Sunday School outing to Saundersfoot — the man hit the woman, the woman nagged the man, and they lived with an alligator. That was no good at all, thought Wilfred, getting back on his bicycle and freewheeling down the last stretch of the road to White Hook.

He coursed down the lane, weaving from side to side. It definitely wouldn't do to marry someone unkind. And every man wanted to marry a woman who was a lady, although it had occurred to him that he didn't want his wife to be a lady all the time. Wilfred could imagine occasions, more private occasions, when he would enjoy it if his wife was a little less decorous.

It was a sultry day and the leaves on the trees along the lane created a dappled shade. Wilfred took his hands off the handlebars and leaned back. There was only one corner to cycle round and then he'd be there. Wilfred knew hardly anything about this Miss Flora Edwards. Except that she was not like other women, seemed more ordered within herself, perhaps wilder in her expression. And did she take photographs? How modern. She was mysterious to him. Surely you shouldn't marry a woman because she was enigmatic? There was that children's hymn that they'd sung in Scripture lessons, the one about the parable: 'The WISE man BUILT his HOUSE upon the ROCK'. Mystery wasn't a rock, it was a foundation of sand, and as that parable explained, if you built your house on the sand, it collapsed.

He reached the end of the lane and rounded the corner. Grace, Wilfred conjectured, was like a daisy, with her blonde, bobbed hair and pale skin. Flora was more . . . he didn't know what, only when he thought of her he was reminded of the rich, deep scent of the wine-coloured wallflowers that grew freely through the iron railings near the stream. Where Grace had been obvious, Flora was deeper, and was reeling him in.

He arrived at the gate to White Hook and felt

a wave of anxiety in his throat. He was here. He had anticipated this for long days and suddenly he was here. The bicycle wheels crunched on the gravel as he began walking up the drive. Right, he decided, he was going to invite her to the Staunton House Refreshment Rooms in Narberth. It was a popular café, if a bit steamy, and they had an impressive selection of cream cakes which he knew ladies were partial to. But would it be good enough for Flora? He'd taken Grace there once, but Flora was different. Flora was the bee's knees, the cat's pyjamas. Though what if she needed a chaperone? What if her mother came along and sat there like a fire extinguisher?

At the top of the drive he bent to pull off his trouser clips then leaned his bicycle against the kitchen wall with a clatter. Right. He would deliver the invoice for the funeral to Mrs Melbourne Edwards — he had it ready in an envelope in his inside pocket — and once financial matters were settled he would ask Flora if she would care to join him for a pot of tea, at a later date, at her convenience, at the Staunton House Refreshment Rooms in Narberth. Right. Yes, he would do that.

★　★　★

'The service was to your satisfaction, mam?'

'Yes, thank you, Mr Price. And you'll be wanting to settle the bill for services rendered.'

'Ah . . . ' This was always an awkward moment in the undertaking business. Customers had recently buried a loved family member — something they hadn't wanted to do anyway — and now Wilfred was asking them to pay for it. It added insult to injury. What had Mr Ogmore Auden said? 'Be delicate in your business dealings but make sure the buggers pay!' That could be easier said than done in some cases, Wilfred thought.

'I'll write a banker's cheque for the full amount.' Mrs Melbourne Edwards searched for a pen in the drawer of the Welsh dresser but was unable to find one. Wilfred took a risk.

'May I offer you mine, Mrs Edwards?' he said, proffering his fountain pen from his inside pocket. Sometimes people wouldn't borrow an ink pen in case they bent the gold nib with their specific way of holding the pen and spoiled it for the owner, but Mrs Melbourne Edwards accepted his offer.

'Thank you very much, Mr Price. That's most kind of you. Things get mislaid in these drawers for weeks on end. I expect your mam is more organized than I am.' Wilfred smiled politely.

Flora was standing barefooted by the gas stove, her chestnut hair catching the light. Wilfred was agonizingly aware of her, barely able to concentrate with her presence so close.

Mrs Melbourne Edwards flapped the banker's cheque in the air to dry the ink then handed the payment to Wilfred. Wilfred took the cheque in both hands, formally thanked Mrs Edwards and then summoned his courage.

'I was wondering', Wilfred began slowly, 'if your daughter . . . Flora . . . ' this was more awkward than he'd envisioned . . . 'would like to have a cup of tea or coffee.' Why did he say coffee? It was too strong! It sounded completely wrong. He hadn't meant to say coffee; he'd even practised saying, 'Tea and cake.'

'A cup of tea!' exclaimed Flora's mother. 'Tea! At this time? And her father not yet in his grave three weeks. Mr Price, surely . . . ' Mrs Melbourne Edwards looked bewildered.

'Yes, forgive me,' said Wilfred far too hastily. 'I don't know what came over me.' He assumed his funeral face. 'I hoped a modest change of scenery and an anteprandial refreshment might provide somewhat of a relief to your daughter during these exceedingly sad times.' Wilfred was lying: his face turned redder.

'Well, I shall say *Auf Wiedersehen* to you both,' he said, remembering the dictionary definition he had read that morning.

As Wilfred slipped his pen back into his jacket pocket he glanced surreptitiously at Flora. He saw her dignified, straight neck, her head bent down, her abundant mass of brown hair, saw her move the toes of her right foot back and forth elegantly across the slate floor, like a ballerina practising. Her mother had said no but was Flora saying no? Could a mother speak for a daughter? Could Mrs Melbourne Edwards speak for Flora? These were modern times. Flora swayed slightly as she moved her pointed toes gently from side to side, and in her swaying Wilfred read her yes.

4

The Invitation

'You couldn't look smarter if you tried.' Mrs Reece, flushed with vanity, reached up and straightened Madoc's epaulettes. 'Doctor Reece, doesn't Madoc look a picture?'

'Son, you do us proud.' Grace watched as her father patted her brother on the arm, his worn, red fingers against the sleeve of the khaki uniform.

'A Sergeant, Doctor Reece!' Mrs Reece interjected. 'Sidney isn't a Sergeant and he's been in the Fifteenth Welsh Regiment for six years as well. He enlisted just after the war, the moment he was seventeen — and he's still only a Lance Corporal. I was telling Sidney's mother last Monday, 'Well, Madoc's now a Sergeant and has a three-point chevron on his sleeve'. I know for a fact she didn't like it that her son is still a Lance Corporal after all that time — when *my* son is a Sergeant.' Mrs Reece reached up and tugged at the corner of Madoc's collar. 'I did a tidy job of those boots. I greased them with Quikko lamp black. They look very clean.'

Grace looked down at Madoc's Army boots with their thick, serrated soles, tough hardened leather uppers and the extreme black perfection of their shine. They were big boots: Madoc had big feet. He'd always had big feet, to match his

73

large head and his thickset body. Madoc smiled, his blue eyes charming beneath his bushy eyebrows. God only knows what happened to him in the war, Grace thought.

'Mother, now! You spoil me. I'll be back at the barracks before long and polishing them myself. Didn't use spit, did you?'

'Oh, get away with you, Madoc!' Grace watched her mother beam and her father smile at Madoc's teasing.

Grace straightened her pearl necklace, formed a smile on her face and felt a tugging in her chest. Her brother was going off again, somewhere no one had ever heard of in Africa, some camp in a wilderness, full of a mess of green tents and men polishing their shoes and pressing their uniforms, smartening themselves to kill. That's all the Army seemed to Grace, polishing and killing. The Army was men without women and, Grace knew, being without women changed men, made them forget, made them more violent. Or Madoc, at least. Men without women thought everything was a war. Men who had been without women for a long time were dangerous when they returned.

'Oh Madoc, what'll we do without you?'

'Pull yourself together, Mrs Reece,' Dr Reece admonished. 'Our son is a grown man with a job to do: let him go in peace. He's not a child any more.'

'You take your lunch tin with you, now, for the train journey. I've made you cucumber sand-wiches. Don't forget to eat properly.'

'Mother!' said Madoc, grinning. Then Grace

74

watched as he bent down and picked their mother up in his arms and swung her round.

'Madoc!' Mrs Reece cried out jubilantly, her long woollen skirt sailing out. Grace could see that her mother was delighting in her son: his strength, his humour, how he tended her.

'Madoc now, put your mother down,' Dr Reece said, smiling and speaking quietly, knowing Madoc didn't like loud noise since he'd come back from the Battle of Mammet and the trenches.

'You're light as a feather, Mother,' Madoc commented, her wooden clogs tapping against the flagstones as he set her down on the floor.

'Madoc,' Mrs Reece said, taking her hanky from the pocket of her pinny and dabbing at her eyes. She was wearing her best pinny, the one Madoc had given her for Christmas.

Grace watched her father's eyes moisten. Her parents were genuinely happy to be here with Madoc, but some of their cheerfulness was false; some of their red-faced animation was because they knew that their son might go away to the Army and get killed. They all knew that. It was quite possible that Madoc would board the boat to that world of men he lived with, and for another man, from somewhere else, to point a gun at him and accurately, precisely and intentionally and immediately, kill him. There would be a grave. And that would be the end of Madoc. In this parting there was the image of his death.

'Grace . . . ' Madoc said. She stood there quietly.

'Grace,' prompted Dr Reece, 'say goodbye to your brother.' Grace looked down.

'Don't be getting all emotional,' her father chided. 'Madoc will be back. There's no need for anyone to get upset. What are you getting upset for?'

Madoc held out his hand and Grace shook it, still looking down.

'Hold yourself together, please, Grace,' Dr Reece said.

'Don't go annoying the bees,' Madoc said to Grace. For reasons Madoc hadn't explained and no one understood, he hadn't gone near his bees since he'd come back from the war. 'I want to come home and find them all alive, every single one of them. I'll be counting!'

'Oh, Madoc,' Mrs Reece said. 'Don't tease!'

'Your suitcase is in the back of the motorcar. Come along now, young man. You've got a job to do.' Dr Reece patted his son on the back. He had put on a maroon and navy Welsh Guards tie to mark the occasion.

Mrs Reece rushed to the kettle, which was whistling hysterically, filling the kitchen with steam.

'No time for tea, Mrs Reece,' Dr Reece decided.

'Oh, Doctor Reece, we can't be seeing Madoc off without a hot drink!'

'No time at all, Mrs Reece. Madoc, Mother's put some Bara brith in your case. Give Ishwyn Thomas a slice when you arrive. And give him our best regards.'

'I will, Da.'

'Tell him I saw his mother. She came to the surgery last Thursday. I examined her knee joint and it is my opinion that she is walking much better.'

The back door was open; it was still early in the year and the air was chilly. Grace wrapped her wool shawl around her shoulders, holding herself within it. The hooked ham was swaying and the clean laundry hanging from the ceiling was flitting in the breeze.

'Right,' her father said, swelling out his chest. 'One mustn't keep His Majesty's Army waiting.'

Then, almost immediately, Madoc had left and the house had a new emptiness — and Grace wondered if Madoc was really going off, or if a part of him stayed always here, always with them.

From the parlour window she watched him walk down the front path to the wrought-iron gate, his broad shoulders emphasized by the epaulettes, his brown leather belt buckled firmly at his waist. The iron half-moons on the soles of his boots hit the stone path with a tight, hard click. At the end of the path, he put his cap on his head, one hand at the front, one hand at the back, straightened it, then opened the gate, which squeaked discordantly. He walked sharply, backbone stretched exaggeratedly in the way men in the Army were taught to walk. He looked distinct, smarter, more powerful and purposeful than the other people milling around on Narberth High Street. He seemed ordained and restored by Her Majesty, or God, to a higher purpose, one of deciding and presiding over the death of others, one who fought evil with the goodness of rationality.

Grace sat on the windowsill observing Madoc stride up the street, past the dust cart, jovially doffing his peaked cap to people, being slapped on the back, ruffling the hair of a small child as if he was a hero among Narberthians, leaving for a quest. Her father followed behind, taking the long route to the car, the public one, past houses and carriages, a cart and pedestrians. Madoc stepped off the pavement on to the road, passed the Star Supply Stores and was gone. And he might not return.

★   ★   ★

A few days later Grace was standing by the kitchen door because her mother had called her. Her father was sitting squarely in his usual place at the head of the table, her mother hovering tensely nearby. In the centre of the table there was a boiled fruitcake.

'Now then, Grace,' Dr Reece began, putting down *The Lancet* and peering over his glasses, considering her.

The problem, Grace realized, with having a father who was a doctor was that he was practised at observing, and right now he was observing her.

'Grace Amelia, your *father* is talking to you.'

Grace didn't answer her mother; instead she walked over to the stove and began re-folding a starched tea towel to keep her hands — and her mind — occupied.

'Grace . . . ' her father began solicitously.

'Your father and I are perfectly aware that you are down in the mouth,' her mother interrupted, before slamming her hand down hard on the tabletop to kill a bluebottle. The teacups rattled in response. 'Look what you've made me do, Grace Amelia. There's tea spilled everywhere!'

Grace placed the now neatly folded tea towel back over the stove rail.

'Is it . . . might it be to do . . . ' her father enquired ponderously. 'We thought it could be to do with Wilfred.'

Wilfred. Grace knew they would know, that they were only pretending to guess. Wilfred, her now ex-fiancé, who was supposed to have been besotted with her, marry her and then provide order and respectability.

'Wilfred hasn't set foot in this house five weeks on Saturday,' her mother pronounced indignantly. Her father removed his gold-framed spectacles and began polishing them with a clean white handkerchief.

'It is not what is to be expected by a young man of sensibilities who has declared his affections,' he offered.

'Madoc would *never* behave like this,' Mrs Reece declared, sawing a slice from the loaf, 'and that's because I've brought him up properly.' She wiped the blade of the bread-knife with the dishcloth. 'I've taught my son right from wrong. He knows how to behave.'

Her father, pointing at the fruitcake, said to his wife, 'Now, Mrs Reece, pull yourself together. Madoc will be back before you know it. And best cover this fruitcake with a net, or there'll be flies landing on it. We wouldn't want it to spoil.'

Grace lowered her head and stared at her shoes, trying to focus. Her father was a highly educated man, but also a practical one. Doctors had to be practical. She knew that he would make a suggestion — a realistic, workable one that would hold within it a path forward. That was what he did for his patients; he gave them a way of coping.

'Have you actually *seen* Wilfred?' her mother called accusingly from within the pantry where she was selecting a cake-dome. Grace inwardly winced at her mother's directness and also cringed at her last meeting with Wilfred. Narberth was a small town; someone would have seen her shaken and tearful at the bottom of Sheep Street or walking desolately to the castle where she had sat forlornly on the hefty broken wall of the keep, swinging her legs and crying. Someone would have noticed and told her mother.

Grace was quiet, waiting for her father to speak, knowing he would.

'I have a suggestion,' he said, leaning back. 'I shall invite Wilfred to come here for lunch this week, on Thursday. I shall use the telephone and ask him myself. What do you think to a shoulder of Welsh lamb with mint sauce and some mashed potatoes, Mrs Reece? Or perhaps a rabbit pie? Grace, perhaps you can make one of your Madeira cakes. Then at least you young people will see each other.'

'Oh!' said Grace's mother, her eyes sharp and

shining. 'Now there's good.'

'I expect he's overcome with sheepishness,' her father surmised, 'being an undertaker and all, and more used to funerals than weddings.'

★   ★   ★

Wilfred was leaning on the kitchen table reading his notice in this week's *Narberth & Whitland Observer*:

Mister Wilfred Price.
PURVEYOR OF SUPERIOR FUNERALS
Motorized Hearse
(with glass sides and wood panelling)
11 Market Street, NARBERTH
Telephone for all inquiries: Narberth 103

Superior sounded honourable, although he could hardly advertise himself as *Purveyor of Inferior Funerals*. What would that mean? Burying the living? Dropping the body? That had happened. Trying to break a stiff corpse with rigor mortis so as to lay it flat in its coffin? No. *Superior* Funerals were the right words, the apposite words, for W. Price, Funeral Director, Narberth. And with a motorized hearse, despite the cost, all the polishing and the occasional temperamental behaviour from the engine, Wilfred was on to a winner. *Adamantine*, Wilfred said to himself: his motorized hearse was adamantine in the sun from all that polishing. He'd learned that word this morning.

Wilfred went to the shelf and looked for

something to eat. He grabbed the end of a loaf and the tin of Griddles Old-Fashioned Black Treacle, dipped a spoon into the treacle and spread it on the bread. Mind, a bit more custom wouldn't go amiss. Not that there was much he could do about that; business was in the hands of the Lord.

He took a bite off the corner of the bread and moved his dictionary to one side. Mr Ogmore Auden had said, 'Everyone in Narberth is a potential customer, Wilfred. Treat them well. A corpse has yet to come through the front door and ask for a funeral.' Wilfred tried always to be polite and was mindful of his pleases and thank yous, but beyond that he could hardly go around committing murder to acquire corpses. He licked the spoon clean. January and February — his busiest months, when it was cold and dark and more people passed away — were over and it would be quiet for a while now. Even worse, the weather was fine. That never helped because people didn't kick the bucket half as much when it was sunny. He had heard though, that Mrs John Howell-Thomas, Kilgetty way, had a funny turn last Tuesday. But Mrs John Howell-Thomas was a tough old boot. And her sister had been ninety-four before she'd fallen off the perch.

Wilfred rubbed the stubble on his cheeks thoughtfully. It was a long time since he had finished his apprenticeship and he ought to be extending the business. There was no shame in having been an apprentice. An apprenticeship was a very honourable path. His father had agreed to it: it would keep his son busy. Idle hands made work for the devil, especially for young men — and Wilfred would be exempt from conscription — and so his son was apprenticed to O. Auden, Funeral Undertakers, Wheelwrights & Cabinet Makers of Whitland, six miles away.

Wilfred licked the back of the spoon. It had been easy for him to choose undertaking for his trade, what with his da being the Narberth gravedigger and — well . . . most of what he knew of the world was death. Perhaps it was because his mother had died when he was so young, only an infant, that Wilfred had gone into the funeral business. It was an unusual profession for a robust young man in rude health, but it was what Wilfred had always wanted to be — a craftsman and a businessman. A businessman: Wilfred felt pride when he said the word to himself. He rolled up his sleeves purposefully and took a big bite of the bread.

Wilfred remembered how he had lodged six days a week with Mr and Mrs Auden, all the while becoming versed in the art of funerary. He had learned about the oak, the beech and the pine, and how to rub planks with a brick until they were smooth and splinter-free, and he'd made coffins, measured for drawers, hinged doors, glued veneers, dovetailed corners and, eventually, did inlay on cabinets.

Wilfred remembered how he had returned after four years, full of hope and ambition, to Narberth to offer the services of coffin-maker whenever the Revd Waldo Williams, MA, popped round to visit his father with news of a death in the parish and the need for another grave. Old Tom Wheeler in the High Street, who made tables, chairs, dressers and coffins retired when Wilfred came back, and Wilfred was blessed with no competition, and these days, experience was making him increasingly proficient. Nevertheless it would make good sense to extend the business and, to that end, he was wondering about turning the parlour into a paint and wallpaper shop. It would improve his prospects, he would be better able to look after his da and it would keep him gainfully employed and perhaps even make him more eligible. Yes! The parlour would do splendidly as a wallpaper shop! He put the spoon down on the table decisively and stretched his arms along the back of the chair. Shelves along the rear wall. The counter facing the door so he could greet the flood of customers when they came in.

He wouldn't spend much money on the initial stock — he knew that was a common miscalculation that amateur businessmen made. 'Young men can get too big for their boots,' Mr Ogmore Auden had cautioned once, 'have fancy ideas about their little businesses and get on their high horse. This is Pembrokeshire, Wilfred, not London.' Wilfred had never left Wales and been up the line to England, and he was certain that Mr Ogmore Auden hadn't either, but he suspected his apprentice-master was right. It was true that a Welsh gentleman, Mr John Lewis, had a department store in London, on a road called Oxford Street. So did Mr D. H. Evans, but they hadn't started out as undertakers. When Wilfred opened a wallpaper shop, he would begin modestly, although he would need to place a new advertisement in the *Observer*:

Mister Wilfred Price
Funerals and Wallpapers of Distinction

No, that wasn't right, he realized. It sounded like he might wallpaper coffins.

'*Bora da*, Wilfred. Post here for you,' the postman shouted through the open front door.

'*Bora da*, Willie. What have you been up to, then?'

'Well, Wilfred, that'd be telling. But it's wonderful what you see when you haven't got a gun.'

'How's the wife?'

'Right as rain.'

Wilfred checked his pocketwatch; it was a quarter past two. The third post was as punctual as ever since they'd installed central heating in the general post office. There had been some concerns about that within Narberth, what with the installation costing sixty pounds.

'I's put the post here now for you, as usual, Wilf,' the postman stated, pointing to the corner table in the hall with the telephone on it. 'What are you up to, then, standing in the front room like a man with no sense?'

'Business being as it is, I'm thinking of turning the parlour into a wallpaper shop,' Wilfred explained.

'There's tidy,' the postman said. 'Wife can't get enough of the stuff. She's talking about wallpapering the scullery. Have you ever heard of such a thing? Wants to do it in cherry blossom. Nonsense on stilts. Too dull to fart, she is.' He adjusted the bulging postbag on his shoulder, 'Picture postcard for you, Wilfred. Can't make any sense of the message on the back.'

'Thank you, Willie. See you now.'

Postcard? Wilfred thought, measuring the back wall for shelves and putting the ruler back in his trouser pocket. Eight foot long — that would be a good-sized shelf.

It was a postcard with a photograph of the sea and two cottages. That's on the way to Amroth, Wilfred thought. It showed a young woman in a large bonnet holding the saddle of a bicycle, and there was a man's cycle propped up nearby on the grass. The Welsh sea was calm in the background.

Wilfred turned the card over. *The cottage, the cove, Saturday afternoon.* No name, no signature, not even, *Dear Wilfred.* Was it for him? Yes. It was addressed to *Mr Wilfred Price, Esquire.* Who could it be from? Wilfred was flummoxed. Could it be from . . . *a woman?* But it was no good running away with fancy ideas. It could only be business. Had a person popped their clogs in one of those cottages and wanted the body removed and buried? He hadn't heard of anyone being ill down Amroth way, nor of any ladies expecting. It wasn't the usual way to contact the undertaker: mind, some of these farming folk had their own ways, weren't quite up with the modern world and telephones.

Wilfred began to mentally prepare. He would

86

need to take the motorized hearse with him just in case; he couldn't carry a body on his bicycle. And he'd have to press his white shirt. Thank goodness for a bit of business, thought Wilfred with relief, putting the postcard in his pocket — when the telephone trilled abruptly. Even more business, he thought with excitement, walking briskly and with a sense of purpose through to the hallway and picking up the receiver of the telephone. It was always an occasion when the telephone rang.

'NARBERTH 103. WILFRED PRICE, FUNERAL DIRECTOR speaking.' It was necessary to shout into the receiver, as reception was extremely poor, especially when it was raining. Wilfred thought sometimes it would be more efficient to stand at the front door and bellow the conversation.

'Afternoon, Wilfred. DOCTOR REECE here. This is DOCTOR REECE speaking.' Dr Reece, Wilfred thought and then, with excitement at the prospect of business: *somebody has died.*

'Wilfred. You are invited to COME ROUND FOR DINNER. ON THURSDAY. THIS THURS-DAY COMING. With Mrs Reece and myself. And our daughter, GRACE.'

Wilfred was confused. The line crackled frantically with static.

'You don't have a FUNERAL, do you?' Dr Reece enquired, filling the pause. 'Do you, or do you not, have a FUNERAL, Wilfred?'

'No . . . ' replied Wilfred, forgetting to shout. There were never funerals on a Saturday. Saturdays at St Andrew's Church and the

Bethesda, Calvinist and Tabernacle Chapels were kept for weddings.

'That's settled, then. Look FORWARD to it. We'll see you at ONE on Thursday, Wilfred.'

'Pardon?' Wilfred shouted but he heard a click and the line went dead.

That man! Why couldn't he just stand up to him? And why did Dr Reece think he would want to go to lunch with Grace on Saturday when he was no longer engaged to her? Wilfred ran his hand through his hair. But then it occurred to him — Grace hadn't told her parents. Which meant Wilfred would have to tell them himself.

★　★　★

On Thursday lunchtime, Grace's father carved the joint with the steel carving knife. He prided himself on his precision and the Welsh lamb flopped in even slices, each a quarter of an inch thick. His years of wielding the scalpel and performing small surgeries on lumps and warts and toes meant he was a confident carver of meat. Grace saw the lamb was lightly bloodied: in the middle of each slice was a large red spot. 'Not properly cooked,' her mother would have muttered critically if Grace had roasted the joint. But her mother said nothing. She wasn't one to draw attention to her own failings or shortcomings in the kitchen.

'Move the tureen of vegetables out of my way, please, Grace,' her father requested, and she lifted the heavy tureen further away from the carving platter.

'Thank you,' her father replied. 'And the gravy boat, please. It is also in my way.'

Wilfred was supposed to be here. An extra tablemat and a silver knife and fork had been laid for him in Madoc's place. Her father had invited Wilfred by telephone — had shouted the invitation down the line. Grace had heard him while she was upstairs. Wilfred no doubt had shouted back his acceptance. They had waited three-quarters of an hour until it was a quarter to two, by which time the boiled vegetables had long since stopped steaming and started to toughen. Now it was painfully obvious to her, and to her father and mother, that Wilfred had proposed — but not meant it — and said yes to dinner — and not meant it. Was there a word for this, Grace wondered. Jilted? No, jilted happened at the altar. This was being jilted before the altar was even in sight.

'Is this lamb from Green Grove Farm, Mrs Reece?'

'It is,' her mother replied curtly. There was the sound of the knife sawing into the bone. A small pool of thin blood gathered on the platter. Raw meat was dangerous. When a patient rushed to see her father bent double, clutching their stomach, and the sound of their retching filled the whole house, her father lectured them on what he called food hygiene: 'The cleaner you are, the healthier you are,' he was fond of declaring, and advised his female patients that it was better to singe the pie or burn the joint than to undercook it. 'A burned dinner is safer than a raw one,' he'd state. But now at the dining-table he was unforthcoming in the face of the uncooked lamb, unwilling to provoke his snappy wife.

Grace was trying hard to keep her thoughts under control and, to distract herself, began studying the picture decorating her dinner-plate. It was the Willow Pattern. Grace had read about it in her *Olive Wadsley's Weekly* magazine: the blue man and the blue maiden, Chang and Knoon-shee, were crossing a bridge, Knoon-shee carrying her box of jewels, leaving the pagoda, fleeing her enraged father because he forbade their love. But Knoon-shee's father would catch them and set the couple's wooden house alight while they were sleeping. Her own father would do that! The two doves at the top of the plate were their spirits, flying to the realms of eternal happiness.

'Mrs Reece, the dinner-plates, please,' her father commanded, stroking his beard. Grace's mother collected the plates and her father put a slice of meat on each one.

Grace looked again at the three fragile figures on the bridge printed on her side-plate, and it occurred to her that perhaps, instead, it was the father and the daughter who were chasing the young man. Perhaps Chang was fleeing from imprisonment in an unwelcome marriage. Perhaps he was looking to the Sugarloaf Mountain ahead, to his freedom and his future in a blue and white landscape, while the father and Knoon-shee were running futilely, doomed to never reach him — always chasing, never catching.

'Pass the gravy, Grace,' her father requested. 'You've made a wonderful meal, Mrs Reece. Most pleasing,' he said to her mother, adding appeasingly, 'Delicious, just what the doctor ordered!' He smiled artificially at his joke, trying to cajole his wife to smile. Mrs Reece gave a taciturn half-smile.

Thin blood seeped out of the undercooked lamb and over the bridge, the sea, the pagoda and the hills on Grace's plate, then her mother slapped down a lump of grey mashed potato covering the tiny figures. Dinner finally began, although no one touched the meat, it being raw.

'What an utter waste of food! This shoulder of lamb cost good money,' her mother complained, addressing the empty seat, her voice high with annoyance. 'If I'd have known I wouldn't have bought it. I won't give Wilfred Price house room from now on.'

Grace, in earnest hope, was wearing her yellow dress again, believing the sight and memory of her clothing would inspire and ignite Wilfred's love and passion. Now she felt silly, pretending the lamb wasn't raw, eating dinner in yellow silk, with each mouthful she ate emptying her plate until more of the Willow Pattern and another unhappy family were exposed.

'You've had a long face on since we sat at the table, Grace Amelia; no wonder Wilfred doesn't want you with a face like that.'

Grace cut into a piece of honey-glazed carrot. She thought of the queen bee in her hive with her hundred, hundred lovers — all unswervingly devoted to her for the one whole summer of their short lives. But she wasn't a queen bee and Wilfred wasn't a drone.

'Grace Amelia, sit up properly. No man will ever look at you if you slouch like that.'

Perhaps Wilfred was held up by a sudden death, a body to collect, Grace thought, straightening her back.

'Would you think Wilfred has gone to collect a body?' her father asked, as if reading Grace's mind. He too, must be searching for a simple, practical answer as to why Wilfred wasn't here.

'Who could that be, now?'

Grace suspected her father was going through the names of his older and frailer patients. But it was unlikely, Grace knew, that there would be death in Narberth that her father didn't know about. Usually within minutes of someone dying people rushed to her father, rapping on the front door, calling out his name, even when it was obvious their loved one was dead, not ill. It was as if they hoped the doctor could do something, cure mortality the way he cured sickness.

'I don't know what I've done to deserve this,' her mother stated.

Grace squashed the cold leeks against the silver fork. The sense of insecurity that had resided in her these last few weeks now grew bigger and quivered within her and she felt nauseous.

'What will the explanation be, I wonder?' her father said aloud. 'What could it be?'

It was now late Thursday afternoon, lunch with her parents and without Wilfred was over, and the light was fading. Grace was watching Mrs Hilda Prout who, with a sense of ceremony, drew the heavy, tasselled drapes.

'Not a soul must see,' Mrs Prout mouthed, opening a portmanteau and taking from it an engraved box. Grace had heard rumours that Mrs Hilda Prout kept a crystal ball though no one Grace knew had ever actually seen it. Motes of dust leaped in the air as she opened the box and unwrapped a crimson scarf. Grace was surprised at how large the crystal ball was.

'There were whispers you had a crystal ball,' she remarked, crossing Mrs Prout's palm with silver. Mrs Prout held the ball in both hands as if it were a divine entity.

'I have had it since I was a small child — not that I used it then. My grandmother taught me to keep it hidden from human eyes and never gaze into it until I could endure a mystery. Until then, all one can see in a crystal ball is empty glass, fingerprints or nightmares . . . '

Mrs Hilda Prout put her face close to the ball, then closer still until her eyeball was against it. Grace winced squeamishly. Was Mrs Hilda Prout not right in the head? Many people came to visit her because she was a charmer and known in Narberth for curing warts by rubbing them with a live black snail while murmuring her rhyme,

Wart begone on this snail's back,
Go and never more come back.

Not that there was anything at all unusual about being a charmer. But crystal balls? They were for gypsies, not Welsh women who read the Bible and attended the Bethesda Chapel. Somewhere a door banged. Grace felt uneasy.

'I see you are now woman enough to keep a secret,' Mrs Hilda Prout stated, staring Grace straight in the eye, and Grace very slightly flinched.

This afternoon in Mrs Prout's darkened parlour with its wallpaper of trellis roses and the ornate Victorian furniture, Grace didn't think about what the Revd Waldo Williams would say. Grace wanted answers, certainty, and her future known. And she wanted normality. Mrs Prout had said she would marry Wilfred, and she wanted to hear her say it again — reassure her in clear, certain, straightforward words that she was loved by Wilfred and would be married to Wilfred; to know that everything somehow would be all right.

Mrs Prout rolled the ball in her hand until it was smudged and greasy with fingerprints. Did Mrs Hilda Prout already know about Grace's life and was now seeing some unknown future world with Grace in it, without Grace saying a word? Were there people who could grasp the truth, guess it, divine it, without being told?

Mrs Prout was hidden away from the bright world of science and modern medicine with its new vitamins and vaccines, and she earned her living charming shingles, warts, jaundice and dropsy. This was the ancient custom and it went unremarked upon and accepted in Narberth.

Grace asked self-consciously, 'What do you see?'

Mrs Hilda Prout ignored her and gazed into the depths of the ball, then blinked tightly.

'I was hoping to ask you about Wilfred Price . . . '

'Ah . . . your affianced. *'There is a willow grows aslant a brook'.'*

'Pardon?' asked Grace, not understanding. 'A willow? I don't understand.'

Mrs Prout stared intently at her. 'Were you expecting to understand?' she asked harshly, brushing her brittle grey hair back into its bun.

Grace didn't want riddles; she wanted a fact about the future, something she could hold on to, pin her hopes on.

Mrs Prout turned her back on Grace, wrapped the translucent orb in the scarf as if wrapping the relic of a saint, and locked it away in its case. She tucked the key down her bosom, drew back the curtains then sat down opposite the girl, saying nothing.

'I didn't hear from Wilfred . . . and . . . ' Grace desperately tried to explain. 'You said I would marry him.' There was a quivering note of panic in her voice but Mrs Prout ignored her.

'There's rain coming. I saw that.'

Grace didn't know how to respond. Is that all? she thought.

'Take your brolly. Don't forget.'

'Did you see anything in the crystal ball that

might . . . help me?' Near-hysteria was welling within her as her hopes were dashed.

'Yes, but there is very little to say about what I saw,' said Mrs Hilda Prout, 'except to say that all mothers are healers.'

★ ★ ★

'Grace, bach,' Dr Reece called gently that evening, knocking on his daughter's bedroom door. Grace watched her father come in. He looked ill at ease, which was unusual; she almost never saw him like that. As the only doctor in Narberth he was always the more confident one, the one who wasn't in pain, the one with all the answers. He never needed his patients the way his patients needed him.

'Grace . . . ?'

Grace was waiting for his answer, which she knew — as was his habit — he would provide.

'Would you take this?' he asked soberly.

There it was — the answer, Grace thought. He placed a blue bottle of medicine on her dressing-table, the bottle clanking loudly on the curved glass covering the dressing-table top. The bottle, with its viscous liquid, stood next to the gilded hand mirror her grandmother had given her when she was twelve. Dr Reece gently put his hand on his daughter's shoulder and left it there for a few moments.

'You may find it is of assistance,' he continued, 'for the heaviness you are experiencing.' He avoided her eyes and Grace looked at her patchwork quilt. What did her father know? She crushed the thought.

Once her father had left the room and she'd heard his solid footsteps on the stair linoleum, Grace picked up the bottle. It was unlabelled. Her father hadn't said how much to take. She could ask him, but she knew she wouldn't.

Grace thought of Mrs Prout's comment: she didn't know if all mothers were healers. Her mother? Her accusing, rejecting mother? No. When she or Madoc had been ill in childhood it was their father who paid a visit to W. Palmer Morgan, the apothecary, who waited while the pills were made and then who dispensed — with exactitude — the treatment. It was true that very occasionally it had been her mother who had wrapped the laddered silk stocking around her or her brother's neck when they had sore throats and who had lit the camphor lamp that burned through the night when Grace had tonsillitis, and had thrust teaspoons of Invalid Bovril into her mouth, but it had been at her father's instruction.

Mrs Hilda Prout was wrong — completely wrong. Her father, with his thick grey beard and piercing eyes, was the healer — not that he would have called himself such; he would think that word was mumbo-jumbo. A healer was what he would call 'antediluvian', whereas he, Dr M. H. Reece, MD, was a man of science, a man of rationality, a man of answers.

Grace held the cold, glass bottle in her hands and thought of her bees. There were those people who believed bee stings were medicine, people who covered themselves, leaving only their arthritic knees exposed before annoying a hive. The bees landed on their bare skin, stung it, and the arthritis was improved, cured even. But that was old medicine, not the modern twentieth-century science her father practised. What her father knew came from books. This bee remedy was learned from the garden and the forest, among the green leaves and the seeds and flowers. Doctors who studied text books would never believe that the insects and the lavender, the birch trees and the roses had something to teach them. Her father would think it was all nonsense. He'd say, 'It's all medieval mumbo-jumbo left over from the Dark Ages and the time of Pwyll. These people live as if the Age of Enlightenment had never happened.'

Grace didn't have a teaspoon in her bedroom so she unplugged the cork and took a swig, almost desperately, like a drunk. It tasted so bitter she retched, then forced herself to swallow again. Her eyes watered and her stomach convulsed. *Swallow. Just swallow*, she told herself. Mrs Hilda Prout was right: Grace kept a secret. But mothers as healers, that was beyond her experience — for now.

5

The Cove

Thursday morning was the first warm day of the year. No one had known where Flora was going. That was the joy of cycling away and not a soul in the whole world having a clue where she was. At the cove Flora could be silent and in solitude: there would only be the green sea and the endless parade of waves for company. Yes, she would bicycle to the cove and she would be restored.

Flora freewheeled down the last hill before the cove, taking her feet off the rubber pedals, her tin mudguards rattling noisily, her camera in her basket. Most people preferred Saundersfoot to the cove for its promenade of beachfront shops with the Welsh Dresser Bakery and the Lollipop Sweetshop, the sound of the accordion player with the monkey chained to his epaulette rising up, and there was Saundersfoot harbour with the blue and white fishing boats bobbing but anchored. The cove, though, was much quieter and most often Flora would have the whole wide bay with its scalloped sea entirely to herself.

She left her bicycle lying by the roadside, took her camera and clambered down the boulders on to the beach. This was perhaps the reason the cove was nearly always empty: it took

99

balance and dexterity to climb over the great granite stones that lay between the road and the sand. Flora, though, was deft at moving across them; she had been doing so since she was a child, when she would come here with her father. As a small girl wearing galoshes she had played in the stream by the crumbly cliffs, filling her bucket with sand and building dams while the crystal-clear water babbled down from springs in the hills and filled her wellingtons with icy water.

Flora began to walk across the cove towards Amroth, so as to forget the world, but inevitably she began to think of Albert. Most of the time she tried not to think of him and usually succeeded. But it was hard not to think of someone. When she told herself, 'I won't think of Albert,' he appeared in her mind's eye: his sandy hair with its attempt at a side-parting and the curls he tried to quash with hair oils. Albert in that spring and summer of 1918, when they were engaged, traipsing through fluid fields of grain before they were harvested, his trousers the same colour as the wheat. And his agility: walking backward, showing off, doing press-ups, jumping the stile. He climbed the Wych elm. He picked pears. Once she'd photographed him standing high in the branches of a cedar tree.

She remembered Albert laughing when he was swinging exuberantly on a rope swing and her sandal had flung off, making a large arc and landing in a bush. They'd searched in the green hedge, laughing, Albert reaching in and getting it. She remembered being free and alive then, with her shoe curving through the air purpose-fully. That was Albert unbuttoned.

Then there was her photograph of Albert holding his formal, military stance — but that was acquired, taught: Albert buttoned. She thought perhaps Mr and Mrs Bowen had been most proud of that Albert: backbone straight, unnaturally so, chest out, gold buttons arranged in groups of five on his uniform tunic, and the three-feathered plume in his bearskin cap. That was the young man she remembered from the silver-framed photograph, not the Albert she remembered from life. That young soldier hadn't been the only Albert. It still made her chest feel tight. So she wouldn't think about it.

A seagull landed nearby, accompanying her a few steps before flying away. Flora watched it disappear into the distance, and began looking in the sand for shells that she could photograph. It had been six years now since the telegram with its three short sentences. *Bang. Bang. Bang.* Like bullets.

Then there had been Christopher, Albert's friend in the winter of 1918, only four months later, sitting in his Welsh Guards' uniform on Mr and Mrs Bowen's settee, the teacup clattering in his shaking hands. She had listened mutely, intently, as had Mr and Mrs Bowen. Christopher said it had gone in his side. It had been very sudden. They were crouching, almost standing really and getting ready to go over the top of the trench. Albert was crouched lower. It had been unforeseen and very quick. Oh yes, Christopher was certain of that. It had been over in a moment, Mr and Mrs Bowen, Christopher could tell. There had been no suffering at all. None.

The room fell silent.

'That is a comfort to Mrs Bowen,' Mr Bowen said eventually.

'Yes,' Christopher replied. He stared into his teacup. He kept knocking the buttons of his uniform against the saucer with a clack. The Army doctor had said that the bullet had entered the liver and there could be 'no hope' — those were his words — 'for a man with a bullet in his liver,' Christopher said. Mr Bowen sat dumbly. Flora picked up the bone china teapot and offered Christopher more tea.

'No, thank you kindly; I'll be getting off now. Catching the train back to Swansea, you see. Got to get back before it's too late.'

'Oh yes, of course.' They understood. It had been very kind, too kind to mention, Christopher coming all this way to tell them, so that they would know there had been no pain at the end.

'A great reassurance,' Mr Bowen had said.

Flora sat on a rock, shook her hair and looked out at the still sea. She tried not to think about Albert and the life they would have had together, kept on trying to shake the shock and the sadness out of herself. For years it seemed as if her very bones had been glazed with grief, though she was becoming aware of a new warmth growing within her and the need to embrace life again.

★ ★ ★

It was Thursday and Wilfred was spending the day in his workshop. What was it with his customers, he wondered. Mrs Howell-Thomas's fingernails, poor bugger, hadn't seen a nailbrush for a while. It was hard washing a corpse's hand. Some cooperated but others lay there like a sack of potatoes with a look of consternation on their face, like a small child who didn't like being washed. Wilfred went to the door of the workshop to get a couple of breaths of fresh air, feeling grateful for the business Mrs Howell-Thomas had provided.

'Nails are in a bit of a state here, Mrs Howell-Thomas. Not like you, what with you keeping your house so spick and span.'

Mrs Howell-Thomas was certainly proving less compliant in death than she ever was in life. But it was like that. These elderly Welsh ladies who spent their life distributing hymn books at the door of the Bethesda Chapel and making lemon curd for the Harvest Festival — as soon as they popped their clogs, that was it, couldn't get them to do anything you wanted. Christian values went out the window once they'd kicked the bucket.

And what was he going to do about that ring? It wouldn't budge. The *rigor mortis* had faded and all the fluids had sunk to the bottom of the body, turning Mrs Howell-Thomas the usual waxy colour associated with the recently deceased. It was a pleasant shade of mushroomy-white and the colour that meant that, when the family saw the departed, they were under no illusion that their dearly departed had indeed departed. It was the colour that proclaimed 'dead'.

'Daughter coming this afternoon, Mrs Howell-Thomas,' Wilfred said slowly and loudly, as if the deceased were deaf. 'We want you to look nice for her.'

The air was getting a bit rich in here; he'd have to get the viewing done early this afternoon, then nail down the lid as soon as he could. He opened the workshop window.

'Bit hot in here today, isn't it?' he remarked.

Hopefully after the viewing the family would say that the deceased 'looked at peace'. 'Indeed, indeed,' Wilfred would answer meaningfully. It was essential for business, Wilfred knew, that the dead must look at peace, rather than rotting. So he 'did the necessary', as Mr Auden delicately phrased it. It meant the deceased didn't smell and the coffin didn't leak. A dab of face powder, sometimes a shave, even a smear of lipstick — and dentures; dentures were always essential — and the faces of most were palatable. An undertaker was in the business of lying about death. Even the poor devils who had passed away in great pain from cancer looked at peace once Wilfred had finished with them. Those corpses smelled — especially the ladies with tumours on their breasts, like a bunch of big, black grapes. Of course, *nobody*, least of all the undertaker, ever revealed that a person had passed away with cancer. It was a terrible secret, because if the neighbours knew they would be terrified of catching it.

Peering into Mrs Howell-Thomas's coffin, he

realised he wasn't going to be able to get that damn ring off. He looked more closely at her fingers which were already purple and bloated, and wondered if Howard Carter had had this problem with Tutankhamun.

'There was a tomb that Tutankhamun had!' he remarked to Mrs Howell-Thomas. 'Absolutely magnificent!'

'What are you talking about in there, Wilfred?' said his da, who was sitting on the flowerbed wall, drinking his tea. 'Are you talking to a corpse again?'

'Oh! Da . . . Just about to touch up the coffin with some varnish. Just thinking about how magnificent it will look . . . when the varnish is on,' Wilfred said, poking his head out of the workshop door.

'There we are then,' said his da, somewhat sceptically.

'Varnish is magnificent,' Wilfred added self-consciously.

'Oh yes. It is.' There was a pause.

'Better be getting on,' said Wilfred.

He leaned on the coffin, stumped as to what to do with the ring. It was on his mind that he had to go to lunch at the Reeces' on Saturday. He would call around and speak to Dr Reece later and explain the engagement was off. Grace must have been, understandably, too frightened to explain to her mother and father what had happened. She no doubt felt humiliated — no one ever liked being unwanted. He sighed. He wasn't looking forward to it, but it must be done. In fact, he was dreading it, which was why he'd procrastinated. It would be that much easier all round to send a note. Grace wouldn't have to see him and have the rejection compounded; a visit might add insult to injury. Perhaps he would pop a note through the door this evening. Wilfred knew he would have to act soon.

He looked at Mrs Howell-Thomas's wedding ring. It was made of reddish Welsh gold and half a century of wearing had scratched and rubbed it smooth. It was part of Mrs Howell-Thomas's body now, like her marriage had been part of her life, and it belonged to her and was with her in death and, as in life, she would not forsake or relinquish her husband. It was often like this with old ladies, that he couldn't remove the thin, clogau gold band that had been given to them on their wedding day, at some point in the last century. They had put it on as a quivering and smooth-skinned maiden standing at the altar, and they had never, ever taken it off again.

'Excuse me, Mrs Howell-Thomas, while I . . . ' he commented as he jammed soap under the ring. Then he rubbed the finger with castor oil and finally engine lubricant, but it wouldn't budge. Mrs Howell-Thomas, so compliant in life, so stubborn in death! Ruddy ring was stuck tight. Wilfred gave it a final tug but nothing was doing. He would just have to mention to her daughter later — in the most delicate terms — that the ring was stuck fast on the deceased's third finger and wouldn't come off, even with quite a lot of force applied.

He could say, perhaps, 'In preparing the body

106

of your dear, departed mother it would seem that Mrs Howell-Thomas's finger has bloated up dreadfully . . . ' No. Perhaps, 'Your mother has ended her pilgrimage and entered eternal peace still devoted to your father, and as a sign of her everlasting devotion she has chosen to be reunited in heaven with her beloved Mr Howell-Thomas still wearing her wedding ring.' That sounded like a bit of a fib to Wilfred, especially as Mrs Howell-Thomas and her husband had argued hammer and tongs. But he didn't want to suggest hacking off the finger, although that was an option which the very poor would sometimes choose. Usually relatives liked to pretend the deceased were still alive, only sleeping. And one would never want to cut off the finger of a sleeping person; you just wouldn't do it.

'The bereaved, Wilfred, want to be spared the details of their loved one's corpse,' Mr Ogmore Auden had stated. 'Talk about the deceased as if they were alive and kicking. Don't let on they're dead, dripping, dribbling and smelling in the workshop. Dress them up in their Sunday best and act as if you've got them round for tea. No one wants to know about their mother's anal cork, Wilfred.'

'Yes, Mr Auden,' Wilfred replied, flabbergasted. So Wilfred had learned to soften over the details of death, to ease the grief for those left behind so they could move from the memory of their departed when they were warm, alive and at home, to — after the funeral — imagining them sitting in an armchair, drinking tea or perhaps tending a garden in those ever-illuminated Welsh hills of heaven.

* * *

All of a sudden, Flora woke. She reached for her alarm clock and it rattled lazily. Three o'clock exactly. She lay back between the sheets, under the blankets, and moved her legs to loosen the bedding. It was inconvenient to be wide-awake in the middle of the night and she would be drowsy tomorrow, not that she had anything much to do apart from wandering around the darkened house, waiting for the months of mourning to pass, although she could take some photographs, perhaps of the aspens. As her eyes adjusted to the dark her pictures on the wall slowly emerged, the photographs delineated by their elegant black frames. She knew why she had awoken. She only roused in the middle of the night when the deepest part of herself wanted to be listened to.

It was that man, Wilfred Price. He had smelled of Brylcreem and something spicy; he had the scent of a formally dressed man. He had touched her arm. Had he touched her lower back? He had put his hand near there, a couple of inches away — though it had felt as if he touched her. She lifted up her nightie and put her own hand there in the gentle curve of her lower spine. It might have felt like this, she thought, only his hand would have been stronger, more powerful. He had square nails. Flora had noticed his hands with their reddish

108

hue, watched how they'd steered the car.

He could have put one hand on the small of her back and then he could have put his other hand . . . where could he have put his other hand? Where would she have liked him to lay his hand? *Here*, she realized with a shock. But then they would have had to stand close to each other, near enough for him to be able to touch her breast. If he had bent down slightly, their hair would have brushed. And where would this happen? In the transept of St Andrew's Church? At her father's funeral? The reality of her grief came to her, slapped her, chilled her. Flora moved to lie on her side, smoothing her nightdress back down over her hips, then tugged the blankets up. Death felt so close to her; close as a small child peering into her face, too close.

Ribbons of moonlight rippled through the gap in the curtains and her photographs of the cove were rendered visible. Despite her grief, she could still feel this feeling, one she didn't think she would ever have again after Albert died. This feeling was like a thinly woven thread within her, was the desire to see and to be with this man again.

★   ★   ★

On Saturday lunchtime, Wilfred knocked on the door of the first cottage in the row: if it wasn't this one then it must be the other one because they were both pictured in the postcard.

'No,' the woman who answered the door said. She wiped dough off her hands on to her apron.

'No one has gone to meet the Good Lord in Amroth.' The woman was holding a battered spatula in her swollen hand and Wilfred could smell Welsh cakes; she would have heated up the family bake stone and be making cakes for the Sabbath.

'No. I don't know anything about that now,' she said warily, pushing her thin grey hair behind her ears. She was uncomfortable, as if Wilfred was the Grim Reaper turning up unannounced and asking her to bring out her dead.

'But I'm to pick up a body at the cottage in the cove. A message was sent,' Wilfred replied.

'The cottage? You mean the one at the top of the hill? That's been empty these last — oh, six or seven years. You'll not find anyone up there, by damn; they're all long dead and gone. Buried already! Are you certain you've got the right address?' she asked.

'I don't know,' Wilfred replied. 'I'd better get up there and see if I can find out what's happening. Thank you for your help, mind.'

Wilfred knew the cottage the woman meant. It had run to rack and ruin and used to belong to a father and son who'd not come back from the Front. The mother had died a while back — probably of heartbreak, Wilfred thought. That was very common, to die of a broken heart — he saw it often in his work. The husband went first, quick as a flash, then the wife followed, sometimes a year to the day. Most often — Wilfred didn't know why — it was two years later that the wife got sick and gave up the flesh.

Wilfred left the Super Ford at the roadside

and walked up the hill and through the copse. It was a slippery, muddy path and he had to concentrate on balancing. The light was flickering through the new leaves. There were many bluebells, daffodils and yellow primroses. Butterflies flitted around the nettles. Someone had called to him, Wilfred realized as he trudged up the hill. The front door of the cottage was lime-washed green but the paint was now bubbled and flaked. He pushed the door open and there, sitting in the dusky light among the grass and moss and dandelions that were growing through the damp earth in the now ownerless and empty cottage, was Flora. Flora, whose father he'd buried this last month, whose mother had forbidden him to take tea with her. It was Flora who had called him. He was startled all over again by her beauty. She looked vulnerable sitting on the ground; it was her courage, Wilfred realized, in asking him here that was making her vulnerable.

Wilfred opened his mouth to say something then understood that this wasn't a time for talking. Flora had initially met his eyes but was looking away now. How could a woman, Wilfred marvelled, be so demure and so desirable all at the same time? A man could never do that. And what should he do? It was slightly chilly so he took off his suit jacket and walked the few steps towards the blanket; Flora moved over to make space for him. Before sitting beside her, he placed his jacket gently over her shoulders. They sat for a moment while the door of the cottage rattled in the wind. Wilfred got up to secure it with a large stone that lay near the entrance — he could barely keep still because he was so excited. He sat down again.

He turned to Flora. Flora met his gaze and he gently put his hand to her hair and stroked it until the clip of her silver earring came undone and the earring fell on to the blanket by her leg. Wilfred picked it up carefully and put it in Flora's hand. This is the first time I am touching her hand, he thought.

Wilfred positioned himself round and lay back, suggesting with the pull of his hands that Flora lie down with him. She lay down willingly. Now Wilfred was on his back and Flora was on her side, her head on his shoulder, and in his arms.

Wilfred traced the outline of her ear beneath her hair. Stroking her hair he was reminded of a poem he had learned at school by that Welsh priest, Manley Gerald Hopkins — was that his name? — no, that wasn't right. The poem had a line he liked, *Every hair is, hair of the head, numbered*. He remembered it again.

I walked into a cottage and the woman I am so drawn to was waiting for me and she has lain down with me, Wilfred thought. He could feel the swift beat of Flora's heart against his chest. This beautiful, raw woman still in her mourning clothes, had called him. He lay there stroking her hair, which was smooth and fine. Perhaps it is me, he thought, who has died, and gone to heaven.

★ ★ ★

Flora lay in Wilfred's arms and breathed in the male smell of his black woollen waistcoat and the spiciness of his hair oil. His arms were solid around her. She hadn't intended to lie on her back, or even lie down at all, but when he pulled her down she went down with him; lay with him, close to him. Flora noticed how Wilfred breathed regularly: inhaling, then exhaling confidently. This man was not Albert, but this man was alive. This is Wilfred, Flora thought. Beyond that, she knew very little about him, the barest facts — that he was the undertaker from Narberth. Flora had a sense of him and that was enough: his mind was alive, questioning, forging, deciding, and she knew instinctively that she was safe with him.

Lying there with Wilfred there were so many possibilities, so many ways they could go. Flora rested serenely, safely, waiting to see what would happen.

★   ★   ★

When they had left the cottage at the end of the afternoon, Wilfred stood to the side of the doorway and let Flora go out first. Then he had pulled the door to, using some force so as to close it completely and Flora, serenely, shyly, without speaking, had got on her bicycle and cycled away quickly, down the muddy lane, past the hazelnut trees and bluebells and back on to the empty road. Behind her she heard the sound of the engine spluttering and the car driving away along the deserted road in the other

113

direction. She wondered if Wilfred would come to the cove again.

When she reached the road she stopped, pushed her hair from her face and was struck by a thought: why did she like this man? Why Wilfred and not another? Flora didn't know. There were many men: the two men she had loved, her father and Albert, both now dead. There were other men, the boys in Stepaside with whom she'd gone to school, the farmers' sons who had brought their horses to her father for shoeing, young men at church. And all the men who had been killed not so long ago, whose names were chiselled on the new war memorial, each letter precise and neat, every name representing a young man and a whole world that had come and gone. All those men. So why Wilfred? And why now, in this dislocation between her father being dead and Flora feeling peaceful about his death?

She began to cycle past Wisemans Bridge, steadily at first then harder and faster, almost as hard as when she had raced to the post office when her father had collapsed, only this time she felt alive, not panicked. It had been years since she had felt this exhilarated. She held the handlebars tightly, feeling her strength. It was windy and the air was carouselling around her.

My father is dead, Albert is dead, but I am alive, she told herself. She forced her hands around the rubber handlebars and dug her thumbnails into the skin of her first fingers, stood up on the pedals, pushing down furiously with all her might. The wind was surging into her. Her face flushed and she kept shaking her head to fling strands of hair out of her eyes. Her lips tasted tangy from the sea air. She could feel her pulse beating in her wrists. She wanted to throw back her head and scream it all out, all the suppressed passions and frustrations of those quiet, deathly years without Albert. She wanted to scream away the dull, dusty deathliness that had befuddled her mind and coddled her body when, all along, she had been surrounded by the sea, endless plashy waves, the great sky, the sharp rocks and the smooth pebbles — though she had seen or felt none of it. She glanced around but there was no one to be seen so she threw back her head, lunged down on the pedals, looked up at the crystal blueness of the sky and said aloud with abandon and certainty.

'I am alive!'

She cycled wildly until she reached the middle of the cove, where she stopped, took her camera and pointed it at the sea and the sky, framing the immense seascape for a photograph. Framing the view, she remembered the postcard she had sent Wilfred, a photograph of this beach, with its unadorned message: *The cottage, the cove, Saturday*. The postcard had been a seed, like a plum stone — small, hard, and capable of so much — planted in fertile ground. Perhaps, with time and patience, the seed would grow into a blossoming and fruit-bearing tree. She had taken a risk, hoped for happiness, something beyond grief. She clicked the shutter and took the photograph.

Flora turned her bracelet around on her wrist.

If Wilfred came to her, if he came to the cottage next Saturday, she would respond, she would be present with him, talk with him, be alive with him, together, in the world of living people and green trees and warm houses, busy shops and tended farms.

★ ★ ★

Wilfred snipped the advertisement from the *Radio Times* with a pair of nail scissors. This was just the thing! What an invention! A wireless set you could walk around with in your arms while listening to the British Broadcasting Corporation. Who ever had thought of that? Heck, people were clever these days. He looked at the illustration again. Mind, the wireless looked quite a weight. He'd have to walk with it, he couldn't run, but nevertheless, he could now take a leisurely drive to Tenby after a day in the workshop and sit on a blanket on the west beach with the Pye Portable Radio next to him and listen to the *Six o'Clock News* broadcast. He could scarcely believe such a thing was possible. He was awed.

'What's that you're reading there, boy bach?' his father asked, coming into the kitchen.

'Da, you'll be surprised when I tell you about this. A wireless set you can walk around with.'

'Well, I'll be damned,' his father answered, putting his cap down on the dictionary. Wilfred read on. The advertisement declared the Pye Portable Radio was for *the strong and silent type*. Wilfred thought he could be the strong and

116

silent type; he was certainly silent when he was listening to the radio, and he could be described as strong, what with carrying all those caskets.

'What poor fool would be wanting one of them, then?' his da asked, reading the advertisement over Wilfred's shoulder. 'Nothing wrong with a wireless sitting on the sideboard. Who'd want to walk around carrying a great big thing like that? More bloody noise, all the time. What is the world coming to! Cup of tea, Wilfred?'

'There's fresh in the pot, Da.'

'Wilfred, are you taking it into your head to get one of those radios? Get away with you! You're like a fart in a colander.'

Wilfred looked at the advertisement again. His da had a point. Wirelesses were very heavy — but the man in the drawing was swinging the portable radio in one hand: he looked very dapper and not at all burdened.

'Perhaps these newfangled radios don't weigh much,' Wilfred remarked hopefully.

'Mark my words,' said his father, looking for a teacup in the sink, 'it would be easier walking around with a coffin. Look, it says here it weighs thirty-one pounds.'

Thirty-one pounds was certainly quite a weight, Wilfred thought to himself, though he was easily strong enough to carry it. But he didn't want to be plodding around Narberth with the wireless set. He was going to place it in the back of the motorized hearse — when there wasn't a body in it — then drive to the cove and take the wireless into the cottage and they . . .

Flora and he . . . would have music. Well, it occurred to Wilfred, they might have music. And dance. Mind, they would have to meet when a music programme was being broadcast. He would need to look at the *Radio Times* to check. It would be no good if it were the news broadcast on the airwaves. He didn't want the Prime Minister's voice in the background when he was lying on the blanket with Flora — that wouldn't do at all. No, one couldn't hold a young lady with Mr Ramsay MacDonald droning on about the Labour Party in the background. The Prime Minister in London was a sober and important man but his voice wasn't conducive to kissing. Wilfred didn't know much about these things but he knew that much.

★   ★   ★

The following Saturday when Wilfred entered the cottage, Flora was standing. Wilfred had pictured her resting on the blanket again, but this time she was standing in the centre of the cottage, wearing a simple linen dress, her dark brown hair held high on her head. And she was here, she had come. The message had said, *The cottage, the cove, Saturday.* Wilfred had hoped, rightly, that the message meant more than just that one, first Saturday last week.

'Hello, Flora,' he said, and he was surprised by the sound of his own voice. Last Saturday she had been mute apart from a gentle, 'Oh,' when her earring had fallen into her lap. She had neither greeted Wilfred nor bade him farewell.

118

She had sat serenely and patiently and then left by bicycle.

'Hello, Wilfred.' Her voice was fresh and cool with a strong Welsh lilt. They could speak to each other! Wilfred realized. There could be even more than the rich silence they had when they met before. There was a whole world of talking to Flora. But then there was a pause, a silence after the enormity of their first words — and the silence moved into awkwardness as Wilfred tried to think of something to say. It was a charged pause, difficult to shift. Now they had spoken to each other once, it was possible, necessary and natural that they should speak again. But what to say?

Wilfred's mind reeled, increasingly panicked. He knew the men in the Rugby Club would have suggestions: 'Make a joke,' the lads said. 'Make her laugh and take her dancing.' It seemed good advice, but this wasn't a dance in the Queen's Hall and Wilfred didn't know many jokes — cracking jokes wasn't part of the undertaking trade. He could only ever remember two riddles: What's the difference between an onion and an accordion? No one cries when you cut up an accordion. And: What's got a mouth but can't talk? A letterbox. No, thought Wilfred, that wasn't funny at all. And Flora might think it was rather an odd thing to say, like that, out of the blue: 'Hello, Flora. What's got a mouth but can't talk?' Flora might think he was a bit deranged, not quite the round shilling.

As an undertaker he liked to be able to have something to say at solemn occasions and this was a momentous occasion. But it wasn't a funeral. Wilfred was beginning to realize that the profession of undertaker wasn't much use to him when it came to matters of romance.

'Hello, Flora,' he repeated. It wasn't a very imaginative piece of conversation, but then he heard himself say it again: 'Hello, Flora.' A third time! His self-consciousness grew to enormous proportions. She would think there was something wrong with him. With nothing to say for himself! And him owning a business! He glanced at her and saw that she was smiling and there was a warmth in her deep-set brown eyes.

'Hello, Wilfred.' They smiled at each other and Wilfred took in Flora's beauty. It was difficult not to stare; the soft down on the nape of her neck, the gentle way her body was held together and the silkiness of her. She was so lovely, he thought.

Wilfred reached out and placed his hand around Flora's shoulder. Then he stood beside her, accidentally bumping her slightly. It was difficult for men — he knew this because he had thought about it — to touch women gently and easily. Men's bodies were for rugby, for great, big, clumpy movements and bashing into people. And he, like most men, had large hands. Craftsmen made intricate objects with their hands, he himself did dovetail joints on coffins, but compared to the refined quality of Flora's downy skin and the grace of her body, his hands would always be large and clumsy, his touch would always seem butterfingered. Women — apart from the really old, fat ones, and the ones from Carmarthenshire — were nearly always daintier than men. With Flora he felt like a dog trying to touch a china figurine with its paws. But Flora was smiling; she liked his hand stroking her arm, self-conscious though Wilfred's gestures were.

When Flora spoke, Wilfred was startled all over again.

'I have my blanket.' She went to the fireplace where there, as before, was the same simple cream blanket buckled in a leather strap. She leaned down and began to unroll the blanket, placing it on the floor then smoothing it with the palms of her hands. Wilfred saw it for what it was: an invitation.

Wilfred knew the recently bereaved sometimes wanted to take a lover immediately. Or else they wanted a dispute. Some of them, the drinkers especially, looked for fisticuffs. This was not something Mr Ogmore Auden had talked to Wilfred about — it would have been undignified. Mr Auden had maintained a discreet silence about the matter, but it was well-known in the undertaking trade in Pembrokeshire that some young widows — and he was sure it was the same for widowed husbands — needed love, reassurance, affection and sometimes something more, and would seek it out and accept it much sooner than people would imagine.

Wilfred felt moved by this: the very human need to be held and to be intimate. As an undertaker, he saw that the recently bereaved needed to feel they were still alive, that their body and sensibilities hadn't died along with their loved one. And while the Scripture said, *In the midst of life we are in death* — something Wilfred had heard repeated many times in funeral services — it was also true, Wilfred knew from his work, that in the midst of death we are alive. And what better way to know that and feel it in one's living body than by sexual congress? The newly bereaved know that instinctively, Wilfred thought.

Wilfred understood. He didn't judge it. The bereaved were a lost and broken community, and making love would — must — help them find their way back to life. Flora, Wilfred knew, belonged among them. She had the white face, chilled fingers and the sad eyes that the recently bereaved had for the first few months. She was open and broken because her father had passed away. She needed gentleness and affection, and she needed to be held, and he wanted to give her whatever she asked him for.

6

Half in Leaf, Half on Fire

'What are you doing up there, Grace Amelia?' Grace's mother called shrilly.

'Reading, Mother.'

Grace had never stood on a book before. She'd been taught not to fold over the corners of the pages but to use her leather book-mark with the picture of St David's Cathedral embossed on it, and also never to break the spine despite the satisfying crack it made as the glue broke and, while nobody had told her so, she knew putting her feet on books was unconscionable: equal probably only to burning them, something that had happened during the Crusades, a long time ago, in darker, more violent times. Imagine burning books — they were so precious, more so than herself. She would take her shoes off first; that would make it somewhat better, but her parents would be shocked, nevertheless, that she had stood on books.

Grace took some volumes from the shelf and placed them in a small, exact pile. She looked up at the ceiling beam, calculating its height: six books — two piles of three — on the dressing-table should be enough. She was going to choose very carefully. The books she would put her feet on were important; they would be the ones she stood for and the ground she stood on. She looked at her bookshelf, reading the spines. *Jane Eyre?* Jane Eyre was well intentioned, just in difficult circumstances. *People in History?* Boudicca was Amazonian and strong-armed, riding her chariot and fighting for freedom. There was Madoc's copy of *Beekeeping: A Discussion of the Life of the Honeybee and of the Production of Honey* by Everett Franklin Phillips, Ph.D? George Bernard Shaw's new play, *Saint Joan?* But Joan of Arc was impossibly pure, and a martyr. *This Side of Paradise* — Madoc's friend Sidney had given her that.

Then there were her childhood books: *Anne of Green Gables, Heidi, What Katy Did Next, Pollyanna* — stories about girls who were good. All Pollyanna had ever done wrong was ruin her parasol. Beth in *Little Women* was so perfect she was only fit for heaven. Why were girls in novels exemplary, almost saintly? Grace preferred adventure stories, histories and romances about what to do if you were damned and female, tales about women who were kind, likeable and believable, who escaped unpunished. No thin Quakers with lace caps. No beatific consumptives coughing delicately. No unloved, eternally jolly orphans. Grace craved books about girls like herself: good women, normal women in a world bigger and more powerful than themselves.

Suddenly a fragment of memory burst into her mind. She heard herself speaking in an urgent, desperate whisper, so frightened her parents would overhear what she was saying and equally terrified he wouldn't hear her. '*No, no, don't, please don't!'* she pleaded. *'Please don't, please don't, please don't!'* They were in the bedroom. Next to the *stairs!* Her mother and father came up the stairs. He was here again, charming, neat, handsome, personable, his shoes squeaking on the linoleum. *'Please, oh please don't!'* That was all she had said. And she had meant it, *really* meant it. Perhaps he thought she hadn't meant it — or didn't care. And while it was happening to her, what filled her mind's eye was the brown wallpaper: she focused on the intertwining lines of the raised shapes, she saw the exact tone of the slick, dark brown paint on the paper and the delicate six-petalled daisy trapped in the arms of one square of Anaglypta.

'Grace Amelia!' her mother squalled from downstairs, interrupting Grace's thoughts. 'You've been up there too long; you'd better be doing something productive. I'm going to the Mothers' Union Thursday Club for the afternoon. And I'm expecting you to have finished knitting those dishcloths before I get back.'

'Yes, Mother.'

Grace heard the front door click and her mother walk out. The house was empty. She took the jar of cold cream and talcum powder from her dressing-table and put them on to the floorboards, then dragged the dressing-table into the middle of the room so it was hard against the bed. There was a dead bee under the dressing-table, so she picked up its weightless, papery body and dropped it out of the top of the sash window. A memory came to her as if on a wave and she felt herself overcome with its reality. And shock. She would not, *would not* think of it.

If she pushed the dressing-table to the left . . . she'd have to take the glass cover off first otherwise it would be slippy . . . Would the piece of furniture take her weight? The pile of books needed to be high enough and level — one more big book should do it. She remembered her copy of *The Mabinogion* and took it out of the drawer in her bedside cabinet where it was always kept. *The Mabinogion*, the very first Welsh book, began with a story in Narberth. When she took that step off the dressing-table, right under her feet would be the book she loved most. She dusted the wine-red cover then opened it at the first page and read, *And he saw a tall tree by the side of the river, one half of which was on fire, from the root to the top, and the other half was green and in full leaf.* Grace felt like the tree in *The Mabinogion*, the one that had stood by Narberth Castle nine hundred years ago, the tree that was half on fire and half in green leaf. That was how she felt, both burned and oddly budding.

Then again, in her mind's eye, she saw the wallpaper. She blinked tightly, desperate to crush the memory away. She tried extremely hard never to think of those moments but it happened without her wanting to. And it was impossible for her to think clearly about anything to do with it, except that she must be the only person in Narberth, in Pembrokeshire, perhaps in the whole world, to have this happen to her. Her face was pushed against the paper on the wall; she saw the intricate daisy held safe and sound in the square. It was a square with rounded corners. A perfect memory of one patterned square. She knew it had happened because she remembered the bedroom wallpaper. It was true but it wasn't convincing. It wouldn't stand up in Narberth courthouse:

'*What do you remember of the event in question?*'

'*I know it happened because I remember the wallpaper.*'

'*What else do you remember?*'

'*Only the wallpaper.*' No one would be sent to Swansea Prison because of the memory of wallpaper.

The six books were chosen now. She placed them in two piles in the middle of her dressing-table. From its drawer she took a silk scarf. The midnight-blue fabric was beautifully, imperceptibly woven; it seemed almost impossible that thread could be so fine and that a craftsman — or probably a machine — could weave it so delicately. She had been given this neck scarf by her nana for her twenty-first birthday, had chosen it herself from the display in the shop window at Mrs Hewyll Russell's Haberdasher's & Draper's, liking the white fleur-de-lys against the blackish-blue background. She wore it when she wanted to feel like an adult, a woman, and appear more sophisticated, more knowing, than she felt.

The practicalities were proving more awkward than she had imagined. Her silk scarf felt sleek in her hands and she was concerned the knot wouldn't hold — she had washed the scarf two days ago for this purpose and it was very silky. What if the knot slipped out? Should she sew the scarf around the beam — Grace wasn't sure she would be able to reach that high — and would the stitches even hold? Grace didn't want to put stitches in her beautiful neck scarf, didn't want to pierce the finely woven fabric that her nana had bought for her. Did she need rope instead?

Grace picked up the Lily of the Valley talcum powder from the floorboards and twisted the lid open and shut. She didn't have a choice. Secrecy wasn't possible, her body wouldn't allow it and it was naïve to think so. She had hoped for a few weeks that perhaps she would have some luck — but her luck was lousy. It was not that she wanted to die; it was that she didn't know how to endure what was now her life. She wouldn't think about what she was going to do, she would just do it.

There was the verse in John, chapter eight, *And ye shall know the truth, and the truth shall set you free.* Her mother had embroidered it as a sampler and it hung in an unvarnished frame opposite her parents' iron bed. What if Grace told the truth? Her mother would scream — if she didn't die of shock. Or kill Grace. What would the neighbours say? No one would believe her. And if they did, they would tell her to lie. Say she'd gone mad. It was more than people could sympathize with, too real for people to bear. And too real for her to endure.

She held the scarf to her face and breathed in the faint aroma of lavender from the muslin bag of dried flowers she kept among her clothes. Perhaps Wilfred . . . ? If she told Wilfred, would he understand? He had loved her once, if only for an afternoon. Grace had tried to be light and airy for Wilfred, to pretend that she, her situation, was simple when the truth was bleak, complex and barely utterable, never mind explicable. And if she explained, would anyone, anyone, understand? Her world would be different if she knew that only one person would understand.

Grace took *Moll Flanders* from the bottom of the neat pile on the dressing-table and sat in the window seat, scrunched herself up tightly and opened the book randomly but soon put it down by her stockinged feet, unable to read. A desk, six books and a silk scarf. Or honesty. It was a stark choice. 'Speak plainly,' was what her father said to his patients as they struggled to explain their symptoms when they were embarrassed, ashamed and guilty. 'Speak plainly so that I can understand.' Perhaps, then, her father would have an answer — he seemed to have an answer to a hundred illnesses. But to this? Did this happen anywhere else? Surely not in Narberth.

There must be an answer. There must be a way out.

Grace looked up to the ceiling and the creosoted beam above her dressing-table. There was a way out in the roof. She climbed on to the dressing-table. *I will lift up mine eyes to the Lord from whence cometh my help*. Is that what King David meant: a pile of books on a dressing-table and a silk scarf around a beam?

Wilfred's da had work to do. He looked around at the graves in St Andrew's churchyard, many of which he had dug. Gravedigging required strength, a cheerful disposition and a robust state of mind. Wilfred's da had taken to it over twenty years ago, enjoying the toil of digging the earth whether it was frozen in the winter or full of rainwater in the spring. He felt at peace in the graveyard with its view of the green curvaceous hills.

As he began digging he thought of his wife — Wilfred's mother — who had died after giving birth to their son. Wilfred's da didn't know a woman, least of all his quietly spoken wife, could make sounds like that — the screams and the bellowing — for almost five hours. He had waited in the kitchen and then in the yard listening to her. At ten past six in the morning his wife's screams had been replaced by Wilfred's crying, and then for four endless days, his wife's incessant moaning for water, finally followed by the quiet of her death room, overlaid by the mewling of the small baby. His sister, Blodwen, had given Wilfred goat's milk from a glass bottle and the baby had sucked vigorously. 'He wants to be alive,' he said in Welsh to Blodwen, and then to his tiny son, 'you suck like you want to live.' Wilfred had learned all this from his Auntie Blodwen who had been at both his birth and his mother's death.

After his wife's death, Wilfred's da had been a broken man, at a loss as to how to live and go on

130

without his wife beside him. It had taken a good two or three years, until Wilfred was up and toddling about, before his father had been able to find a way forward. By day his father worked as a labourer on Clunderwen Farm, but at night he would go and visit his wife, sitting tranquilly by her grave. It gave him a sense of peace and soothed his grief, which was more intense and painful than anything he had ever known. It was during these nights that he met the gravedigger, a now elderly man of fifty-nine; too old to do his work well. The gravedigger had befriended his father, understanding as he did the nature of grief — his father hadn't been the first person to sit through the night by the granite gravestone of a loved one — and accustomed to the solemnity and madness of the bereaved. Wilfred's father had begun to help the older man to cut the sod and dig the graves, and had eventually taken over the position himself when the gravedigger's arthritic spine prevented him from working.

Wilfred's da felt blessed, as he dug the new grave, to like his work. He toiled in the day tending to the grass and the hedgerows in the graveyard but he liked to dig graves at night by moonlight, to be free and alone with the stars and the planets. He took satisfaction in being outside, casting an eye for Cassiopeia or the three stars in Orion's belt, and was pleased when he recognized the familiar and distinctive light reflected by Jupiter. Every couple of months he borrowed *The Constellations of the Stars for the Enthusiastic Amateur* by Ferdinand Nell from the Mechanics' Institute Library, each time

131

reading about a different constellation then searching for it in the night sky, mapping it out and watching it, over the months, cross the heavens.

When there was a death in Narberth or Templeton, as there was earlier today, he would go unbeckoned, the wind flapping at his coat, a lantern on a stick, to the graveyard at St Andrew's and measure the plot. He left home at nine o'clock at night, after a pint in Mrs Annie Evans's public house the Conduit, then dug until four o'clock in the morning. It took him seven hours — one, he said, for every age of man — never less, never more. He would put an hour of sweat into the earth for every decade of a man's — or woman's — allotted time in the world whether the deceased had had a full lifespan or not. It was different for a child; a child's grave never took long.

Wilfred's da knew this earth, he knew the different textures of the soil in the graveyard: where the roots of the blackberry bushes matted the mud, where the whitethorn grew, how the shale at the bottom of the graveyard was waterlogged in spring and mottled with moss. He was acquainted with where the magpies nested, where the red squirrels built their drays and where the moles would likely make their crumbly molehills. He remembered when to expect the swarms of swallows and the murmurations of starlings and he watched the swifts flicking and dashing, marvelling at how — some birdwatchers said — they could stay airborne for years without landing once.

132

From his work, Wilfred's da carried the aura of death about him, more so even than Wilfred, and for that reason some of the town's inhabitants slightly shunned him, were wary of him, as if by conversing with him they would need his services sooner rather than later, for surely he would be the one who would dig their graves. Sometimes the simpler folk in Narberth even confused him, in their mind's eye, with the Grim Reaper, despite the Grim Reaper being of an altogether different nature. People were shocked, especially the young, that the gravedigger was not horrified and terrified, the way they were, by the empty, pitch-dark graveyard at night. 'If the buggers didn't hurt me when they were alive they won't hurt me when they're dead,' he told anyone who had the courage to ask if he was frightened. That was true — to an extent, the person who had asked the question would think. But what about the other worlds — the Afterworld and the Underworld — didn't they swim around in graveyards? And weren't all graveyards populated by corpses? Sometimes dancing corpses?

For over several decades, Wilfred's father had dug many graves, from the very tiniest to the grandest, cutting into the earth with certainty and precision to shape with the blade of his spade the grave's four edges. The spade's ash handle was worn smooth by his hands and kept oiled by the grease and sweat from his palms. It was an old tool but they were the best ones, his da knew. It was made of cast steel from the steelworks in Flintshire and, of a morning after a night of digging, Wilfred's da would, without fail, fill a pail with icy water from the water pump opposite the Conduit Stores and wash the blade and shaft with a chamois leather full of holes. The implement would then be dried and the metal polished on a piece of clean lint he kept especially for the purpose. His spade was precious to him: 'You couldn't have a gravedigger without a spade,' he'd say. Indeed, as he dug, he felt that the tool was an extension of his very body. It was as if his back and shoulders, along his arms and into his fingers, flowed into his spade and they worked as one.

And as Wilfred's father laboured he thought about how he was cutting the good Welsh earth, the fields of which had fed his family for generations and which he would in turn nourish with his own body. He felt at peace with his work; it was part of a great cycle — and it gave him a sense of repose to work within it.

★　★　★

Grace had barely slept, but in her snatched sleep she had dreamed of her father, and in her dream she found a way to survive. She felt giddy all morning and faint through lunch. Enormous waves of anxiety rippled through her and her throat kept contracting.

She put down the book she had just started reading, or looking at — her mind wasn't able to focus. It was *Moll Flanders* again. Moll Flanders was a fallen woman: what was going to happen to her? A lot, no doubt. More, Grace hoped, than would happen to her, her mind racing. It was as if the atoms of her body were dissipating and could no longer find a centre, could no longer hold her together. It would be the truth. She would tell her father. He was a doctor and he was capable of being kind. She would break her father, her good, upright father, with the truth. Right now — in the hope that he would help her. She would tell him immediately. I cannot die, she thought to herself, not now, especially not now. I want to live. I want to stay alive. Whatever I have to live through, I will live through, Grace thought to herself. She was decided.

Grace straightened her dress, pulled it down at the hem so it was hanging straight and not bunched up at the waist, and retied the belt. She thought about Joan of Arc. Joan of Arc had been pure, true, wronged against. But Joan of Arc had been burned at the stake. Grace expected that in the past women were burned alive for this, but at least she wouldn't be put to death, not in 1924, in Narberth. Things were different these days, at least a little bit.

I will tell him now, without waiting, she told herself. Grace combed her blonde bobbed hair, her hands shaking, and then drew a line with the tail of the comb to make a straighter parting. Combing her hair always made her feel slightly more in control. She smoothed her hair and put it behind her ears then turned back the cuffs of her cardigan. She looked neat, ordered. Out of her small bedroom window, the sky was a pure blue and cloudless: the sky was neat as well. In her mind's eye she suddenly saw the brown wallpaper, but forced it from her thoughts. She swallowed. I shall put on my shoes to tell him, Grace thought to herself. While she didn't need shoes to walk downstairs to her father's surgery, as her slippers would suffice, she had an intimation she would need them afterwards. She buckled the pearl buttons on her shoes and looked for one more thing to do, to delay herself a few short seconds. She straightened the sleeve of her cardigan and pulled up her beige stockings, which had crinkled somewhat at her ankles. She looked presentable. She would go and tell her father and it would be the end of an innocent world. She walked downstairs.

Grace knocked on the surgery door tentatively. 'Father . . . '

'Come in, come in,' Dr Reece said cheerfully.

'Father . . . '

Grace went to stand in front of his large, imposing desk and next to the simple chair for his patients. On his desk she saw the fat blue paperweight with the air bubbles inside, trapped. Air trapped in glass. The paperweight was heavy — she knew that from when she was a little girl and her father would let her hold it. She had had to sit up properly in the leather armchair first, hold her hands open and her father would bring it to her.

'Here you are, Grace, bach. Mind you don't drop it. Daddy doesn't want glass all over his surgery, does he now?'

'No.'

Her father would carefully place the weight in her small, unformed hands so Grace could hold

136

it and put her face close to the glass. There was the big bubble in the middle that looked like a jellyfish, and then teensy-weensy baby bubbles around it. The bubbles didn't pop, Daddy said, because they were stuck in the glass for ever.

'For ever?' Grace would ask.

'Aye, for ever. Or until the glass is smashed.'

'We would never smash it, would we, Daddy?'

'I would hope not, Grace. What would I do with all my prescription forms? The wind would be blowing them.'

For as long as Grace could remember, the paperweight had sat on her father's desk. She looked at her father.

'What is it, Grace?' her father enquired.

'I'm having a baby.' She said it. The room turned vivid and perfectly defined: the wine-red carpet, the black ink blotter, the white clock-face with each capital letter absolutely clear: S. BELL CLOCKMAKER SAFFRON WALDEN. The silver-framed family photograph of the four of them, Madoc in his uniform. There were great gasps of time between each sharp tick of the grandfather clock. Perhaps the house will fall down now, Grace thought.

Her father placed a broad palm against his forehead, his other hand held his fountain pen loosely. Ash-grey, he stood up, went to the coat-stand in the corner, pulled on his herringbone coat and picked up his doctor's bag. There he stood, lost, before walking back to the armchair and collapsing down heavily.

'Wilfred,' he said simply. 'Wilfred Price.' And with that he rose and walked out of the room.

Wilfred popped a red and white aniseed ball in his mouth and put the hearse into third gear. This was good news — well, of course it wasn't good news, it was terrible news, very, very sad for all involved. Mrs Cole had kicked the bucket. Wilfred had almost given up hope! It had been such beautiful weather, the leaves on the trees were out, full and bright and green, and there were bluebells everywhere: no one was going to pop their clogs on a day like this. Good old Mrs Cole! She'd had a decent innings as well, sixty-five. That was Calvinism for you. Husband already gone — he'd buried him a couple of years back. Wilfred negotiated the corner into Kilgetty, and the pine box in the back slid slightly, despite the cotton bands holding it in place.

'Hold on tight there, Mrs Cole,' he called over his shoulder.

He moved the aniseed ball around his mouth with his tongue. Wilfred hadn't thought Mrs Cole would ever kick the bucket: she'd had more funny turns than the Waltzer at Tenby fair. Mustn't poke fun at the dead, Wilfred remembered. Oh no, mustn't be making jokes. But it was felicitous that she'd conked because he needed the money. And now the old dear was in the back of the motorized hearse and dead as a dodo, he'd get her straight back to the workshop and start on making a coffin.

'Soon be there, Mrs Cole,' he said solicitously, glancing in his driving mirror. 'Don't you worry, now,' and he pressed down on the accelerator. 'Steady on, Wilfred, lad,' he heard Mr Auden say. 'This is not Pendine Sands and you're not Malcolm Campbell trying to break the world land-speed record. Fifteen miles per hour is more than enough for a corpse.' Wilfred put his foot on the brake as he negotiated the sharp bend at Cross Hands, remembering something else Mr Auden used to say: 'Cars can easily provide work for undertakers.'

'I'm driving carefully, Mrs Cole, don't worry,' Wilfred reassured the corpse, putting both hands on the steering wheel. 'Did you read in the *Narberth & Whitland Observer* that there have been three motorcar collisions in Narberth in only six days, all at the Commercial Inn and Coach and Horses corner. It said in the paper that Aunrin Rogers's car was knocked completely over, and Mr Edward Evans and Miss Henton were *extricated from a perilous position*.' Wilfred checked the speedometer and pressed slightly harder on the brake.

He'd have to measure the poor dear for her small coffin; she wasn't that big and had shrivelled in old age. He liked preparing the coffins. In his workshop, which he'd built in the yard behind the house, Wilfred decorated the caskets, screwing in the brass handles, the nameplate and the occasional crucifix, then trimmed the box with deep purple drapery — white for the very young — by tacking the material to the four sides. He positioned the bodies: dabbed lines of blood from the corpses' mouths, combed dead hair and placed stiff lace handkerchiefs over waxy faces. He arranged for the photographer to come — only when the family asked, of course, and some did, especially the more old-fashioned ones. Then the photographer, Arthur Squibs of Tenby, would make a glass plate of the corpse. On occasion Wilfred even upended the coffin, as the next-of-kin requested he do, so that the body was standing upright, the head leaning heavily against the side while the photographer did one long, four-minute exposure.

'Arthur Squibs is coming to visit you this afternoon. We'll have to get you looking your best.'

He'd better get going, too, on preparing Mrs Cole's body what with the weather being so warm. The *rigor mortis* would leave by the day after tomorrow. Good grief, these aniseed balls are strong! thought Wilfred, taking the sweet out of his mouth and throwing it in the glove compartment. And he'd tell Da to get digging.

Wilfred glanced over his shoulder to check that the plain box he used for collecting the body of the deceased was in place; he didn't want it slipping out of the back of the hearse. The engine purred reliably, almost musically. He rolled up his sleeves. On Thursday evening he'd put a polite note through the Reeces' door declining Saturday's dinner invitation, saying it was no longer appropriate to accept their hospitality in respect of the now changed relations between Grace and himself. He had worried about how to decline the invitation all

140

week and had felt much better after doing it. He felt relieved and was feeling dapper; business was flowing again. But it wasn't only that. It was because of Flora. He had held her dear, soft body in his arms and stroked and kissed her hair. That's all. There were many more things they could have done, might one day do, but each moment had been precious to Wilfred.

He tried to think about the proportions of the casket but his mind kept turning back to the cottage. He swerved round the corner past Templeton and saw the purple Preseli Hills in the distance. The hearse rolled down the hill smoothly. This hand here, he thought, looking at his hand on the steering wheel, touched Flora's long hair. And my shoulders, that's where she rested her head.

Wilfred folded down the top of the window, rested his broad arm on the ledge and reclined back in the dun leather seat. The air was fresh on his face and he felt himself expand and soar. That exquisitely gentle afternoon with Flora had marked his life. There had been an intimacy between them and although that intimacy wasn't fully realized, such closeness had nevertheless been unimaginable to Wilfred before he had experienced it. This woman, Flora, who was smaller than him, with her slender waist and dark, flyaway hair: her life, her body, was precious to him. He had felt her preciousness, and perhaps, it occurred to Wilfred, this was what love was, this preciousness. Even her shoes, her slightly scuffed, brown leather sandals were precious to him because they were *her* shoes.

Wilfred looked up at the cloudless sky. He could see clearly now.

★ ★ ★

'And how is Mrs Reece?' Wilfred's da asked. By damn, this was getting awkward — that was the third time he'd asked after Dr Reece's wife. She was well half an hour ago; no doubt she was still well now. And he'd asked after Madoc twice and then Grace and then Madoc's friend Sidney who was in the Army with him, yet Dr Reece had only nodded. But it was a bit trying, sitting here in the middle of the day — a nice day as well, and no rain for once — with Dr Reece at the kitchen table with not a word to say for himself. And the wireless off. It was usually the other way around: when the undertaker came to visit he was supposed to dampen the proceedings.

Wilfred's da brought the mug of tea up to his mouth. Dr Reece had been sitting at the kitchen table waiting, silent as a Sunday, for the past nearly three quarters of an hour and counting. Well, clearly something was up, that much Wilfred's da was certain of. No one he knew of was dead, apart from Mrs Cole and that wasn't too great a surprise. Wilfred had gone to collect the body and should be back soon. It could only be that someone in Narberth had taken their life in their own hands and Dr Reece didn't want to say a word about it until Wilfred was here. Terrible thing that, terrible thing.

'I'll wait. I'll wait for the boy,' Dr Reece had

142

stated ominously when he arrived, keeping his thick wool coat on, despite the sunshine, and his doctor's bag tightly in his hand. He looked disturbed.

'You'll excuse the mess,' the gravedigger apologized. Dr Reece snorted. Wilfred's father moved several old copies of the *Weekly News*, the book on the constellations, the blue teacup and the dictionary from the kitchen table and on to the windowsill. The kitchen was none too tidy, Wilfred's da knew, but Dr Reece would have seen worse: after all, he looked after Mrs Hugh Pugh and gave her daily injections, and she was known for her filth and her twenty cats.

Dr Reece wouldn't have a cup of tea so Wilfred's da had offered him a custard cream biscuit then a Jacob's Cream Cracker, but Dr Reece had frowned his refusal. It was a solemn occasion then; as well it might be with someone in Narberth taking their life, and no time for biscuits. But there was no knowing exactly when Wilfred would be back, and on a fine day like this, it was going to be a long wait and a stuffy afternoon.

'It's been pleasant weather now for a couple of days,' commented Wilfred's da, attempting one last time to lighten the atmosphere. Dr Reece harrumphed out of his nostrils. So Wilfred's da joined his visitor in sitting wordlessly. Without conversation, Wilfred's da was left to his own thoughts as to who it could be, which sad soul had done such a dreadful thing.

★   ★   ★

143

'Da? Da!' Wilfred called, bursting through the front door of 11 Market Street later that afternoon.

'Here's the boy,' his father said with relief. Dr Reece stood up tall and waited while Wilfred walked along the passage into the scully.

'Wilfred,' stated Dr Reece portentously.

Dr Reece must have read Wilfred's note declining the lunch invitation and had come to acknowledge it — or perhaps more likely to admonish him, Wilfred thought. His stomach dropped to his feet, but whatever the man had to say, Wilfred knew he had done the right thing by breaking off the engagement.

'Hello, Doctor Reece. How are you?'

The doctor's face was set sternly, and Wilfred noticed the puce colouring of his cheeks. Wilfred held out his hand. Dr Reece didn't shake it. Instead he stated, 'You'll marry Grace on Saturday. At the register office.'

Wilfred stared at him.

'At two o'clock,' he added. Wilfred was trying to understand. 'There'll be no honeymoon, of course.' Dr Reece looked around the messy and humble kitchen with disgust. 'You'll be living with Mrs Reece and myself from Saturday.'

'Married?' asked Wilfred's da.

'But,' Wilfred said incredulously, his eyes wide open, 'I sent you a note explaining . . . '

'This is no time for protestations! I'll not be having any protestations. It's too late for those, boy.'

'But . . . ' Wilfred repeated.

'What's done is done,' Dr Reece stated.

144

Wilfred was flabbergasted. Dr Reece was trying to make him marry Grace and they weren't even engaged.

'We're not even *engaged*,' Wilfred declared earnestly.

'Well, you are now,' Dr Reece replied.

It was Wilfred's father who spoke next. 'Doctor Reece,' he said, 'surely, now, Wilfred needs an explanation?'

'He's made his bed. Now he must lie in it,' was the man's terse answer, the muscles in his jaw flinching.

Wilfred looked at the slate floor. A register office? That could only mean one thing, especially with the Reeces being such respectable people. There was only one reason people in Narberth got married in the register office.

'Now listen to me, Wilfred Price. You'll be in that register office at five minutes to two this Saturday. No doubt about it. You put right what you've done — quickly. Saturday.' And with that Dr Reece picked up his doctor's bag, turned and walked out, the door banging behind him.

7

What Was Known

'Has anything happened recently that we should discuss?' enquired Mrs Annie Evans, wiping the steam from her wire spectacles. The ladies of the Mothers' Union Thursday Club were having their weekly meeting at the Staunton House Refreshment Rooms.

'Before we start,' stated Mrs Reece forcefully, 'I'd like to say something. I have some news. I had a letter. Yes — it came today. Willie delivered it in the second post. Doctor Reece and I are delighted.'

'My Willie does a good job with the post,' Mrs Willie the Post told the two other ladies loyally.

Mrs Reece pursed her lips, before stating, 'Madoc's doing us proud. He says it's like an oven in Port Said. The camp's thermometer was at a hundred and thirteen degrees Fahrenheit. Can you believe it?'

'I can't believe it,' said Mrs Willie the Post. 'Is it nice, that custard slice, Mrs Evans?'

'Absolutely delicious,' Mrs Annie Evans murmured. 'I've eaten two now and I'm as full as an egg.'

'Well,' said Mrs Willie the Post, 'I won't have one. I'm on a weight reduction diet. Look at me!' She patted her stomach. 'I put on a stone in a week at my mother's in Carmarthen. Willie said I'm as fat as a wardrobe.' She breathed in and sat up straighter.

'Get away with you, you daft brush! You're thin as a stick,' Mrs Annie Evans replied, telling a blatant untruth.

'Go on, then, I'll have one,' said Mrs Willie the Post. 'You know, something happened the other day: Willie got a letter for *Edith, Narberth*. That's all it said, *Edith, Narberth*. No address. He showed it to me. Couldn't believe it. And he went to Edith Lewis in Wells Street and said, 'Edith, is this for you?' And she said, 'Yes, it is. It's from my auntie in Merlins Bridge who's lost her address book — and her marbles.' Then Edith Lewis said to Willie, 'Oh, Willie, you're the best postman in the world.' She was in seventh heaven to hear from her aged auntie.'

'Madoc always addresses his envelopes properly. With commas — and full stops,' stated Mrs Reece, adjusting the artificial wreath of forget-me-nots in her hat.

'Oh, there's posh,' said Mrs Annie Evans.

'And a stamp from Egypt.'

'Oh! Get away!' said Mrs Willie the Post. 'Willie would have had a good look at that stamp; I'm surprised he didn't show me.'

'Madoc was saying he's in charge of twenty-three soldiers. They have to take orders from him.'

'Now there's good,' said Mrs Willie the Post.

'Pass me that napkin, please,' said Mrs Annie Evans, who wanted to wipe a dollop of custard from the lace on her blouse. 'By damn, this custard tart is tasty.'

'He makes sure they make their beds properly — you know, with hospital corners.'

'Do they do hospital corners in the Army?' asked Mrs Willie the Post. 'I would have thought they did Army corners. By the way, I saw some lovely wallpaper in T. P. Hughes in Carmarthen. Oh, it was . . . it was . . . ' Mrs Willie the Post looked up at the ceiling with inexpressible delight. 'Blossoms, like the spring. So beautiful the flowers were, you could almost smell them.' She closed her eyes and sighed, adding, 'I hear Wilfred Price's taken it into his head to turn his parlour into a wallpaper shop, isn't that right, Mrs Reece?' she said, daring to mention Wilfred's name.

'Seems he could,' Mrs Reece replied, snapping her handbag shut. 'Madoc has his work cut out in Egypt, what with all those Egyptians.'

'Oh, there are a lot of Egyptians in Egypt,' said Mrs Willie the Post.

'But if the Spanish Influenza comes again,' remarked Mrs Annie Evans, 'Wilfred Price will be rushed off his feet. He won't be able to set up a wallpaper shop then because he'll be too busy sawing wood for coffins.'

'Mind, that's where a wife is handy,' said Mrs Willie the Post, smiling knowledgeably. 'Grace can help sell the fancy wallpapers.'

'Grace will be too busy with housewifery to be working in a shop,' said Mrs Reece, sniffing.

Mrs Annie Evans, feeling brave, said, 'There's a beauteous comely veil in *Embroidery Weekly*: Grace will look pretty as a picture in it. White it is, with yellow daisies. She'll look like Lady

148

Elizabeth Bowes-Lyon when she married Prince Albert last year.'

'Yes,' said Mrs Reece.

'Oh, Mrs Reece, you must be proud — a son in the Army and a daughter about to marry an undertaker who might one day have a paint and wallpaper shop as well. And I heard Wilfred will be living with you, in your house. There's good. There's not enough room in 11 Market Street for Grace, and I know you'd never let her live in all that mess. Nice and clean in your house it is, Mrs Reece, and plenty of space,' complimented Mrs Annie Evans, eating the last, crumbly mouthful of her custard slice. Then, unable to stop herself saying what everyone was thinking and no one dare mention, said, 'Not long to the wedding. You don't want to be waiting around and planning these things for ever.'

Mrs Reece pursed her lips.

'Have another cream slice, Mrs Reece,' encouraged Mrs Willie the Post quickly. There was an awkward pause in which no one could think of anything to say.

'Well, I think the meeting of the Mothers' Union Thursday Club can draw to a close,' said Mrs Annie Evans, embarrassed by her comment. She put her dessert fork on her tea-plate, self-consciously adding, 'We've got a good bit done today.'

★   ★   ★

Wilfred stood on Mrs Russell's Haberdasher's & Draper's doorstep, cleaned his shoes on the mud-scraper, collapsed his umbrella and shook it before ringing the bell.

'The plain white with the yellow fleck is most becoming and not overly ornamental,' he could hear Mrs Russell advising a customer.

'Wilfred. What a surprise!' she exclaimed, swinging open the door. Wilfred came regularly to Mrs Russell's Haberdasher's for the purple tape which he glued over the tacks that held the material in place inside the coffin. Mrs Russell ordered the reels especially for him from a stockist in Neath. He bought five rolls at a time, each of 150 yards.

'I'm afraid I can't let you in,' whispered Mrs Russell, peeping out from the shop door.

'Why ever not, Mrs Russell?' Wilfred asked, tying the strap on his umbrella. 'I've come here to collect my tape order. You said it would arrive by the last week of April.'

'I did indeed, Wilfred. And it's here.'

'Well then, surely I can come in and collect it, rather than waiting out here in this dreadful weather.'

'No! You most certainly can't.' Mrs Russell was now standing on the step of her shop with her hand behind her holding firmly on to the brass door handle.

'Mrs Russell, I have never in my born days been denied entry' — these are big words, Wilfred thought ' — into a haberdasher's and draper's. Whatever have I done? You sound adamant, Mrs Russell,' he added. *Adamant*. Wilfred thought to himself proudly.

'You have it on my word of honour that you do not want to come into this shop. A certain young lady and her mother are at this very moment in the back room selecting netting.'

Wilfred was perplexed. 'You already have some customers, Mrs Russell, and that's the reason you don't want me to enter?'

'Yes. Exactly,' said Mrs Russell, somewhat amused.

'But aren't I your customer, too, and have been these last seven years?'

'Indeed,' she replied, smiling. 'Wilfred, it's not just any customer I have in the shop.'

Wilfred's heart lurched. He understood. Grace and her mother were in the back room now, selecting material, material for . . . He suddenly had a dreadful sinking in his stomach and his insides flopped over. This was too definite, too conclusive. Preparations were being made: buying, cutting, sewing, stitching. His proposal, that little question, was being turned into something concrete, something big.

'Oh,' he said gravely.

'Custom prevails, Wilfred. You can't see the dress or the veil now, can you? There would be a thing! Mustn't be having you glimpsing the outfit. What would the Mothers' Union say?' Mrs Russell whispered conspiratorially.

'No.'

'Not yet. Not before the day.'

* * *

Wilfred put his empty teacup down on the chair. It was Wednesday morning, almost exactly four days since he was last with Flora. He was going

151

back to the cottage in the cove. He'd cycle the seven miles on his bicycle and wheel it up the lane to the quiet, forgotten corner hidden from Narberth. Flora had been in the cottage on Saturday, as he'd thought she might be. Maybe, *maybe*, she would be there now. He was looking for Flora and perhaps something of her would linger there. He needed to feel her close. There was no one in the world he wanted to see as much. Wilfred splashed a couple of teacups of cold water on the hearth to put out the fire and left home.

On the way, near the cove, a bi-plane flew overhead, the quiet buzz of the engine high above Wilfred. The plane was moving east and into the huge expanse of the sky. Wilfred, craning his neck, watched it flip upside down, flying for a couple of seconds with the cockpit hanging down before righting itself. The pilot was playing; he was free, impossibly free, to do whatever he liked. Wilfred waved, stretching both hands up, like someone who was drowning and wanted to be rescued, signalling to the plane that was so very high above him. The aeroplane headed further into the distance, and when it was almost at the horizon and over Pendine Sands, it wheeled round in a great circle. That is a free man and that is what free men do, Wilfred thought enviously. They twist and turn and go where they will. Nothing holds them down, not even the earth. I would like to be out there with him, he thought.

When he arrived at the cottage the green door was closed, and as Wilfred pushed it open, he had a moment of almost pure hope that there inside would be Flora, exquisite Flora. She would be asleep on her cream blanket, the one she had brought last time, her brown eyes closed, her hair ruffled around her warm face, lying on her front, sleeping serenely. And he would lie next to her, pull some blankets out of the ether and over them, and take her beautiful, feminine body in his arms. There can surely, Wilfred thought, be nothing better in this whole wide world, nothing lovelier, than being held and holding close and warm the woman you love. No, there was nothing better.

But the cottage was dank, damp and, most disappointingly of all, empty. Flora wasn't there. The cottage, Wilfred — everything — felt achingly desolate. It was hard for him to imagine he had felt such warmth and excitement in this dark, dilapidated house. He sat on the cold, earthen floor — the chair had woodworm and only had three legs — and put his head between his knees. He was a man condemned.

★　★　★

Grace scraped the honeycomb with a knife; she was always astonished by the perfect regularity of the hexagons on the honeycomb. She would filter it overnight through clean white muslin to remove the dead bees, and so there would be fresh honey for the wedding breakfast.

Her father — reliably — had spoken to Wilfred, and as far as she knew made Wilfred acquiesce — and now there was only one day

153

before the appointment at the register office ceremony. She hadn't heard from Wilfred, didn't expect to judging from her father's mood when he returned from the Prices'. Her father must also have used his status to force the register office to bring the wedding forward sooner than was legally allowed.

A bee landed on the netting over her temple. She brushed it away with her gloved hand. Obviously a white wedding dress was completely out of the question. Even cream was unthinkable. Her wailing and hysterical mother seemed to consider black the most appropriate colour. Or scarlet — though she had made Grace a simple veil. Grace no longer cared what she wore.

Through the kitchen window, she heard her mother slamming the mixing bowl on the table and beating the currants into the cake mixture with true fury.

'Grace Amelia?' her mother called angrily.

Grace was collecting the honey so it could be spread on the Bara brith along with pats of butter. Grace — if her mother would let her — would take the warm butter and press it into the intricately carved moulds, and then place rectangles of ice around them to harden the butter into solid yellow sheaves of gold. Then the wedding breakfast for her and Wilfred, her mother and father and Wilfred's father would have cold butter on hot cake and there would be fresh honey from her hive. This is what she would bring to the wedding breakfast. And new life.

'*You'll marry him,*' Mrs Prout had said. The key had turned in the Bible. Now she was marrying Wilfred, but she hadn't imagined it would be like this.

'Will you hurry up?' her mother shouted. 'I can't be in here working all day on my own with you out there gallivanting around with a beehive. What on earth are you doing?'

'Collecting honey.'

'Well, hurry up! I don't know what you want honey for, anyway.'

'You heard your mother,' her father said.

The bees were swarming above the hive — they could sense her agitation and were reflecting it back to her. Grace puffed the smoker. They knew. They had been around for millions of years, much longer than people; they must have seen everything before and knew there was nothing new under the sun. Bees were intelligent. What would it be like, Grace wondered, to be a satisfied queen bee, to sit eating royal jelly, the very best of foods, and to be adored by all the drones, not merely one drone, but every drone in their tight, boxed world. To be queen of a universe. Instead of what she was now — abandoned, an outcast despite the wedding. She felt like little more than a larva made of squishy, unformed mush, sealed in a small case.

'You'll be the death of me,' her mother implored.

Grace touched her neck gently with her hand. Her skin was downy but the muscles beneath felt strong; she imagined the bones in her neck were strong too. Necks were beautiful things — fragile, supple and expressive. It was *her* neck and she nearly broke it, snapped it with a rope and the weight of her own body

Grace removed her beekeeping hat and veil. Saturday would be hard, practical and joyless. A dismal wedding with an unwanted bride and an unwilling groom. Wilfred had surely been coerced and rushed by her father because of the situation she was in. Her father was a quiet bully — probably all doctors were. But there would be cake, chilled butter and new honey afterwards. Grace knew it was a poor bargain, but she was alive within it.

★   ★   ★

'The usual?' the barber asked, tilting back the chair. He rubbed a mass of foam into Wilfred's neck in vigorous circular motions, almost engulfing Wilfred's face.

'Wilfred! I was walking past and I saw you through the window,' Jeffrey announced, coming in the shop. Wilfred moved his eyes to the side without moving his head — the barber had a cutthroat razor to his neck — and nodded in Jeffrey's direction as much as he dared with the blade against his throat.

'I'll wait while you get seen to,' Jeffrey stated and sat on the bench against the barbershop window. When, ten minutes later, the barber wiped the lather from Wilfred's jaw, Jeffrey could see the devastation in his friend's face.

'Come on, Wilf, come for a walk with me,'

156

Jeffrey suggested when Wilfred stood up to have the shavings brushed from his jacket. 'It's my lunch-break.' Jeffrey worked at Lloyd the butcher's on the corner of Market Square and he had that pink raw look that butchers often had.

'Let's go up the Doggy Drang — it's much quieter,' he said, seeing how dark and troubled Wilfred looked.

As soon as they went up the Doggy Drang, Jeffrey said, 'You're marrying her, then.' There was no use beating around the bush now.

Wilfred nodded, unable to speak.

'I heard,' said Jeffrey. 'Unlucky, old chap. These things happen to the best of us.'

Wilfred looked at his shoes.

'It'll be all right, Wilf,' said Jeffrey, wanting to console his childhood friend. 'She's a nice girl . . . nice legs . . . and they've got plenty of money.' He didn't know what to say. Jeffrey wondered if Wilfred was going to cry.

'Don't fret now,' he soothed, as much at a loss as Wilfred to know how to deal with the emotion that was flooding Wilfred's dark blue eyes. They walked up the back of the Conduit Stores and leaned on the wall of the pigpen belonging to Mrs Annie Evans.

'And she'll be kind to your da and that's something. Say you'd met a girl at a dance from Carmarthen or Cardigan — from a long way away — what would you have done about your da? At least you'll be near him and be able to look after him.'

'Aye, there is that.'

'You's got to be careful when you do the

business,' Jeffrey added, philosophizing on the situation.

Wilfred looked at his hands.

'We'll still be able to go for a pint at the Rugby Club,' Jeffrey offered. 'Doctor Reece full of the wrath of God, is he?'

Wilfred smiled resignedly.

'Don't worry about that Mrs Reece — perhaps she'll die soon!' Jeffrey jested.

Wilfred sighed.

'That will be one dry old stick you won't be sorry to bury. Say something, Wilf. You're normally so chatty.'

The pig grunted and waddled over to be near them. Wilfred watched its fat snout with delicate grey hairs sniff the air.

'Be Wilfred Price and Son now, will it?'

Wilfred said nothing, noticed a dark cloud in the sky above.

'Don't fret.' Jeffrey gave Wilfred a friendly thump on the arm, his own eyes moist. 'Everything will be all right, it always is.' The pig oinked greedily and snuffled the squelchy mud.

'Stinks here!' exclaimed Jeffrey, nodding at the pig. 'Mind, he'll smell lovely sliced up in a frying pan.'

'Ever the butcher,' Wilfred murmured, rousing himself.

★   ★   ★

I shouldn't be wearing this suit, Wilfred thought, knotting his necktie in the mirror. This was the suit he wore for funerals; it wasn't a wedding suit. But it *is* a funeral, he realized. It's my funeral. I'm being buried alive.

It was a quarter to two, the ceremony — or the execution as Wilfred wryly thought of it — was due to start in fifteen minutes.

He pressed the knot to make both sides symmetrical but it was an uneven four-in-hand knot so he undid it and began again. All week he had been in an ever-deepening panic, unable to think clearly. He didn't seem to be able to find the courage within himself to know what to say or do. He had wanted to talk to someone, perhaps to his da, but he and his da didn't talk about these things. His da was married to his mam, and even though his mam had passed away, Wilfred knew his father had stayed faithful to her, *forsaking all others*, as it said in the wedding service. He couldn't talk to Mr Ogmore Auden. Even if he drove over to Whitland to pay him a visit on the pretence of having a cup of tea, he still wouldn't know how to broach the subject. Wilfred tried to remember if Mr Ogmore Auden had ever mentioned anything on this topic, apart from his advice about refraining from lewd thoughts around the deceased. His apprentice-master had avoided such crude conversations. And besides, the advice he most usually gave was about undertaking, and the last thing Wilfred wanted to do was bury Flora. But Mr Auden often said, and reinforced it through his own example, 'An undertaker does the right thing.' Jeffrey? Jeffrey would listen and try to understand, but Wilfred needed someone older and wiser. He could go for a drink at the

Narberth Rugby Football Club and perhaps talk to someone there, but if Wilfred said anything to one of those boys, well . . . the members of the Narberth Rugby Football Club were not known for their social delicacy.

He pulled on his jacket, smoothed the shoulders and began brushing the dark wool with a clothes brush. Surely a man couldn't get married because his ex-fiancée was having a baby by someone else? And who was it? Grace lived a coddled life, she wouldn't have that many chances to meet lads. Wilfred had realized, with a rush of indignation, that Grace had been seeing someone else — when they'd had that picnic in the garden! When he'd proposed. Seeing someone indeed! Seeing all of them, more like. While all along he, Wilfred, had thought she liked *him*, had worried — *worried* — about hurting her feelings by breaking off the engagement.

He expertly combed his hair, slicked it with Brylcreem then brushed some lint from his collar. Over the previous six days it had become obvious to Wilfred that he was being trapped, that Grace had known all along she was expecting, that some rascal had left her in the lurch and Grace had hoped that Wilfred would marry her and get her out of her quandary. Which meant Grace would have had to have done *it* with Wilfred soon, before they were supposed to have got married, to cover her tracks. Wilfred's head hurt from trying to understand so much duplicity.

'Well, there's a predicament.' That's what Mr

160

Ogmore Auden would have said, had Wilfred been so coarse as to tell him the ins and outs of it all. And he would be right and all. It was a predicament.

He started brushing the front of his trousers with his clothes brush. There was something he could do: he could say it wasn't his, by damn, and not marry Grace. The relief at the thought. He could stand at the altar or whatever they had in register offices and shout, 'It's not mine! It's not mine!' But nobody would believe him. His ex-fiancée was having a baby — his ex-fiancée, Dr Reece's *daughter* no less, was having a baby and Wilfred was saying it wasn't his. Unless the baby was Oriental-looking, no one would believe him. And no one would ever again permit Wilfred to bury a member of their family; he would never put a body in the ground again. It would be too disgraceful for any family to use his funeral services. He'd have no trade and no money. He'd have to join the Foreign Legion — or something.

Late last night, in utter desperation, sitting up in bed, his shoulders collapsed, he had turned to his red dictionary — had taken it from the top of his chest of drawers and opened it randomly to look for one word, a chance word among the thousands of precise, tight definitions. This was called, he had recently learned, *ad aperturam libri*. Perhaps one word, one profound definition, would give him the answer.

He'd opened the book quickly, decisively. It was in the *D* section. But which word should he choose? He closed his eyes, placed his index finger tentatively on the page, then looked:

Diamond.

Diamond? Wilfred thought, puzzled.

Diamond. *(Noun) a hard gemstone. Made of* carbon.

Diamond? Ruddy dictionary, thought Wilfred. What help was that? Well, that would teach him to lose his commonsense.

8

The Wedding

'Grace, a carnation.'

'Thank you, Mother,' answered Grace.

'Wilfred, a carnation,' said Mrs Reece with barely concealed dislike. Wilfred accepted without thanks the delicate flower with its fluted petals. Her mother, in a spasm of last-minute enthusiasm, and finally stirred by the occasion of her daughter's wedding, had cut carnations from the garden and she, Dr Reece and Grace were wearing white corsages. Wilfred had sternly accepted the carnation when Mrs Reece had given it to him and had pinned it to his lapel with what had looked like solemnity, but Grace wasn't fooled. As she watched him pierce the flower stem and pin it into the heavy serge of his suit, she thought that perhaps he felt like that green stem, stabbed by something sharp and unnatural, until it died. And Wilfred was wearing what looked very much like his funeral director's suit.

'A corsage is a pleasant addition for the occasion, Mrs Reece,' commented Dr Reece.

Grace adjusted the shoulder of her dress. Her yellow dress — bright and optimistic, sunny even — had been deemed appropriate by her mother. Nor did her mother consider the occasion of Grace's shotgun wedding a reason for a new dress, not under these circumstances; all she needed was a cheap, homemade veil. Her mother would have liked to have seen her married in a sackcloth and ashes and crawl penitently along the aisle on her knees. Only it wasn't an aisle, it was an office in which she was getting married to Wilfred, with few guests, no gifts and no celebration because there was precious little to celebrate. And Wilfred was intimidating as he stood ramrod straight: it was clear that his will had brought him here and not his heart

'If the guests could come through in half a moment,' announced the office clerk cheerily, popping her head round the door of the register office.

'Stand up properly,' her mother hissed. Grace stood up and pulled her stomach in.

Wilfred's da patted his son's arm. Grace, standing next to Wilfred in his top hat and tails, pondered on how upright they must look as a couple. We are not upright, she thought to herself, but it matters that we look as if we are.

The clerk, Mrs Pritchard of Sheep Street, doing the job of master of ceremonies, announced, 'Doctor and Mrs Reece, Mr Price Senior, please enter the register office now.'

'All right, son?' Wilfred's da said as the guests moved forward.

Wilfred and Grace were alone in the wood-panelled auditorium. Wilfred stood as if all the hope in the world had deserted him. A strange sound came from his stomach. Grace smiled apologetically but Wilfred looked thunderous. She unclipped her bracelet, dropping it in her bag; she felt overdressed as if she was

164

making too much of the occasion by wearing it. Wilfred was perspiring and looked as if there was a violent struggle taking place within him, something unspoken and unformed fighting for consciousness and voice. She smoothed the pleats of her dress and noticed that the thin laces of Wilfred shoes were knotted very tightly.

'It won't take long,' she said brightly. She wondered if she might vomit everywhere, all down his suit and splatter his shoes. She swallowed hard. From behind the door, some music played.

'It's hot for a suit,' she said, feeling stupid the moment she said it.

'The groom, please, in you come!' said the registrar chirpily, popping her head round the door.

★   ★   ★

The room, when she entered, was small, crowded with chairs and a table, but there was still an emptiness within it. Her father turned back and smiled formally to see her come in. Wilfred was standing by the table, waiting for Grace. Grace walked towards him with as little aplomb as possible, passing her parents, her father standing with his hands behind his back, like a sentinel of righteous living. Wilfred looked enraged in his top hat and tails, and like a Greek god with a hidden thunderbolt who wanted to destroy the world. Grace smiled appeasingly and breathed in.

'Move in a little,' the registrar told Grace, who

stepped sideways lightly, almost skipping, her dress flaring as she moved. Wilfred looked down at his hands while Grace waited politely for the registrar to speak. She had her answers ready.

'Do you take this man, Wilfred Aubrey Price . . .' The registrar began reciting, finishing with ' . . . until death us do part?' Grace agreed, said yes; it was easy to promise, she liked Wilfred. This would do. Wilfred said his vows gruffly. Though she stood next to him she did not feel close to him: he had — she could tell — armoured himself with rage and hate and unwillingness.

'You may kiss the bride!' said the registrar with a levity. The clerk looked up, watching everything, her eyes glittering with excitement. Grace's pearls clacked as she removed her veil. Wilfred kissed her dryly with a stern face, as one might kiss the dead, as if kissing her was against life and possibly dangerous to one's health.

'Just a few papers to sign and it's all written in stone,' said the clerk, and she lifted the needle of the gramophone arm and placed it on the disc. 'Shall I play the gramophone music?' she mouthed to Mrs Reece.

'That's enough,' said Mrs Reece, putting her hand to her diaphragm.

To Grace the wedding ceremony felt like a stiff ballet, a slow dance without music, in which their fates were sealed. She gave Wilfred a relieved smile and breathed out. She was a married woman. It was done.

'Mr Price, if you would like to come back to the house to join us, we have some refreshments,' offered Dr Reece.

'Oh, that would be lovely,' Wilfred's da replied, his voice catching with feeling.

Grace smiled encouragingly at Wilfred, but doubted he would feel encouraged. She knew him to be hurt. Wilfred was like a stone monument who wouldn't dance in this *pas de deux*, wouldn't move but stood lifeless, like a prop. But at least some of it was all right now. And some violence, something dark she had once experienced, that she would never let herself think of again, would soon be glossed over, forgotten and ignored for ever. Relief flooded and opened her face.

★ ★ ★

The wedding breakfast that afternoon was the first time in a week her mother hadn't slammed the crockery on the table; propriety in front of guests wouldn't let her, and the welcome confusion of tea and cake had conferred a certain decency on the day.

During the wedding breakfast, Grace was complimented by Wilfred's father on the quality of the honey.

'Is this the honey from your bees? It's very sweet, now. And rich.' He was wearing what was clearly his best suit. 'Do you have a lot of lavender in your garden?' he asked. 'Is that the reason why?'

Grace replied that they had, that they were mature plants now.

'Bees like lavender, can't keep them off it. And lavender makes good honey,' Wilfred's da added, smiling and looking round at the others.

Grace felt her face slightly flush with withheld tears. These were the first genuinely kind words she had heard all day. Wilfred, of course, had vowed to cherish her — worship her even — but his words had failed to move her. They were words without feeling — words he said but didn't mean. Her mother, as well, had smiled and almost gushed since the marriage — she had even offered everyone a Meltis Duchess of York Assorted Chocolate. She was smiling because she was the mother of the bride and that was what social correctness expected. Grace knew she was privately enraged. The register office was not St Andrew's Church. A yellow dress was not a bridal gown and she, her parents and Wilfred's father did not constitute a wedding party. No, Grace knew that for her mother, it had all gone far, far too wrong.

But Wilfred's father — that quite watchful gravedigger — spoke gently. He had the humility of the broken. And he knew, surely, that his son was an unwilling groom. Whatever he knew, Grace thought to herself, he understood that she was hurting; he saw that and he reached out with kindness. It had been a small gesture but a powerful one to Grace after these recent loveless, hopeless months.

*   *   *

Grace stood outside what was now their bedroom. She had chosen to wear her favourite white nightdress. It reached almost to her toes

168

and the cotton was fluffy. She had had it several years now and imagined it would last almost her lifetime. And it was demure. She knocked on the door very lightly and waited. There was no answer from inside the room.

She knocked on the door again then pushed it open and entered quickly. She stood by the door and wondered why Wilfred had married her earlier in the day. She knew why. He had been her fiancé — everyone in Narberth knew that. So everybody knew, or would know by now, he had to be the reason why she was in the condition she was in. If he hadn't married her, had refused, he would have had absolutely nothing — they both knew that. No one would have used his funeral business again: to use the services of a man like that when there was a death in the family, people just wouldn't. It wouldn't be respectable. He would no longer be a man around town and that was what Wilfred wanted to be. He would be ruined. And the gossip would last for generations, definitely three, at least four. It would probably take five generations before people in Narberth no longer talked about Wilfred Price.

Grace unclasped her pearl necklace and took off her dressing-gown, hung it on the hook behind the door and sat nervously on the bed. It had been a long day, too intense, and now this, her wedding bed, the honeymoon, such as it was. The first night. She smoothed her nightie down over her arms then lay down self-consciously and pulled the blankets over herself. This was the first time she had slept in the attic. Madoc's room with its bigger bed had been allotted to them because her mother decreed it was more suitable than Grace's childhood bedroom.

Grace was now on the left side of the bed, Wilfred on the right, nearest the door. The blankets fell into the gap between them. It was very strange to be in bed with another person. Grace didn't know what to do. She knew what was supposed to happen on a wedding night, but that was the wedding night of a wedding that the bride and groom had wanted to be at. This is what the first night is like, she thought, of a married person who doesn't want to be married. Suddenly she saw the brown wallpaper but she quickly cut the memory from her mind.

Grace lay awake. She knew Wilfred was awake too, both of them staring at the white ceiling. And out of the corner of her eye, she saw Wilfred wipe a tear from his face.

★   ★   ★

Wilfred had never been in bed with a woman before. He had thought about it, imagined that it would be very cosy. Not only cosy; he had hoped it might be something more than that. Perhaps that is what a loved and wanted wife gave to a man: sanctuary from the harshness of being male — but this iron bed wasn't a sanctuary. People who were sleeping in the desert in Arabia with a stone for a pillow were right now more comfortable than he was. And getting a better night's sleep. The bed was an altercation of a wedding bed in an austere room. Did he have an

170

acrimonious marriage? There were many A words that applied to his marriage.

Wilfred lay stock-still. To take his mind off things he began thinking about his work. He was surprised when he began to tot up how many funerals he must have been to — at least a hundred — and in each and every one of them he had maintained what Mr Ogmore Auden had called 'a composed and serious demeanour'. Even when he was only fourteen, when he began his apprenticeship and was very excited by his prospects, he'd still just about behaved in a sober manner around the departed.

Sometimes it had been hard — what young man doesn't want to fool around sometimes? Nevertheless he'd managed to stay solemn, even in 1922 when Narberth won the Rugby Cup, or when they'd done a funeral the day before Narberth carnival, even when the lisping vicar from Princes Gate gave the peroration and stroked the lectern with his hand the whole time; Wilfred had still maintained the proper demeanour, though he had been desperate to laugh. But today he had felt more desolate and more burdened than he had ever done in any funeral he had attended, and this, his own wedding day. His one and only wedding day. Wilfred's heart was full of misery.

That morning he had barely been able to get out of bed; his legs had felt like lead. He almost couldn't be bothered to shave. He didn't eat breakfast. But he'd been at the register office at five to two as Dr Reece had told him to be — commanded him to be, more like. Dr Reece was a bully, Wilfred thought. He had married Grace because her father was a horrible, hectoring, browbeating bully. If he hadn't been so intimidating Wilfred might have been able to explain. Why didn't people listen to one another? Wilfred thought hotly. Why didn't they just listen! If people could explain themselves, then there could be understanding. But no, some people — quite a lot of people even, Wilfred thought — were bullies. They wanted other people to do what *they* wanted them to do, and if they had the power, like Dr Reece did, then sometimes they used that power, bossed people around and messed up their lives. It was appalling. It was audacious. It was an abomination. Wilfred struggled to find the words, big, powerful words that would express the big, powerful feelings he had now that he felt so small and powerless over his own life. Marry Grace! Marry Grace. He had. Now they were in bed together. What had Dr Reece said? 'You've made your bed. Now you lie in it.'

★   ★   ★

The kitchen was smoky and smelled of fried food. Wilfred had come home for breakfast every day of his married life so far, and today Wilfred's father had cooked his son's favourite meal: fried eggs and cockles, with bacon and sausages, and slices of fried potato they called Specials. Wilfred had loved Specials since he was a tiny boy and his Auntie Blodwen had taught his father how to cook them: 'Peel the new tyatas, slice them into

172

thick circles,' Auntie Blodwen instructed, 'then fry them in a lump of lard till they're golden brown. That'll put some fat on the boy. He's got legs on him like a flamingo.' His father eventually mastered the recipe and, ever since, Wilfred and his da had eaten Specials every Sunday morning, on their birthdays, after a night at the graveyard or whenever they needed strengthening.

'Eat up, Wilfred, lad,' his da encouraged, but Wilfred was pushing the black pudding around his plate, his body slumped, his head resting in his hands. He wasn't even reading the *Undertaker's Journal* in front of him.

'Wilf, you'll be a bag of bones if you don't eat. And no good to anyone. You'll make yourself ill, now.' Wilfred's da could have added, 'Think of your wife,' but he knew well enough that thinking about his wife was the reason Wilfred couldn't eat.

'Don't you want to eat breakfast at the Reeces'?' his da asked gently. 'Mrs Reece is a tidy cook.' Wilfred pushed the leftover Specials to the side of his plate.

This was the first time Wilfred's da had ever known his son not to speak. Wilfred liked to talk, always about his work. He could talk for Narberth, could Wilfred. If it wasn't making chitchat about his funerals he was wanting a conversation about the wallpaper shop and paper-hanging. Wilfred was even more of a talker since he'd been reading the dictionary every day, had even more to say for himself. What was that he'd said to him now the other day? He wanted to 'augment' the funeral business with a

173

wallpaper shop. Augment, by damn. Well, there wasn't much augmenting going on for Wilfred now, his da thought, whatever augmenting was.

Wilfred would have to say something soon, it was his way. Wilfred's da knew his son was a thoughtful young man who was eager for his life to happen; no, he wouldn't be able to keep quiet for long.

'Eat up, boyo,' his da said again. 'There's a good lad.'

★ ★ ★

Wilfred had been in his workshop for the last four days. He'd started making the coffin the day after the wedding even though it was the Sabbath and the day of rest. It was a standard size of 28-inch width and 84-inch length for a large man, around 6 foot and 12 stone, about the same size as himself. Not that there was anyone specific he could think of who might die soon, but he would keep the casket ready and waiting for one of the whiskery old men of Narberth to kick the bucket. It would save him making one in a rush.

'You've been in that workshop for days, Wilfred,' his da had said. 'What are you doing in there? Anyone would think you were making a coffin for Tutankhamun.'

He was filling time, staying in his workshop because it was familiar, safe, the place where he had spent the last seven years working. He looked around him — the sawing had created a lot of sawdust, which lay like a thick yellow blanket on the tins of varnish, over the boxes of coffin handles, his dictionary and in the furrow of his workbench where he kept his tools. He should sweep, but what was the point of making the workshop spick and span when he felt so dejected and old, as if life itself was over? The tin dustpan and brush in the corner remained unused. He remembered that Mr Ogmore Auden had been clear:

'Sweep up, boyo. Sweep as if your life depends on it.'

'Yes, Mr Auden,' Wilfred would reply immediately and dutifully. Indeed, sweeping the workshop floorboards had been his very first task on that first awe-inspiring day of his apprenticeship.

'Brush up that sawdust,' Mr Auden had said on that first morning. 'And you'll be sweeping up too, every day, at least three times a day, for the next four years.'

Mr Auden hadn't been kidding. In the first year Wilfred thought all he was ever going to learn was how to use a dustpan and brush, and that the nearest he'd ever get to an actual corpse was getting down on his hands and knees and sweeping up the shavings beneath a coffin. But as Wilfred proved himself capable and assiduous at keeping the floorboards spotless, Mr Auden responded by giving him more challenging tasks until Wilfred came to understand that the more thoroughly he swept, the more real work Mr Auden would give him. With time, Wilfred began what he thought of as his proper apprenticeship, beginning with how to identify wood by colour, from white and pale yellow to red, purple and black, and by open or closed grain, and also by pattern — the stripes, the circles, the waves and the curls, ripples and eyes. He learned that the preparation he needed to be a funeral director depended on how enthusiastically and humbly he swept the floor.

'One spark on all that sawdust and we'll be up in flames — indeed, in-double-deed. We purvey other people's funerals, Wilfred, not arrange our own. You sweep up those wood chippings, there's a good lad, and mind you do it properly now. No cheating or we'll all be down the crematorium and it won't be me who'll be driving the hearse.'

'Yes, Mr Auden,' Wilfred had said. 'Yes, Mr Auden,' were the words he said most frequently over those four years of his apprenticeship, and as Wilfred's respect for and obedience to Mr Ogmore Auden grew, the more he meant it when he said, 'Yes, Mr Auden.'

Wilfred looked around his workshop. There was at least an inch of sawdust and chippings on the pile of old copies of the *Weekly News* and he knew that Mr Auden would be appalled.

'What are you doing here!' Wilfred imagined him exclaiming. 'Are you trying to kill us all? Hell's bells, Wilfred. This'll go up in a puff of smoke, just like *that*.' Wilfred could hear Mr Auden click his fingers.

Wilfred didn't care. A quick fire, hot flames, death from the smoke; it wouldn't matter to him now. He'd sweep up the dust, perhaps tomorrow.

He heard Mr Ogmore Auden again: 'A man needs something to look forward to.' Mr Auden had always been clear on that. 'Whatever happens, Wilfred, have a plan. Might not work out — poor bugger in the back there had a plan' — they had been on their way to a funeral when his apprentice-master had delivered the homily — 'but you've got to have something to aim for, especially when things turn out unexpectedly, as they do.'

Wilfred knew he would keep going. Perhaps he'd keep reading the dictionary, though the last definition he'd read was *Apillera*: a pictorial Peruvian wall decoration stitched on to sacking backcloth — that wasn't a very useful word. Maybe one day he would even finish turning the parlour into a wallpaper shop. But he couldn't imagine ever feeling happy again. Would he ever adjust, get used to his new life? He brushed the dust off a wooden chair with the side of his hand and sat down. He'd spend his days in the workshop, and eat at home with his da as he had always done. At night he'd sleep at Dr Reece's house. Life would go on, he'd go on, and then one day he, too, would be laid out here in his own workshop, in a coffin no doubt of his own making, and then this dreadful mess would be over.

★ ★ ★

For two weeks now Wilfred had clung to the very edge of the bed on what had become his side, the side by the door. He slept curled up. Grace hadn't imagined he would be so unhappy that he would stay hunched up all night long; his legs tucked together, his hands held close to his broad chest. She had always thought of Wilfred as a confident young man about Narberth, able to ask for what he wanted. After all, he had asked her to marry him — he'd been confident and robust then. And he'd been almost brutal when he'd stated — or more like blurted out — that he didn't want to marry her, that day when they'd been standing in the rain outside the Angel Inn. Grace had thought Wilfred was strong and quite unafraid to speak his mind. But in the dark, here, now, he lay tight, making himself smaller than he was.

Lying in bed, awake and sleepless, she thought back to a vague memory of Wilfred as a young boy, running around the town moor, playing cricket on the cricket field with a band of boys, including Madoc and Sidney. That was a long time ago. She'd forgotten about the young Wilfred. But glancing at him, clasped, restrained, locked in his own world, she was reminded of him when he was much younger.

He was, she thought, resolute, granite-like in his determination to sleep alone and untouched in this double bed under the eaves of the attic. He acted as if she wasn't there. And day-by-day, as she got almost imperceptibly larger, he seemed to be getting smaller and tighter, almost as if he was diminishing. He was thinner than he'd been a fortnight ago, his neck was smaller and his face less square. Grace hadn't seen him smile or heard him laugh, nor had he spoken to her since he'd pronounced his wedding vows, promising to stay with her until he died. It looked as if he was beginning to die already.

Did people *die*, rather than stay married, Grace wondered, actually let themselves fade away rather than live in wedlock? She had got married for the opposite reason: to stay alive. But Wilfred hadn't fought, hadn't said, 'No, I do not take this woman, Grace Amelia Reece, as my lawful, wedded wife. I do not love her. I will not cherish her until death us do part.' Wilfred had not spoken the truth at their wedding. He had lied, Grace realized. All his vows were a lie. He didn't fight the vows and he didn't fight the wedding because he knew he wouldn't win, and now, here in their marriage bed, he was lying down as if some part of him was dying. Grace didn't want him to die. Grace had wanted to live, but she didn't want Wilfred to die in her place.

She reached out her hand across the bed, across the gap between them that had been maintained each and every night for the fourteen nights of the marriage, and touched his arm, leaving her hand there for a few seconds; it was a touch devoid of sexuality or passion, desire or wanting. It was the touch of one broken person reaching out, in recognition, to another.

★   ★   ★

Wilfred was curled up on his side, looking at the bedroom door. Neither of them had moved into the middle of the bed. This is what they must mean by a no man's land, Wilfred thought, a land no man wants to go into. In a normal marriage, the centre of the bed was where the coupling — the marriage — would take place, the space into which the man would invite the woman. Eventually, over years, the weight of both of their bodies caused the bed, its springs and lattices, to squeak and sigh as if it were aching along with the couple's bodies. In the middle of the bed the marriage was made. But not in this bed. This was Dr and Mrs Reece's old bed in Grace's brother's old room in Dr and Mrs Reece's house at 32 High Street, Narberth, Pembrokeshire. That's whose bed it was. Wilfred didn't think of it as his wedding bed.

Wilfred had once kissed Grace under the jasmine in the wood, before it flowered and when it was still in bud, and he had put his hand up her skirt and on to the velvety, fleshy pad of her thigh — and that had been the extent of it, that Good Friday, a few months back. He knew she would never let him touch her breasts, so, with some courage he had stooped to put his hand under her petticoat and along the ridge of her thigh. There she'd stopped him, put her fingers over his; her hand was over the cotton, and his hand was under it. Wilfred had understood, pulled his hand away and concentrated on touching her lip with his tongue. The embrace had taken minutes and it felt to Wilfred now as if in those minutes he had spent the whole of the rest of his life.

But I didn't do anything, Wilfred wanted to say. He hadn't done anything, had he? He had thought about it, he remembered that quite clearly. But that wasn't the same as actually doing anything. Had he? He had touched her leg, that time. Perhaps Grace had sat on a toilet seat. But everything was spotless in Mrs Reece's house. Wilfred was at a loss. He didn't know about these things, no one spoke plainly about them and there were no books that he knew of, not in Narberth. There were rumours that contradicted and left him confused and unclear. He'd kissed her, once, when they went for a walk — had that been it? No. You couldn't make a girl pregnant from kissing her — that was a load of old nonsense, surely? I'm innocent, he thought. But, he realized, Grace wasn't.

But he hadn't done *that*, hadn't put himself there. Good God! If women got pregnant that easily, from men merely touching their legs, well, there would be babies everywhere and there would be millions, billions, of people in the world. Wilfred didn't know much about these things but he guessed that what he used to hear in the Narberth Rugby Football Club bar was just about right, if a bit exaggerated. The rugby lads liked to exaggerate, especially when they had had a few pints, but he suspected they spoke something near the truth. A man could learn all he needed to know about women if he went to the Narberth Rugby Football Club bar for a drink and listened.

Wilfred felt hot, almost fetid, between the flannelette sheets and beneath the weight of the heavy, woollen blankets. There was even an eiderdown on top. It looked like Mrs Reece had sewn it from exact triangles cut from her family's old clothes. Wilfred felt smothered. He wanted to kick away the bedding and the blankets.

It was as Wilfred was lying there perspiring, worrying, that he felt Grace's hand rest on his forearm. It shocked him. He had never expected her to touch him; he didn't want it, crimped himself up to the edge of the mattress every night to avoid it. It had been unthinkable that Grace would touch him. Now her touch felt like a taboo being broken. Didn't she know that they weren't married, not really? That he didn't even want to be married? Didn't they both know — and they were the only two people who did — that it wasn't him? Well, another man *knew*, whoever he was. And everyone else had assumed it was him because he was married to her, but Wilfred and Grace alone knew. Between them, they knew.

Grace, Wilfred had seen out of the corner of his eye, was wearing a long white nightdress. She had worn that bloody yellow dress on their wedding day. Both the nightdress and the dress left Wilfred cold. She had to wear something though, he supposed. Not that she'd worn any clothes with somebody! Wilfred was still shocked. She'd taken off all her clothes with someone. That was certain. But what Wilfred didn't like to think about, couldn't think about, lying in the double bed in the stuffy attic of Dr and Mrs Reece's house, what he couldn't even contemplate, because he knew it would cause him more pain than he could bear, was the thought of Flora.

9

The Sea

Flora laughed. 'On the back of your bicycle? It'll buckle the wheel.'

'Let's go quickly. Hop on,' Wilfred said. 'I'll cycle. The tide will be out soon.'

Saturday had come again and Wilfred and Flora were outside the cottage door. Flora climbed carefully up on to the saddle and Wilfred stood on the pedals. They set off precariously, veering from side to side along the winding lane from the cottage.

'Won't someone see us?' Flora asked.

'I don't care,' Wilfred replied.

'Mind the hydrangeas. Mind the hydran — ' Flora called. Wilfred steered the bicycle sharply to the left, just missing the bush, though a couple of the pink flowers brushed against them.

'Oh!' exclaimed Flora as the hydrangeas fluttered against her face and bare arm, pink petals scattering. She smiled.

'Sorry, dear,' Wilfred called over his shoulder.

'I'm fine,' Flora replied, her chin resting on his shoulder. 'I like wild hydrangeas.' He called me dear, she thought.

It was sultry and would soon be scorching. The sky was utterly cloudless and a bold mid-blue. They were saved from the heat of the sun by the shade of the hawthorn and lime trees beside the path, but when they reached the sea road there would be no protection. Flora had an arm around Wilfred's waist and with her other hand she was holding on to her cloche hat as the bike hurtled in the direction of the sea.

'Slow down!'

'No!'

Flora stretched her legs out from the bicycle, asking, 'Do you drive the hearse like you ride a bicycle?'

'I never get any complaints from the passengers.'

'You're laughing,' Flora said. She took her hat off, putting it under her arm, and wrapped both arms around Wilfred's solid body, laid her head against his back and held on tightly.

The bike clattered and bumped down the steep hill to the cove and Wilfred steered it skilfully, avoiding jagged flints and dry dips that had recently been puddles. They cycled over twigs that snapped sharply and the bicycle bell jingled and the mudguards rattled.

'Yahoo!' Wilfred shouted as they jolted over the lip of the road and freewheeled down the lane and round the corner. When they reached Heane Castle, Wilfred stopped the bike. 'Off, my fair lady, while I make adjustments to our carriage.'

'Is the wheel buckled?' Flora asked.

'No, Raleigh bikes are sturdy.' Wilfred straightened up the handlebars, stepped over the bar, put his feet on the pedals and said to Flora, 'Your carriage awaits!' He bowed down low and made a flourish with his hand.

Flora had never seen Wilfred playful before. She'd seen him stiff and formal at her father's funeral, seen him serious in the cottage — he had even held her as if it was a serious matter — but today he was different, free, light: it was almost, Flora thought, as if he was careless.

'I shall lead my fine damsel to the enchanted forest. And away we go!' Wilfred announced, cycling again.

The road was flat and empty and they made slow progress now they were no longer going downhill. Wilfred worked hard cycling and Flora said sympathetically, 'I'm trying not to weigh too much.'

'Don't worry,' he replied. 'I'm used to having corpses in the back; one elegant lady is no burden.'

By the time they reached Amroth, the muscles in Wilfred's legs were burning and his face was dripping with sweat. He took out a comb from his back trouser pocket and combed his hair to the side while Flora smoothed down her long hair with her hand and tucked her cotton blouse back into her skirt.

'I think we might find the forest because the tide is so far out, the furthest I've ever seen it,' Wilfred commented. It was getting hotter; it would soon be sweltering. He propped the bike against a large granite rock, adding, 'Shoes off!' While he untied the laces of his shoes, Flora unbuckled her sandals and then took her camera from the basket on the front of the bicycle.

'To the sea!' shouted Wilfred. He grabbed Flora's hand and began running. They jogged towards the water for a quarter of a mile or so, their steps in rhythm. The sand was dry and the running arduous, and grains leaped up in their wake.

When Flora slowed into a walk, aware of the growing heat of the day, Wilfred slowed down with her but held on to her hand. She glanced behind them.

'The sand is soft: we haven't left footprints,' she said. 'No one will know we have been here.'

'We are alone in the cove,' Wilfred replied.

It was true, Flora thought. Amroth was deserted. The day-trippers would be further down the Pembrokeshire coast in Saundersfoot and Tenby and, since the anthracite mine had closed last year, Amroth was very quiet, empty even. She and Wilfred were alone in an enormous space.

'I like that the sea goes out in Pembrokeshire,' Wilfred said enthusiastically as they walked along, wiping the sweat from his brow. He was excited to share his thoughts with her and had imagined and practised this conversation in his head.

'I read that in Spain the tide only goes out a yard or two. Whoever heard of such a thing? What do folks do when they want to go somewhere to have a think? Where we are now, and that rock there, in a couple of hours' time, the tide will have come in and that'll be twenty feet, even thirty feet underwater while right now, it's dry as a bone in the sun.'

Flora looked at him and smiled with her eyes. He was right; the sea would be very deep here before too long. Once the tide had gone out as far as it could, the water would then determinedly, unhesitatingly wend its way back towards the road. It would probably turn quite soon.

'Let's run again!' Wilfred enjoined. He pulled Flora's hand and they went towards the sea.

★   ★   ★

The ancient forest was unearthly: logs of ochre-red, fossilized wood lying on soggy sand, some still standing. The stones were orangey-brown, the colour of a tree trunk.

'How long do you think it has been here?' Flora asked Wilfred.

'I read that the forest is seventy thousand years old.'

'Where did you read that?'

'When I was a boy I had a *Chatterbox Annual* every year for Christmas, and one year there was a full page on the petrified forest of Amroth. There, in my book. I wanted to come and find it, but my da said no one he knew had seen it. My da's da had heard of fishermen who worked on schooners from Saundersfoot who'd spotted it at very low tides, but no one in Narberth has ever seen it.'

Flora touched the stone tree with her fingertips.

'How can wood become stone?' she wondered aloud. 'How can a tree that grew and was green with leaves turn to stone?' She took her camera from around her neck and began to take photographs of the trees. Wilfred gazed at the large stones encircling them, shielding his eyes from the sun.

'The patterns in the tree trunks are very beautiful,' Flora commented, glancing away from her lens.

'What do you take photographs of?' Wilfred asked.

'Shells on the beach, the rocks at the cove — and now fossilized wood. Sometimes people.'

'Who?'

'The people I love — portraits of them.'

Wilfred wondered, with a sharp pain, if there was a man; she might have a man she loved. There could easily be, she was so beautiful.

'I haven't taken any photographs of anyone for a while,' she offered.

Wilfred noticed her looking at him, as if assessing the proportion and angles of his face.

'What do you do with the photographs?' he asked.

'I keep them in an old chocolate box in my bedroom and look at them sometimes. And I make albums as well.'

'Would you like to be a photographer?'

'I would, but I don't know how. Perhaps I could take photographs for postcards or do wedding portraits.'

'That would be exciting. There are very few ladies who are photographers.' There is a world of thought and creativity within her, Wilfred thought.

'To think,' he continued aloud, keeping his thoughts to himself, 'that where we are sitting now, on this flat sand at the edge of the sea, must once have been a wood. Maybe people even lived here.'

'That was many ages before our cottage was here,' Flora replied.

Our cottage, she'd said. Wilfred looked down at the sand. Our cottage. Perhaps if it had been their cottage when this was a forest, instead of water and sand, he could have lived by the cove with Flora for all of their lives, had a different life, a happy one.

'Are you thinking about something?' Flora asked. 'You are frowning.'

Wilfred smiled at her. 'Come and sit by me,' he said gently. Flora moved along on the fossilized tree and Wilfred put his arm around her shoulder. He liked wrapping his arm around her. She stretched out her legs and put her toes in a small puddle of seawater.

'I want to tell you something, Flora. It's not important. But I want to tell you anyways.'

Flora looked up. The sea was still at a distance, but turning; before too long they would have to head back to the road that led to the world beyond. This copse in the sea was magical: an ancient forest hidden beneath the waves. The sea had a secret.

Flora waited for Wilfred to speak.

'It sounds important even though it isn't,' Wilfred repeated. He took Flora's hand in both of his. Her hand was much smaller than his, more papery and delicate.

'It's not important, Flora, but I'm married.'

The waves swished in the distance. Eventually

Flora said evenly, 'But you're not wearing a ring.' She looked at Wilfred's large, square hands. His fingers were bare.

'It's in my pocket.'

'Can I see?'

Wilfred stood up, delved his hands into his trouser pockets and there was the sound of coins jangling. He brought out a handful of money and among the shillings and sixpences was a large, gold band. He picked it up between his fingers and showed it to Flora. It was proof. To Flora the ring was a circle of proof.

'That is your wedding ring?' Wilfred nodded. 'Why didn't you tell me?' she asked faintly. Flora stayed sitting on the log, Wilfred standing in front of her. She felt as if scaffolding was collapsing inside her, planks and poles collapsing and falling down with a distant din. This is betrayal, she said to herself. I am being betrayed.

Wilfred took her hand and pulled her up, put his arms around her. This time he held her to him more confidently than he had before. He placed his arms around her purposefully, with intention, as if he knew what he wanted, and breathed in the scent of her.

It was a couple of seconds before Flora realized she was holding her breath. Then she felt herself imperceptibly curl forward. In her mind's eye she saw an unborn child curling up on itself. Wilfred would not have noticed the movement she made because it was so slight, yet she knew that it was a profound and decisive moment that would mark her for the rest of her life. She felt like an unborn child regressing and curling in on itself.

'Flora . . . Flora,' Wilfred said gently, calling her. She pulled away and looked up at his face: his thick eyebrows, his straight eyelashes, the reddish flush of his cheeks. Wilfred in turn saw the whiteness of her face, how she had blanched since he'd told her, despite her skin being burnished by the sun.

'I wanted to tell you — I *want* to tell you because if I only speak the truth to one person, then I want it to be you.'

Flora looked out at the sea and noticed it was coming in fast. They were a long way from the road; the tide in Pembrokeshire was unexpected and the water could have fractured patterns and strange eddies. Sometimes the sea made islands of sand as it came in, islands it was possible to be stranded on until the sea came in. It wasn't only this dead wood that was drowned by the sea. They were silly, stupid, to have come so far out. She could swim a little but the sea was strong. Anyone who lived by the sea quickly learned to respect it.

'The sea is coming in fast,' she said. Wilfred had forgotten himself. He, too, saw the sea, its small waves heralding powerful, more wilful ones.

'We need to go back. Come on, best if we run.' Wilfred took Flora's hand, and began to pull her towards the cliffs.

They had been looking out at the sea but the sea had come in behind them: where they had been sitting on the beach was now a sand dune.

The sea has come in already, Wilfred realized with horror. There was water between them and the road. It was an inlet, and would be deep already. Could they wade across it? Could Flora swim? How wide was the inlet? Ten feet. No — more. Twenty . . . thirty feet. It was hard to see the further edge clearly in the shimmering light. The sea was surging into the inlet from both sides. It would be getting deeper by the second.

'Run, Flora, come on!' He clasped her hand and she took great paces, pushing her feet against the sand.

'Look!' Flora exclaimed. 'It's come in already!' She felt panic, fear. They were at the edge of the water.

Wilfred unbuckled his belt, yanked down his trousers, pulled off his shirt.

'Take your clothes off now! They will pull you down.' In her panic, Flora couldn't undo her buttons so she ripped them apart and tore off her blouse.

'Your camera as well!' Wilfred grabbed her forearm with his muscular hand and dragged her into the water. It was cold. A few steps and the waves were at her thighs.

'But I can hardly swim,' Flora cried, resisting. Wilfred, a few steps ahead, tugged her forward. Flora stood on a stone, stumbled, and her face went into the water.

'Quickly,' he insisted, but the water thwarted them and they couldn't run. Wilfred was attempting to cross in a straight line but the current was forcing them to the left.

'It's hard to walk,' Flora replied. 'Shout for help. Help! Help!' But the beach, the whole cove, was deserted. There was no one.

'Hold on to me.' He was still gripping her forearm powerfully. She held on to his arm with her other hand as well and they entered the middle of the channel.

'I have you,' Wilfred stated, surging forward. 'Take deep breaths.' Flora was on her tiptoes now, the water at her shoulders, tight waves slapping her neck and face. The water was thick, forceful, hard to move against.

'Wilfred!' she yelled. 'I can't touch the bottom!' But he kept moving forward though the water was up to his neck. He took more steps and hauled her. She was going under now; with each step, the water was getting deeper and faster. She gasped and swallowed air, then water.

She clung to Wilfred's upper arm and she could feel the certainty of his hold on her, the absoluteness with which he seized her. She could no longer speak, the water stung her eyes, she couldn't open them, couldn't see where she was going, where Wilfred was leading her, didn't know where the shore was, nor which way the sun was, then finally, where the sand was or the bottom of the sea . . .

Breathe! Breathe! She felt an injunction upon her. Breathe! When Flora felt air on her face, she sucked in as much as she could. Breathe! It was an inviolable command from someone, somewhere, who knew what she must do, and each time her mouth emerged from the water, this instinctive voice was commanding her, *Breathe!*

So she opened her mouth and the saltwater and air went into her. All around her was the violence and the chaos of water. There was only the certainty of Wilfred's strong grasp on her forearm then the air on her face, then water, then air, then water . . .

★ ★ ★

Wilfred held Flora as she vomited slushes of seawater on to the sand. She was leaning over, coughing, retching, and Wilfred had his hands on top of her arms. The water behind them was widening quickly, they were barely beyond its reach and they must move soon — now — as the sea was advancing. And there were maybe other sand dunes forming. Wilfred took Flora's hand and began walking swiftly, though she stumbled because of the seawater stinging her eyes, and her limbs were mottled by the cold. She had swallowed whole mouthfuls of sea and the salt was prickling the insides of her mouth. She felt dizzy, jelly-like, could hardly believe there was firm sand for her feet to stand on. Wilfred half-dragged, half-carried her, Flora almost bent double, until they reached his bicycle, still propped up against the boulder where they had left it what now felt like a very long time ago.

They were both shaken and bewildered. They walked quickly, almost ran along the road, Wilfred pushing the bike, Flora hunching her shoulders forward self-consciously. The day was now broiling and the road was blistering on their bare feet, and small gravel stones dug into their soles.

Within ten minutes they had reached the other side of the cove. Wilfred headed into the foliage of the wooded hill and began to lead the way through the bushes to where he thought the cottage was; he hadn't waited till they reached the path, wanting for them to leave the road as soon as they could. Thorn bushes, nettles and sharp sticks brushed against their bare skin and Wilfred held back branches for Flora to pass, to save her being scratched and stung.

In the copse and further from the sea Flora began to feel safer and more grounded; her bare feet on the cracked mud was comforting to her. It was the firm, solid earth; it was where she belonged. The leaves were providing shadows from the brilliant sun overhead, which had burned down on them on the beach and the road.

Wilfred shoved the cottage door open then led Flora in. He pulled the green tablecloth from the three-legged chair and gave it to her. She wrapped it around her shoulders, making a shawl of it. Then he took her in his arms. This time, for the first time, there was no awkwardness in Wilfred's touch, no hesitancy; he held her with strength and ease. This was the body of the woman he had dragged through the sea, had held on to hard and tight while she flailed behind him. When her head went under the water he had found a resolution within himself — one he hadn't known he had. It was as if a force had risen up inside him and it was absolute. She would live — he would make her live, he would not lose her. His grasp was iron-like, welded to her: the muscles of his arm, his knuckles and her wrist were made of iron welded into one piece and he would do anything, everything, before he let go of this woman. His body had never been stronger, his resolve never firmer. He knew a less determined man holding a lesser woman would have loosened his grip. And when she stood slightly beyond the river, in her liberty bodice, vomiting, the nakedness and the physicality of her body were nothing to him, not even a revelation. His decision was made, it had formed within him, was strengthened, then finally forged as he had dragged the nearly drowned body of this woman, Flora, through a river that had almost, *almost*, engulfed them. So, in the cottage when he took Flora in his arms, it was different. He stroked her damp hair, her small shoulders and then ran his hands down her bare arms.

Flora leaned against him, her arms hanging by her side. She had swallowed so much water and vomited so violently, her drenching had been so complete, that she felt as if the water had taken everything out of her. She felt purged: physically, emotionally. In those seconds, or minutes — that timeless space when she could no longer touch the bottom of the sea — Wilfred pulled her forward. When everything around her was water, when she no longer knew which way to find air, against the endless waves was the hard grip of Wilfred's fingers. He had had his hand locked on to her body. Looking down she saw an imprint, an emerging bruise on her skin from his four fingers and thumb, a mark of Wilfred's commitment to her. Wilfred, noticing it, put his hand gently over the darkening skin. He had held on. Wilfred enfolded her, unafraid, then pulled her even closer.

They were alive, they were both alive, he thought. And that was all that would ever matter to him again.

'Come here,' he said, that's all, but the words were spoken with such openness that Flora could feel the warmth within them. No, they weren't married and yes, Wilfred was married to someone else. They lay down on their sides, Flora with her arms folded across her chest. The earth was cool beneath them and the air very slightly chilly in the dusky cottage.

'There,' Wilfred said. After a while when they had both relaxed a little, he had pulled her arm away from her front and placed it around his back. 'There, there, there,' one simple word which he repeated as he held her, a word full of comfort and solace.

* * *

Flora could hear the breeze in the birch trees outside their cottage. She was shaking visibly when she'd come out of the sea and been chilled on their furtive run from the beach to here, but now she was warm. She was wrapped in Wilfred's arms; his body was much bigger than hers and it was warming her. She placed her hand in the thick hair of his bare chest and felt Wilfred's heart beating. It was a strong, regular

197

beat, well-paced — the beat of a heart that wanted to beat, wanted her to be alive.

'There, there, there.'

They slept for the rest of the afternoon. Wilfred woke up, slightly uncomfortable. The flagstones underneath him were hard, and if the day hadn't been so sweltering he would be chilled, but he had Flora in his arms and they were wrapped in the green tablecloth and he was warm. It was still light because midsummer was approaching and out of the low square window he could see a crescent of pale moon against a whiteish sky. He smoothed Flora's hair away from her face where it had fallen and she stirred. She snuggled into him and he saw the lattice on her cheek from where she had lain against the linen and he felt her breath against his neck.

After a few minutes, he noticed her eyes open and that she was looking at him. He smiled and pulled her to him. He kissed her neck gently and ruffled her hair. She took the tablecloth and pulled it over them, making sure it covered Wilfred too.

'Tell me,' she whispered to him. She hadn't heard from him over the last few weeks and had started to wonder what was happening. Wilfred raised an eyebrow and smiled in a resigned way. He felt the curve of her breasts against his chest.

'Well . . . ' he said, then: 'Well, it wasn't . . . ' Then he added, 'I don't know where to begin.'

'Tell me from the beginning,' she said, knowing he was lost in the maze of his own life. 'How did it begin?'

'Well . . . ' Where to begin? 'I am married to

Grace Reece, Doctor Reece of Narberth's daughter.' He saw Flora's eyes close in a slow blink, then open again.

'How long have you been married?'

'Three weeks.'

Wilfred suddenly felt his tongue, which had been tense and swollen in his mouth, begin to say the words that had been locked inside him.

'I was foolish. So foolish.' He tried to put into order all that had happened. 'I was sweet on her and I proposed, out of the blue. Just said it, like that, stupidly. Then she said yes. But I told her, I told her plain as day that I didn't want to get married. I didn't mean it when I proposed. And that was that. Then her father came and told me I was marrying her. She's expecting.' He felt Flora flinch in his arms.

'No. No. It's not like that. I didn't know. She wasn't expecting when I proposed — or perhaps she was. But it wasn't me. It wasn't anything to do with me. And her father and her mother, ruddy Mrs Reece — everybody thinks it's me because I was her fiancé, and it isn't, and the only person who knows it wasn't me is me. And Grace. And now you.'

As all the words poured out, Wilfred felt his mind and body unwind, as if he had been clockwork, wound up so tightly that he might have popped and unravelled with a ping and a clatter of metal cogs and wheels. Now it was as if he was allowed to uncoil and express himself.

'I haven't even seen a woman naked, not a real, live one. I had never even kissed a woman before, never mind had sexual relations. I was once sweet on her at a picnic, that's all.' He paused and stroked Flora's hair. 'If I told everyone it wasn't me, no one would believe me because I was her fiancé for a few weeks. It would have to be me, but they would be wrong. It wasn't me and I don't know who it was. I've racked my brains but it must be someone because Grace is hardly the Virgin Mary and Narberth isn't Bethlehem.'

Wilfred reached out and leaned over Flora. He could feel she was alert and listening intently, like a deer aware of her surroundings.

'So I went to the wedding in the register office, and I've done so many funerals and buried so many people, and that day felt more like a funeral than any funeral I've ever been to. I felt as if I was burying myself alive and no one was noticing.

'And there's my da . . . My ma died four days after I was born and my da brought me up. And if I hadn't married Grace I would have had to leave Narberth, because no one would have let me bury their next-of-kin if they thought I'd left Grace in the lurch and abandoned a baby. And for how many years would they remember what I'd done? I'd have no work and I wouldn't be able to care for my da. It's because of my da. I am his world and we are everything to each other, and if I left Narberth, what would happen to him? Who would look after him? He needs me and I need him.' He looked into Flora's brown eyes. 'And where would I go? I thought of the Army but I don't want to fight or kill. I don't want to kill people; I only want to bury them.

And I couldn't leave Narberth because my da is here and my da will never leave Narberth because my ma is here, buried in the graveyard. And my da sits with my ma every day. No, I couldn't leave, not after all my da is to me. Not ever.'

He pulled Flora to him and rubbed her along the length of her back.

'And if I didn't marry her and I stayed in Narberth, no woman would ever marry me. What woman would marry a man who they thought had left their child? What woman would love a man who had been so cruel?' Wilfred buried his face into the thickness of Flora's hair.

Wilfred, saying it all for the first time, realized that he had thought his life was his own, but it wasn't; he knew now that it belonged as well to his da and to the people of Narberth, and by loving his father and by living in Narberth, his life belonged, in part, to them.

Wilfred could feel the sweat trickling from his forehead as he spoke, seeping out from under his arms and damp on the hair on his chest. Flora was absolutely still in his arms; it was as if she was absorbing Wilfred's words, and he could feel she was utterly attentive.

'So it was because I was bullied and panicked, and because I love my da and because I fancied a woman once at a picnic. And because she was expecting, and because I was stupid and unlucky. And then I met you.'

'Yes.'

'And then your da . . . your da . . . it was your father and he'd passed away and I buried him and I liked you from those first few moments, when you were beautiful and sad and elegant, and I thought you looked like a deer, a graceful, vulnerable, startled deer and I wanted you, this, here, for ever.' Wilfred heard Flora breathe in.

'I planned to take you for tea, and when your mam said no, I didn't know what to do, didn't know what to think. Then I got your postcard — only I didn't know it was from you, and I came here and it *was* you.'

There. It was said. He was spent. The truth was between them like a cloth laid out — she would do with it as she would. He had spoken the truth and he could do no other. Suddenly a gasp escaped from him and the muscles of his face crumpled. Wilfred cried — loud, jerky sobs that wrenched the silence of the cottage. He cried in an unpractised way, as if he didn't know how to cry, and Flora held him in his gaucheness.

When Wilfred's crying had subsided, Flora pulled back.

'Shall I tell you?' she asked.

'About yourself?'

She nodded.

'Yes,' Wilfred said. This was what he wanted, the truth of her.

'Well, there was Albert and we were engaged and I loved him like it's possible to love when your heart hasn't been broken. But it was the war and he went . . . and he never came back. When I saw the telegram, it felt as if a bomb had exploded in my heart. Sometimes I think I died with him at the Battle of the Sambre as he went over the trench. And for a long while, I *wanted* to die with him. But there were years of life without Albert, numb, flat years where all I wanted was the life I'd thought I was going to have with him. Other men came along but I couldn't love them because my heart was too fractured; there wasn't enough of it left to love. Then my father, like that, gone. Nothing is as sudden as death.

'At the funeral it seemed that you knew what to do in the face of death, knew almost how to organize and command it, how to cope with it and still breathe and walk and talk. I had only known how to die when death came near. But you were businesslike about mortality and it was an answer.'

She covered herself in the tablecloth.

'At the funeral I felt your warmth for me and it melted something deep inside me that had frozen, and when my mam said I couldn't have tea with you, I knew that was my life now and that it belonged to me, and that I want to live it before I die, not spend it grieving.

'And there was something else.' She smoothed her hair away from her eyes. 'When I saw my father laid out in his coffin, he looked perfect and dead. His skin was cool and even, his face set peacefully, not strained. And he was lying so still in an immaculate white shroud. He was perfect: perfectly still, perfectly composed, and perfectly serene. I realized then, that the only thing in the world that is perfect is death. Life is like this, here, now — not perfect, not still, not calm, not over. Like us. So I opened up, I reached out, I sent the postcard, and you came and you're married. And I . . . '

She didn't finish the sentence but Wilfred sensed she wanted to say something else.

'And I want to be here with you,' she added. Wilfred put his hand to Flora's face, stroked her cheek and took a piece of grass from her hair.

There was a peace between them born of release, a silence without secrets. The moon was reflecting its pure light on to the cove. Wilfred looked over Flora's shoulder and out of the window, and saw that the sky had darkened somewhat and the stars were emerging, bright and far away, peppering the night with their beads of light. The wind moved in the trees and bats swished across the sky. The tablecloth they were wrapped in was muddy, stained with earth, damp from tears and warmed by their sunburned skin. Wilfred put a hand to Flora's narrow shoulder.

'What will you do?' Flora asked.

'I don't know,' he said.

Wilfred and Flora walked silently from the cove through fields of green wheat, Wilfred carrying his bike, to the low hedge at the back of White Hook. At the bottom of the garden Wilfred picked Flora up in his arms and lifted her over the hawthorn. They parted silently. Wilfred went to kiss her on the lips but Flora turned her face away.

★　★　★

There was a light on in the house, Flora saw — her mam was still up and waiting for her. It was past midnight and her mam must have feared the worst. For the last few weeks Flora had told her she was going for a bicycle ride when she had been cycling to the cove most days to take photographs but then she hadn't returned. Night had come. It was dark and silent by the time Flora pushed open the door and walked through the porch into the kitchen.

Her mam was at the round kitchen table, a lamp burning intensely beside her, sitting mutely, waiting modestly. The fire was low and a breeze was disturbing the green curtains hanging at the kitchen window. Flora stayed still for a few seconds and then she walked across the floor, sat down on the slate tiles, put her head on her mam's knees and cried.

Her mam sat upright, as she had been taught to do in her childhood, and put her now weathered hand on her daughter's head while Flora wept. Mrs Edwards was mature enough to say nothing. She didn't ask where her daughter's clothes were, or why she was in her undergarments, nor why she was wearing the old green tablecloth across her shoulders — the one from her own wedding day almost thirty years ago. She saw the sizeable bruise on Flora's wrist, which must surely be hurting. It looked like fingerprints, but how had she come to get a bruise like that? Her daughter had been somewhere — she didn't know where — and had returned bruised, almost naked and alone in the early hours. Her daughter had returned, her mam acknowledged, but it was as if she had left for good. A moth flew into the lamp, beating its wings against the glass, threatening to burn itself.

Flora's mam knew that something had happened — something profound, perhaps even violent — but she sensed it was best not to ask; sensed that one question, just one, would make her daughter get up and walk away, not merely upstairs to her bed, but to walk away inside herself and never open up to her again.

Earlier tonight, sitting at the pine table, Mrs Melbourne Edwards had felt utter terror that she had lost her daughter as well as her husband, both within the tiny span of a few days. She had sat alone in the family home without her family and felt as if winter had come for ever. Her daughter had gone into the day and she had thought she would never return. Something had happened: her daughter was different, that was plain. Her daughter held something new, unsaid, something unsayable within her, something she would never tell her mam, and something her mam knew she must never ask about. So they sat there until Flora, spent with crying, took her head from her mam's lap, lay down on the slate floor by her mam's feet, curled up and fell into an exhausted sleep.

★ ★ ★

It was well past midnight when Wilfred left Flora and began cycling back down the silent lanes towards Narberth. When he was just past the turning at Peter's Finger he heard a car engine approaching so he pushed through the hedge

206

beside the road, disturbing a sett of bustling badgers, and lay low in a muddy cornfield until the car passed. It was nearing one o'clock when he arrived at Narberth. Instead of cycling down the High Street he trundled his bike through the cow fields encircling the town and then sprinted down Church Street, into Water Street and straight through the back door. That way he had been able to get home, a near-naked cyclist in only his underwear, without anyone seeing him.

His da was in bed, wouldn't have waited up for Wilfred, thinking he would be staying at Dr Reece's, where he was supposed to live now. But no. Wilfred was back in his bedroom and there was his bed. It was with a sense of relief and exhaustion that he took off his tattered underpants, got in between the crumpled sheets and found the worn, almost threadbare, patch where his feet rested on the flannelette. This was Wilfred's own bed where he slept on his back and spread himself out. He hadn't extended his limbs in bed like this, flexed his feet, tossed or turned for many nights. It is good to feel free in bed, Wilfred thought: this is my bed and this is my home.

He could hear his da harrumphing from next door. His da always snored easily and mightily, often waking Wilfred up.

'Shut up, Da!' he'd shout, banging on the stone wall between the two rooms. 'Stop snoring!'

'Eh?' his father would grunt. 'I'm not snoring. I don't snore,' he'd retort, seemingly awake but still wrapped in sleep.

As much as his da's constant snoring had woken him through the nights when Wilfred was young, it had also reassured him and, until he got married, it was all he knew of the presence of another in the night. Lying awake in the nights of his childhood and youth, frustrated by the snoring, a pillow over his head to muffle the noise, he was also reassured, thinking, It is the night, but my da is here.

10

Wallpaper's All the Rage

'The parlour, Da, we'll have that now as a paint and wallpaper shop,' Wilfred announced the following morning. He was frying black pudding, sausages and Specials for them both in the cast-iron frying pan.

'Wallpaper's all the rage,' he continued, turning the sausages over. 'Very fashionable it is, Da, mark my words. Especially the Paisley prints. And Mrs Bell Evans of Sheep Street was asking after some floral paper — orchids or sweet peas, I know that for a fact.' Wilfred cracked an egg against the wall and plopped the contents into the sizzling pan. And if his da wondered why Wilfred had slept at home and not at Grace's, he said nothing.

'Double yolk in the pan! I reckon if we have a wallpaper shop we'll have them coming to Narberth from as far away as Carmarthen to buy the stuff. By damn, I could see it working, Da.' Wilfred lifted two enamel plates from the sink and plonked them on the table.

'Well, Wilfred,' his father replied cautiously, 'I don't know about wallpaper. Houses in Narberth don't have straight walls. There'll be no pasting wallpaper on a lopsided surface.'

'Da,' Wilfred said, slipping some Specials out of the frying pan and on to the plates, 'don't be daft. You can hang wallpaper on anything. Only need a dab of that Henkel wallpaper paste — it's got potato flour in it that sticks it to the wall. You know Margaret White in Green Grove Farm up by Lampeter Velfrey, well, she apparently has even wallpapered the door in her water closet.'

Wilfred rubbed the forks clean on the dishcloth. 'The salt's on the chair, Da. And there's more black pudding in the pan.' Wilfred was ravenous. He'd slept deeply, 'like a stone,' his father would say, and woken with a raging appetite. He ate his breakfast with his face low and close to his plate.

'And don't be worrying about what'll happen to the furniture in the parlour. It will all just about fit in the workshop behind the coffins.' Wilfred's knife and fork clinked and tinged on the plate as he cut a sausage in half.

'Why would you want to turn the parlour into a paint and wallpaper shop when only seven years ago you's turned the back yard into a workshop for coffins?' his da asked, slicing the double yolk of his fried egg with a fork and dipping a Special in it. 'It's damp as anything round here. The wallpaper will be hanging off bedroom walls after a few weeks, and nobody will want that. It might be all right in Carmarthen or London, where people like something altogether a bit different and fancy and the houses are built of bricks, but around here? It'll be a sight.'

Wilfred had to concede his da had a point. Suddenly he felt weary, exhausted. He watched an ant walk briskly across the table and around the tin of Saxa salt. Wallpapering lumpy walls would be difficult. And if he couldn't get paper to stick on a wall, how could he ever . . . He felt too dispirited even to try and put into words the ways in which his life was wrong.

'Is there a knife anywhere?' his da asked. 'Can't eat an egg with a fork.'

'There's a butter knife in the butter, Da,' Wilfred replied, still thinking about wallpaper. To stick wallpaper on the ancient walls of Narberth homes would require strong glue. And to leave the situation he was in with Grace would also need strength. He ate the last of his black pudding, lost in his thoughts, while his da rinsed the butter knife under the tap. Lies had got him into this mess, but the truth would get him out. Yesterday he had spoken truthfully to Flora; now he would speak honestly to his Grace.

'You's been talking to those travelling wallpaper salesmen,' his da commented. 'Tasty breakfast, Wilfred. It's filling a hole nicely.'

What was that phrase? Wilfred thought. 'Wallpapering over the cracks'. He might one day have a sideline to his undertaking business, decorating for the more fashionable ladies in Narberth and the surrounds, but it wouldn't do to wallpaper over the cracks in the walls. To do so would be bad for business. Wilfred placed his knife and fork together on his plate. No, he would only wallpaper on strong plaster and a well-held wall. And nor, he decided, would he wallpaper over the cracks in his life.

★ ★ ★

Grace felt flushed and somewhat uncomfortable in the armchair where she was dozing. Her lower back and hips ached and her limbs felt heavy and swollen. She saw her reflection in the tainted mirror above Madoc's chest of drawers. Her fingers, holding the book, were bloated, and the skin under her chin was fuller. She was getting fatter and she felt a sense of panic. She picked at some lint on her skirt. She had been sitting all morning in the armchair in the attic reading, biding time. That's what she did these days, bide her time, engage with time and forwardness: relentless and ruthless time. Pregnancy was showing her that — that life went one way and one way only. And it took a woman with it. Life was absolute in its forwardness.

Before all this — she looked down at her body — she'd thought her life was fine, good; now that old life, the one where she used to have garden picnics, sing in St Andrew's Church choir and tend her brother's bees, that life had an innocence to it, a perfect wholeness it would never have again. Now her life was formed and set and she was married. There would be the . . . baby, her baby, though it didn't feel like hers. It was a baby that was forced into her, against her wishes. If she had struggled she would have been forced violently. So she hadn't struggled. She had frozen instead. So she had been forced to acquiesce, silently, mutely. *I won't think about it. Don't think about it*, she told herself. She had promised herself she wouldn't think about it. But her body ached. What had happened was with her now — had taken over her life and was taking over her body. Wilfred hated her, her mother was enraged with her, her father was stone cold towards her, and she hated *it* growing within her. 32 High Street was a house of contempt. It was as if she had been filled up with hatred, and now that hatred was seeping out of her and contaminating the circle of people surrounding her.

No wonder she couldn't read Jane Austen. Those girls, Emma, Lydia, Marianne, Fanny, going to balls and dances then falling in love with Colonels. Grace couldn't focus and she put her book on the side-table. She would go and collect honey. But she felt strange, as if something was happening and something was shifting. The air was oppressive, and as she breathed in she felt a quiver of panic run through her. She would collect honey — it would sweeten her bitter mood. She put Jane Austen back on the shelf.

★   ★   ★

The bee had stung her! One of her bees had stung her! Grace had been checking on the hives. There was some honey to collect, not much. These days she was grateful to the bees for their friendliness and lack of judgement. Bees didn't care. All these bees, hovering around the irises and landing on the lavender, had only one wife between them — the engorged and adored queen bee. Of what concern to bees were mothers and fathers, brothers and sisters and husbands and wives? They made honey, fed

213

larvae, found flowers, on and on across millennia, while she floundered, fatter by the day, trapped and unhappily wed day in, day out and even through the night, feeling desperate. Bees had existed for millions of years; she had been alive for twenty-four. These bees' ancestors had lived long before her, and their offspring would be around long after her life was over. Bees, with their eternity of business and productivity, gave her a sense of perspective. They had made honey for what might as well be eternity as far as Grace, with her short lifespan, was concerned.

Grace had been thinking these thoughts, feeling lethargic, when she had been stung. The sting was on her hand, on the fleshy pad between her thumb and forefinger. The bee must have climbed up through the small gap between her sleeve and glove. Feeling itself endangered, trapped and fearing death, it had killed itself by stinging her. It hurt. Grace pulled off the glove and flicked the bee away. It hovered drunkenly. It would soon be dead. Grace saw the dark hook-like barb in her flesh and after a few moments of painless shock, her thumb then her fingers began to throb. Tears came to her eyes, long-held tears in need of an outlet.

She was shocked. The bees had not stung her before — she had been proud of that, boasted to herself that she had never, ever been stung. When patients coming to the house for her father's surgery asked, 'Are you not scared of all those bees?' she had been able to answer confidently, back in the days when she had been confident, 'No, I'm not scared of them.' Then when they enquired, 'Not even when they sting you?' Grace had been able to announce fearlessly, as if commenting on the loyalty of her bees, 'I have never been stung.'

People often asked her about her beekeeper's outfit. Did she wear a hat? Didn't she ever worry that a bee might get inside her suit or under the netting? Didn't bees kill people? Grace answered calmly. She knew it wasn't the protective clothing she wore that kept her safe. Bees were intelligent creatures; if a bee wanted to sting or a whole hive wanted to attack, it would. It had nothing to do with what one wore. Her hive didn't sting her because all twelve thousand of the bees knew who she was, recognized her gloved hand on the cedar slats not as a thief but as a friend. They let her have their honey freely; she didn't steal it from them. If they'd thought she was a thief, they would have unleashed themselves. As she reached out to the bees, the bees reached out to her, landing on the white suit, buzzing calmly around her.

Grace shook her hand to dispel some of the pain. Her hand was reddening and the skin around the sting was swelling into a lump. The bee, now resting on the lawn, had sacrificed its life to sting her with its poison. Its fragile body was agitated. Grace's hand was hurting and she could feel her whole body beginning to ache. All is not well, Grace realized, looking at the nearly still, almost dead bee lying by her foot. All is not well.

'Da! Da!' Wilfred called, later that afternoon. 'Where are you?' A muffled reply came from inside the water closet. Wilfred walked through the house to the yard where the small brick hut with the corrugated iron roof stood. The closet could do with a lick of lime-wash because there was fungus on the outside and the white walls were bubbling with old, mould-attacked paint.

'Da!' Wilfred shouted through the door. His da was in there for an hour every Sunday afternoon and Wilfred didn't want to wait.

'Good God, Wilfred! What do you want? Can't I have a moment's peace?'

'Da, I want to talk to you now.'

'Well, give me a minute, boyo.' Eventually Wilfred heard a bucket of earth being poured down the toilet and the door opened, and his father emerged doing up the buckle on his trouser belt.

'What is it now? What is the world coming to, if a man can't even respond to a call of nature without being rushed?'

'Da, I want to tell you something.' Wilfred breathed deeply. 'Da ... ' But he didn't continue. He kneeled down to do up his shoelace, and when it was done, he stayed kneeling, looking vacantly into the distance.

'You got me off the lavatory,' his da tucked the newspaper under his arm, 'and now you're not telling me.'

Wilfred mumbled, 'Da, there's a woman.'

'Are you talking about Grace?'

'No.'

'Another woman?'

Wilfred nodded, put his knuckles to the ground and pushed himself up.

'So you're telling me there's another woman and it's not Grace?'

Wilfred's eyes met his da's, and he nodded.

'So that's why you've been so unhappy . . . but Wilfred . . . ?'

Wilfred knew his father understood what it was to love a woman and order himself in life around a woman, and how his marriage — even in widowhood — had sustained him and given him joy. When his wife died, his da wanted to go with her. His da lived because Wilfred lived, but his heart was gone into the grave or the heavens — wherever it was the dead went. He only dug the graveyard because he wanted to lie down in the earth by his wife, and he only studied the stars because he was looking for his wife among them.

'But Wilfred, we both know there is a baby coming,' his da said. Wilfred's face clouded. 'You must care for your child, Wilfred. You must care for Grace. It is what a man does.'

Wilfred put his hand to his forehead.

'But Da . . . ' He looked at his father. He had lived at 11 Market Street for twenty-seven years, for all of his life. He and his da had walked around naked, cooked cockles and Specials with no clothes on, each taken a weekly dip on a Sunday evening in the tin bath on the rug in front of the hearth. They had lived in their small home in an unabashed and intimate way, the way a family lived, but they had never talked about things like this.

'What is it, Wilfred, my son?' His da looked at him and watched and listened.

Wilfred's heart felt like a boulder in his chest, like one of those at the cove. His heart felt large and heavy and difficult and impossible to carry within him any more, so hindered was he by the secrets and lies of himself and others.

He looked at his patient, kind da who thought only of the world to come and his wife waiting for him. There was a soft, gentle silence. The door of the WC banged from time to time in the breeze and next-door's pig was grunting in its pigscot. The sky was playing with the clouds. They stood there in their small yard with the pissabeds, the bellybuttons, the moss and the ivy, the vegetable patch and the overgrown and unkempt flowerbed that was a mass of green plants and small flowers. His da was waiting, listening; he wasn't judging him — hadn't even judged him or mentioned it when he understood that Grace was expecting and something was very awry, even though his da saw how unhappy he was. That's what listening was, Wilfred realized; listening was not judging.

His da was so familiar to him he was almost a part of him. His da was just his da and was always there, like the mist on the hills around Narberth that came up from the earth and one walked within it, barely even seeing it. And like the mist, his da had no shape, no specificity; Wilfred had lived enveloped in his gentleness that was safe and familiar. But right now, there in front of him, with his light blue watery eyes, his lined face etched with experience, and his braces hanging from his trousers, was this utterly separate man. Wilfred saw that, after all, they were two distinct men, with two different lives and each with their own woman to love.

Wilfred stood up. He looked at the man in front of him and said, 'It is not my child.'

★   ★   ★

After the revelation, Wilfred did the washing up. Back in the kitchen, he filled the sink with boiling water from the whistling copper kettle, and collected the plates and cups, throwing the loose tea in the bin. He began washing, the bubbles mushrooming out of the white ceramic sink.

'Not your child, then?' his da asked.

'No.'

'No, not your child,' his da repeated. He was tidying up the newspapers on the table, but was too distracted to do it properly.

'It wasn't me, Da,' Wilfred said. 'It couldn't be.' Wilfred was accused but he was innocent. The room fell quiet.

'So it's somebody else's child, then?'

'Yes,' Wilfred said, scrunching up the lid of the salt pack and putting it on the shelf. 'I don't know whose child it is. I have no idea.'

'No. No,' his da said, shaking his head.

'It must be someone,' Wilfred said.

'Yes.' His da nodded thoughtfully. Wilfred rubbed yesterday's dinner-plates vigorously with the grey dishcloth. Steam was billowing up from the sink.

'Grace will know,' his da said. 'Women know who the father of their child is. Women have secrets; they hold them inside themselves, like they hold a child.' His da had never spoken like this before. This was entirely new.

While his father dried the plates, Wilfred wiped the steam from the windowpane above the sink with his hand. He looked out to the green hills beyond, the hills that curved so confidently and easily, like a well-fed woman. Sometimes Wilfred wondered if under those Welsh hills there were great women, giantesses, who had lain down on the earth in ancient times and fallen asleep, and then the earth had crept over them, over their breasts and their hips and the dips of their waists and tapering up their strong thighs. And then the green grass had grown over them, covering them with a fertile blanket of fresh plants that kept them warm and hidden.

'What are you going to do, Wilfred?' his da enquired. His da looked at him, and Wilfred knew for the first time that he was alone and that he, like his da, like everyone else, was utterly alone in the world in the deepest sense that it was possible to be alone. And everyone else was alone, too.

★   ★   ★

It felt wrong, Wilfred thought, as he unhooked his belt, to get into bed with this woman. He stepped out of his trousers, picked them up from

220

the green rug and folded them. It felt wrong to untrouser himself in her presence — too intimate. He pulled his necktie from one side to the other with one hand, tugged it apart then unfastened his black cufflinks and began undoing his shirt. He would undress here this once, then never again.

Wilfred sat in what once must have been Grace's brother's chair, took his socks off and stuffed them in his shoes. There was something easier, Wilfred thought, something more honest about speaking the truth when he wasn't wearing a tailored suit and waistcoat. A suit was armour for a man, in the way that corsets and brassières were shields for women. Barefooted now, he pulled on his striped navy pyjamas. The cotton was soft and yielding; a relief after the hard contours of his three-piece suit. He tied the cord of the trousers then hesitated for a moment. He would get in the bed, he would lie there and — he was determined — he would speak. Wilfred smoothed out then rolled up his necktie and put it on the dressing-table.

He hadn't said anything to Grace and Grace hadn't said anything to him, not for twenty-four days and nights. Wilfred took his trousers off the chair, sat back down and looked at the wall ahead with its brown wallpaper. He ran his hand through his hair. All the words he had learned from his red dictionary — well, the A section at least — and autodestruct that he was, or was it autodidact? — it would still be hard to speak. Wilfred's newly acquired vocabulary wasn't helping much when it came to saying the most important things. Even simple words were difficult to use when the conversation was so enormous. In fact, the enormity of the truth was so great no words seemed big enough to address it.

The chair creaked as he shifted and he noticed Grace's leg move slightly under the patchwork quilt. She was awake, on her side with her back to him, and he could see her right eyelid close and open anxiously. He thought about Grace. She was a woman as Flora was a woman, had the same vulnerability and that same strength. Women, Wilfred thought, had an inexplicable strength, despite their delicacy: it was the strength of endurance. They often lived longer than men; he knew that from his work.

As he sat there on the mahogany chair in the corner of the attic for much, much longer than he had intended to, thoughts came into Wilfred's mind, new and surprising thoughts — ones he hadn't considered before. Had Grace been suffering too? Yes. Perhaps it wasn't that she was seeing someone. Perhaps something had happened. He might imagine if it had, she would be hysterical, but she was too well brought up and disciplined for that. Certainly she'd lied, or not told the truth, and he'd been bullied into marrying her because of her dishonesty, but that wasn't the same as being the sort of girl he had thought she was. Because she had never seemed that sort of girl before, and she hadn't been that sort of girl with him.

He thought back to the picnic in her garden, the bees from her hives buzzing around them, her dress, yellow like pollen, and the feminine way she had served the dessert in the china bowls. There was the care that she had evidently put into the spread: the egg and beetroot sandwiches with fluffy white bread and cold butter, the dainty, precisely-cut triangles with the crusts trimmed off. Really, her dress had been demure. Wilfred felt humbled by realizing the truth. Grace's yellow dress had covered her breasts; it was Wilfred's lust, his own desire that made it seem otherwise. It was my imagination, Wilfred said to himself. I have looked for and imagined what I wanted to see. It was not the dress of what the lads at the Rugby Club would call a hussy. Wilfred didn't think hussies wore yellow. In fact, he was certain that hussies wore knee-length dresses and brassières trimmed with lace. And lipstick — a lot of lipstick. He couldn't imagine that Grace wore underwear with lace; there certainly wasn't any lace on her white nightdress. It was as plain as could be.

Wilfred knew then that while Grace had not been honest with him, he in turn had not been honest with himself. Grace was not what he had painted her to be in his head. Grace was a nice girl, the doctor's daughter, she kept bees — granted that was a little unusual, but it didn't mean she was a . . . was a . . . whore. There. He had admitted it to himself. *Commonplace whore* was the phrase he had used to himself as he stood in the register office. He hadn't been proud of thinking that, but he'd thought it. 'Commonplace whore,' he had said decisively in his mind as Grace had made her vows. It wasn't a nice thing to call her, but he'd thought it, he admitted to himself ashamedly. But what if he was wrong? Wilfred rubbed the stubble on his face.

Maybe that was why Grace was in her condition. Perhaps she had been spooning with some spiffy limey. Or perhaps there had been a man, one who was stronger than her. These were new thoughts to Wilfred and disturbing ones. But who could it be? Surely not someone in Narberth? The boys in the Rugby Club were hefty but they were a decent lot. But then nearly any man could overpower a woman; he wouldn't have to play for Narberth Rugby Football Club. All the young men in Narberth would be stronger than Grace — but that didn't tell Wilfred who it was. He thought she'd been seeing Madoc's friend Sidney, but he wasn't sure. He was confounded. Only Grace knew, and Grace was lost in silence.

Wilfred looked at Grace, giving her more than a glance this time. Her body was folded up beneath the white patchwork quilt that was drawn up to her shoulders, tension emanating from her as if she was trying to hold herself in, make herself thinner and smaller than she was — as small as she used to be. Her curled body was no longer that of the light, elegant young woman who had served him trifle in the garden of this house. This was the body of a woman, another human being who was so strained she would surely snap soon, like a pane of very thin ice trodden on. In that moment, Wilfred's anger with Grace dissolved.

That's all she is: another human being. Like me. She is drowning, too, he realized, as Flora had been drowning. It had been many weeks since Wilfred had felt any softness towards Grace; indeed, his anger for her had felt more like an immovable hatred. He stood up from the chair, stepped across the brown rug and got into the bed. He didn't know what he would say, only that he would speak.

★　★　★

He's going to speak to me, Grace sensed. Wilfred, Grace knew, had for weeks been too enraged to talk to her and so they hadn't conversed once since they made their wedding vows. Grace wondered if this silent fury was unusual. Possibly not. Married life was hard — she knew that now. It could be an imprisonment without love, and some marriages were made in hell just as surely as others could be made in heaven. Grace was trying to lie perfectly still, pretending she was asleep, and her breath against the quilt was humid on her face. She had thought that marrying Wilfred would be an answer, and it was true she was still alive, but she was beginning to realize that it was not the answer she had thought it would be. She was still confined and had been these last three months or so, and it was nothing to do with marriage. People said — some people said, the ones who were probably unhappily coupled — that marriage was a jail. It certainly was for her husband. But for Grace it was her body that was the prison.

She was aware that Wilfred had got into bed but he hadn't curled into a tight ball at the very edge of the mattress as he had every night previously. Instead he was supine, his legs slightly spread. He was unexpectedly taking up his half of the mattress. Grace stayed on her side, her back to him, surreptitiously pulling the white quilt higher until it reached the curve of her earlobe. Wilfred was definitely going to say something. He might want to speak to her but Grace now knew something of what men were like. Men had strength, for better or for worse; men had a power and there were times when they weren't afraid to use it. And Grace felt that soon, in the next few moments or minutes, Wilfred was going to use that strength.

★   ★   ★

On the count of three, I'll speak. One, two, three, Wilfred counted in his head. After three. One, two, three. But still he said nothing. One, two, three. Four. Five . . . The air in the bedroom was charged. He sensed Grace knew he was going to speak. There had been an eternity of silence between them: it was time to speak.

'*Grace!*' His voice boomed against the profound quiet of the night. Had he shouted? Maybe Dr and Mrs Reece had heard him. No, he had spoken firmly, certainly, but no one except Grace would have heard. Now he had spoken once he would have to say more.

'Grace.' She didn't reply. Perhaps she wasn't

awake. Perhaps he had finally said something only for her to be fast asleep, after all that. But then Grace's foot moved slightly and he knew she was alert and listening.

'There is something I want to say.' He didn't mean to sound like that, like an undertaker. This time his voice was quieter. He definitely didn't want Dr Reece and Mrs Reece to hear, particularly not Dr Reece.

'There are matters which it is important that we discuss.' Wilfred paused. Grace was tight and didn't move.

'I am sorry I sound so formal . . . like an undertaker. I don't know how to say what I need to say. Or ask the question I want to ask.' There was a pause. 'But I am sorry, Grace.'

★   ★   ★

Grace knew instinctively from the way Wilfred had said, 'I am sorry,' that he wasn't only apologizing for his inarticulacy. He was apologizing for something larger, for how he'd been, possibly even apologizing to her for her life. He was saying that he was sorry for her, for how her life was now. Tears sprang quickly from Grace's eyes and on to the pillowcase.

There was silence again but it was of a different nature from the earlier, suffocating wordlessness that had lain between them. These last weeks had been chokingly full of Wilfred's unspoken, angry words. This new quietness, though, was peaceable; she could sense the beginnings of a calm within it and even the intimations of an answer, though she had no understanding of what that answer could be.

It was her turn to speak. Wilfred had broken his deep silence, now she must break hers. The silence between them was melting, like the white ice on a frozen river breaking up, cracking violently, then floating downstream to a warmer sea. Yes, she would speak.

'*Madoc*,' she whispered.

11

The Willow Pattern

Wilfred hammered the nails into the wood with fury. The plank would break if he kept hammering like this. *Flam! Flam! Flam!* He threw his claw hammer down on the iron nail with huge force, then dragged his forearm roughly across his brow to wipe off the perspiration with his sleeve. Fat circles of dark sweat bloomed from his armpits. He took off his shirt. The cedar would fracture, shatter. Then the side of the coffin would widen and break. And he would have to replace the whole damn panel again.

I don't care, he thought. I don't care if this bloody coffin splits. I don't care if this bloody coffin breaks its ruddy sides. He had never hit a nail in wood with so much force. Mr Auden would turn in his grave. 'Wood, Wilfred. Treat it with love,' he had cautioned. 'An undertaker caresses the wood in his hands. A hundred years the growing, an hour in the felling, a week in the shaping and an eternity with the deceased.' But right now Wilfred needed to bang and thump, and this wood here would have to take it.

Madoc! he thought. Madoc with his ruddy Army uniform and his marvellous *West Wales Board Higher School Certificate* and his bloody Sergeant stripes. And those bloody fancy-dress costumes he wore at Narberth carnival. Bloody, bloody Army. Madoc? Madoc! Never in all his born days . . .

It had not occurred to Wilfred during those turbulent, wakeful nights as he went through one after another of the players in the Rugby Football Club and eventually every young man in Narberth, that it might be Grace's brother. It simply had not occurred to him. This was Narberth! This was 1924. They weren't Stone Age people. Or cannibals! Sweat from his temples ran into his eyes. He hammered another nail into the corner. The timber creaked, complained and threatened to burst.

Last night when Grace had whispered Madoc's name, Wilfred, in that first split second, decided she was lying — but there was something in the plain and broken way in which Grace had spoken her brother's name that told Wilfred she was speaking the truth.

'Hell of a noise in there,' his da called from the back door. 'What in God's name are you doing?'

'Nothing, Da.'

'Well, it doesn't sound like nothing to me.'

'Making a coffin.'

'Are you killing someone to go in it as well?'

Wilfred held the hammer in both hands, pausing. He took another nail from the box. He rammed it into the wood.

After Grace had told him, he had lain awake perturbed, desperate to understand, while Grace had slept in a way that appeared almost serene, as if released from an overwhelming burden she had been carrying, and relief had given her respite. She slept, but Wilfred was utterly awake; his mind charged and clouded with incomprehension. What would the Revd Waldo Williams say? Dr Reece? *Mrs* Reece? He imagined telling Flora. He tried to lie still, but couldn't. It was too big, the truth of it too enormous to understand or envisage. All night he felt fevered, the skin on his face burned, the bones in his head ratcheted tighter and his legs moved restlessly between the sheets. Madoc. It was all he could think about and he was unable to rest with the truth of it — and he knew it to be true.

Madoc.

⋆   ⋆   ⋆

'Doctor Reece?' Wilfred called. He knocked on the panelled door to his father-in-law's surgery. There was no answer.

'Doctor Reece,' Wilfred stated with more resolve. There was still no reply, but this did not deter him. The man might be a doctor of medicine, he might be older than him, he might even be his father-in-law, but Wilfred would not be intimidated. Wilfred would not be bullied, not this time. That was over now. Unbidden, he opened the door and stepped into the room.

Dr Reece didn't look up. Instead he put the lid on his fountain pen with a snap, replaced the Mont Blanc on his ledger and took his blotter between his hands. Relations between the two men had been exceedingly strained since the early summer when Dr Reece had come round to 11 Market Street and waited a whole warm,

231

sunny afternoon for Wilfred to return home. Since then there had been no small talk — no talking of any kind. Until now.

As hard as it was to imagine, seeing the doctor's aged face, Wilfred knew that Dr Reece had once been a young man who had all the thoughts that all young men have, and that he would have been sweet on Mrs Reece, when she was younger and fleshier. But Grace's father had assumed that Wilfred had had these same feelings towards his daughter and had acted on those thoughts, made them a reality, with the resultant consequences. That, outside the strictures of marriage, was unforgivable.

Wilfred coughed, but Dr Reece ignored him. This man is a doctor, Wilfred said to himself, looking around the dark front room that was the surgery. He must know far more about the birds and the bees. He must have studied such things in books at university. Indeed, Wilfred thought, Dr Reece would know more about the matter than anyone else in Narberth — theoretically, of course. This man here, his arms folded like a shield in front of his chest, sitting at his large, heavy desk, so certain that Wilfred had nothing worthwhile to say, knew more about intercourse than any of the other three hundred or so people in Narberth. But he didn't know about his son. He doesn't know that, Wilfred thought.

'Doctor Reece, I want an annulment.'

His father-in-law looked up at him with his piercing eyes and snorted. He smoothed his hair slowly and moved his stethoscope to the corner of his desk.

232

'From Grace,' Wilfred continued. He was no longer cowed by Dr Reece's silence. Nor would he be daunted if the doctor spoke as if Wilfred had said a ridiculous thing.

'Of the marriage.'

Dr Reece glanced briefly at Wilfred.

'Because the marriage was not consummated.'

It was awkward indeed, to talk about this thing with a man, even a medical man, about his daughter. Awkward? Impolite? Would those be the right words to describe it, Wilfred wondered. No, not really: this was beyond impolite, beyond normal conversation.

'And how will you *prove* the marriage is unconsummated?' the doctor asked, emphasizing the word 'prove'. He was a scientist; he wanted proof. Wilfred looked back at him, held his eyes steadily. Wilfred knew that Dr Reece expected to win, was used to winning. Grace's father was certain of his power and practised in the art of bullying.

'I shan't,' Wilfred admitted. He looked down at the floor. A bird flew past the window, creating a quick shadow. Dr Reece picked up his prescription notepad and moved it purposefully to the centre of his desk. Wilfred could see he had been dismissed because of his perceived ignorance and stupidity, and that the doctor was about to resume his paperwork.

'I won't prove it to you, Doctor Reece, nor to the magistrate at the courthouse.' Dr Reece looked at him as if he was dull. Wilfred continued: 'Grace will admit it.'

The grandfather clock ticked. In a couple of

minutes it would chime quarter past three. Almost time for afternoon surgery. Wilfred looked at Dr Reece but Dr Reece looked away. Feigning disinterest, he picked up his pen again, unclipped the lid and held the nib above the notepad. He is going to write something, Wilfred thought, but the pen stayed poised above the paper for one, two, three, four ticks of the clock, and Wilfred realized that Reece didn't know what to write or what to say.

★ ★ ★

Dinner that evening was the first occasion the four of them had eaten together since the wedding. Oddly, Mrs Reece wasn't slamming the crockery down on the table. Grace had often wondered why the dinner-plates had not smashed, so vehemently in the past week had her mother slapped them on the table, splotting the gravy over the table linen, then wailing at the mess it had made, not once conceding that she had caused the splodges, not admitting her own culpability.

Bone china, Grace thought, looking at her dinner-plate, breaks less often than the bones it is made of, which was good, as her mother's tight, hard grasp would have shattered weaker plates.

Grace knew Wilfred was at the dinner-table not because he wanted to stay married: Wilfred still wanted what he had wanted for several months — his freedom from her. Wilfred was here this evening as he thought her mother and her father couldn't and wouldn't say anything to her while he, her husband, her protector of sorts, was sitting at the dinner-table. Wilfred was different now. He'd changed. He'd become stronger in the way he spoke and in how he held himself. Wilfred had even sat next to Grace. On the other side of Wilfred there was the empty chair for Madoc, her brother. The chair was waiting for when he next came back on leave from the Welsh Guards.

With her husband here, Grace hoped her parents wouldn't proselytize, that there would be no rage — no sharp words from her mother. Grace knew Wilfred was buying her time, sitting with her while her parents, dumbstruck, reeled through the first and worst of their shock. By the time Wilfred had gone, when he was no longer sitting here eating chicken, boiled potatoes and mashed swede, her parents would — she hoped — be slightly calmer. He was protecting her from them. That is what husbands do, Grace realized, even unwilling husbands.

'Please could you pass the salt,' Wilfred said, 'salt for the meat.' Neither Dr Reece nor his wife moved, Mrs Reece pretending not to hear, Dr Reece sitting stone still, like the statue of a biblical king. Grace reached across her father.

'Excuse me,' she said faintly, and picked up the small, three-legged saltcellar.

'Thank you,' said Wilfred, shaking the salt liberally on the chicken pieces. 'Very nice dinner, Mrs Reece.' Grace thought that Wilfred didn't eat proper meals very often; that he and his da probably didn't know how to cook.

Wilfred was the only one around the table able to eat. Grace felt nauseous, as she did continually. Her mother, who was even thinner, even sharper these last few weeks, was pretending to starve herself in protest at the injustice meted out to her through her daughter. Her place setting was empty. And her father? He looked too lost to eat. Her father wasn't used to losing or being told he was wrong, but Grace supposed he knew enough not to fight against a man strengthened by the power of the truth. It would be futile. Wilfred, though, ate his dinner like a man offered a reprieve. He put the last potato on to his fork with his knife, pushed it around in the gravy and put it into his mouth. A lesser man, Grace thought, could be triumphant now because he had been wronged, but Wilfred seemed humble, just hungry.

'Thank you, Mrs Reece. That was very nice,' he said. Grace saw that Wilfred was grateful for the meal and that he had an appetite again. Her mother would have begrudged him the food and its cost. Mrs Reece nodded, unable to lower herself to speak to him. Grace got up to leave the table.

'Right,' said Wilfred. 'If you'll excuse me . . . ' That had been the first dinner she had ever eaten with Wilfred. No doubt it would be their last supper, thought Grace. Wilfred stood up and put his crumpled napkin on the table.

'I'm off to see my da,' he announced.

His heart has been with his da all along, Grace thought, watching him.

'Sit down,' Dr Reece commanded. Wilfred saw

the ropey cords of the man's neck leap out and twitch. 'You're staying here.'

Wilfred instinctively tensed and clenched his fists. Dr Reece was his father-in-law. He was a doctor, he was powerful — it was true. Wilfred knew that it often depended on Dr Reece whether someone ended up dead and in his workshop or not. That was power. But Wilfred was different now. He had met Flora Myffanwy and he had become, to his own mind, through recent experiences and something newly forged within him, something he couldn't articulate but that he could best describe as 'a purveyor of superior funerals'. He was rooted in the world, felt his place in it. In his mind's eye he imagined his feet growing roots that surged into the earth, forming a net of tendrils spreading deep and wide into the Narberth soil, holding him here, holding him upright. Wilfred did not sit down.

Dr Reece's face turned a deeper shade of puce. He put his large hands on the table as if to rise to his feet. Grace averted her eyes and stepped back. Grace's mother snatched the china tureen from the table.

'I am your father-in-law. You will do what I say.' But Dr Reece's words sounded papery and lightweight as if they could dally and float on the breeze.

Wilfred straightened his back. He had his da, his work, his friends at the Rugby Club, the people he knew in Narberth. And there was Flora Myffanwy. He was supported by the strength of those he loved. They would all have something to say — probably not all of them to his face — but they would buffer and hold him. So Dr Reece could bellow in fury — and Wilfred in his health and strength, his youth and most of all, in his rootedness, would not succumb or snap. Wilfred pulled back his shoulders.

'Yes, Doctor Reece, you have been my father-in-law.' He met Grace's eyes. 'But I am my own man.'

Dr Reece leaned right back in his chair and was rendered speechless, seemingly as much by the strength that resonated from Wilfred's body as by his words. Wilfred felt himself to be like a tree with inner rings of new growth that were hidden deep inside, but nevertheless present and holding up a strapping trunk easily and naturally.

'Do as I say.'

'No.' It was the straining of Dr Reece's neck, Wilfred thought. No one with any power ever had to strain their neck.

Mrs Reece was frantically scouring the draining board with steel wool. She repeatedly dabbed her eyes in a fury of self-pity and contempt. Well, Wilfred thought, she could dab her eyes and she could cry. The drama and self-righteousness would feed her for years. She would have an occupation now in her small life.

'Wilfred Price,' Mrs Reece interrupted shrilly, 'what would your mother say?'

Wilfred was thrown: his mother, so absent from his whole life — he hadn't thought what she would say and hadn't known her at all to even be able to have a sense of her response.

'My mother,' Wilfred replied, once he had centred himself, 'is dead.' And I bet Grace

238

wishes her mother was dead too, he added to himself.

'You would have killed your mother with this. And your father broke his back working to look after you.'

Broke his back? Had his da broken his back for him? An image of his da came to him: his da was stooped, it was true. He didn't want his da to break his back for him.

'Yes, see? I am right — I can tell by your face,' said Mrs Reece, with a look that, to Wilfred, seemed like one of utter hatred.

'Worked like a slave for you.' She put the corner of the hanky to her eye.

Then it occurred to Wilfred that he could say, 'It is your son who has caused all this. I know what Madoc did to Grace.' And watch all the veneer of respectability, pretence and snobbery crack and fall away like carefully applied, generations-old varnish. *It wasn't me; it was your son. I would like to inform you* . . . how would he say it? How did you inform people of the most devastating and unacceptable fact that they would ever hear?

Wilfred considered speaking. He looked at Dr Reece sitting at the head of the table, with his power and his title, who had immediately assumed it was Wilfred and judged him harshly. Yet Wilfred knew that somewhere inside that formal façade there was a man who watched over the people of Narberth, who rubbed his hands together to warm them before placing them on the tissue-thin skin of elderly people with arthritic joints, who cared that the people of their small town were rosy-cheeked and sturdy, were born alive, lived robustly and died without too much pain. A man who drove as fast as he could, but also carefully, to patients who were sick at night in nearby farms. A good man, with Madoc for a son.

The dishes clacked as Mrs Reece scoured them in a fever. Wilfred looked at Mrs Reece, deliberating what he would say. She had an empty life of housewifery with nothing to peg herself on but her husband's position and her son's rank. But now there was the agony of her daughter's fall. *Madoc*. Five letters: Madoc — that's all he need say. Suddenly he understood Grace's trust and courage in telling him the raw, skinless truth. And Grace's dignity in not telling anyone else.

Madoc. The name was on the tip of his tongue. No. And he walked out of the door.

★　★　★

If Grace had been surprised that Wilfred had stayed for dinner, she was even more astonished later that evening when she heard the stiff latch on the attic door lift and realized it was Wilfred coming in. He had not come back the other night and there was no need for him to pretend — he could go home to his father's again tonight, to his kind da who loved him so much and to whom Wilfred was the world. Grace, in not speaking the whole truth, had deprived Wilfred's da of his son and of his son's happiness. Grace winced at her cruelty, more cruelty again. It went on and on; intentionally, unintentionally, it didn't matter. The end was the same: broken people left in pieces, lives fractured, love bludgeoned.

She saw Wilfred undressing out of the corner of her eye. Wilfred's father would be pleased — over the moon — to have his son back with him, though Grace doubted he would say anything but instead would keep his counsel, as wise people often did. And even if Wilfred did one day marry, he would be wounded from this failed marriage. He deserves a wife, Grace thought, who loves him and does not use him for her own ends.

She glanced at him as he undid his cufflinks. It occurred to Grace that she didn't know much about Wilfred, not really, despite being married to him. She knew he liked trifle with whipped cream. That he had liked her yellow dress. Perhaps he liked yellow dresses. Perhaps he liked yellow. She knew that at night he put his socks in his shoes, one in each, but Grace suspected all men did that with their socks at nighttime, in the bedroom, ready for the morning. Grace didn't know much that was personal or intimate about Wilfred: he had told her nothing, she hadn't asked anything.

Though she felt as though she was married to a stranger, it would also be true that once their marriage was annulled — when the court had ratified it — she would always have once been married to Wilfred. He would always be her first, probably only, husband. Even in twenty years' time, in 1944, which was unimaginably distant in the future, when this all might possibly — possibly — not be the end of the world any more, it would still be true that she, Grace Amelia Reece of 32 High Street, Narberth, had once been married to Wilfred Aubrey Price, undertaker.

So she felt calm and kindly, resigned even, when Wilfred, her once and soon not to be husband got into their marriage bed — the bed that had once belonged to her brother. And when Wilfred moved into the centre of their bed, that no man's land where neither of them had dared to lie for the whole of their married life, Grace let Wilfred take her in his arms and hold her.

'I'm sorry,' he said.

★　★　★

It was the middle of the night. Wilfred was asleep, but Grace hadn't slept. Over the long hours of the night, her resignation had turned to anxiety and her anxiety into appalling anguish.

Eventually she said, 'Wilfred . . . Wilfred, can I ask?'

He stirred. Soon they were both lying on their backs in the dusky half-light of the room, looking at the ceiling, the eaves, the beam and sickly brown wallpaper. She hated this bedroom, Madoc's old room, with his boxes of Snakes and Ladders and Tiddlywinks on the shelf and his suit hanging loosely, like the clothes of a ghost, in the wardrobe. She hated this room in which her life had happened.

'I am afraid, Wilfred. If you stay, I will be a good wife to you. A kind wife, and I won't be like my mother, and we could have a child together. Children.' Her voice sounded needy and her words were fast. 'I would be kind and good and I would follow our wedding vows and I would be kind always.' She was trying to strike a bargain, like she sold honey in Narberth, to sell him herself and her life as if it were honey in a jar to offer, something that he might want.

'And we could live with your father, I'd be happy to live with your father, and I would look after him and clean and keep the house tidy, and . . . and if you show me how, I can help you laying out the bodies and getting them ready and . . . ' Her words were gabbled, her eyes wide, her heart beating. 'And I would take care of the baby and it would be no trouble and it wouldn't get in the way, Wilfred . . . and . . . and I will pay my way by selling honey. And I could even train to be a teacher at the school because I always like reading. And you wouldn't need to visit my mother, or see any of my family, ever. And I would like you, Wilfred. And I wouldn't carry on with other men. And we could say to my father that it doesn't need to be . . . annulled.'

She put her hand between his legs. He gathered and tightened almost immediately. She sat up, took off her white nightdress and put her hand back where it had been. She heard Wilfred swallow and moved next to him.

'We would be happy, not like my mother and father, but like your ma and da.' She slightly tightened her grip. She had never touched that place on a man before, never even seen it, only glimpsed it once, a part of it, but she *wouldn't* think of that. She took Wilfred's hand and placed it between her legs. Wilfred moved on to his side and faced her and put his hand on her flank. Only once, Grace thought, and the marriage couldn't be annulled. Grace knew that doing this only once with a man could change the world.

An hour or so ago she had crept out of bed and put red lip-stain on her lips, had rubbed it on surreptitiously after combing her hair, even dabbed her wrists with Chanel N° 5, the new French perfume she'd bought for her wedding, before half-undoing her nightdress.

She shifted closer to Wilfred, till her breasts were brushing against the hair on his chest and she felt the muscles in his arms tighten. She pushed aside the flies in his pyjamas, making room for her hand to move. She thought that maybe she should move her hand. She didn't know what to do, but Wilfred was responding to her tentative gestures. He put his hand on one breast, then quickly across to the other one.

'Oh,' he said, as if he was sinking into himself.

He pushed into her and she turned to lie on her back. Wilfred, lying over her, pulled up his pyjama jacket, freeing his stomach, and then he reached down and tried to undo the knot in the cord but he couldn't do it with one hand. He rolled on to his back. Grace noticed the intensity and heat in his face while he tugged at the knot. She had seen once before that look of utter focus, that unconsciousness of everything around him when a man was gripped by the tautness in his body. Men had one vulnerability, Grace thought, watching — that soft, squidgy place, softer than a woman's breast, as honest as a woman's stomach, and stronger in its effect than anything else in the world. Wilfred was still trying to get the knot undone and becoming frustrated, pulling at the cord. It was loose. He yanked down his pyjamas trousers, started to drag his top over his head but it wouldn't go, pulled it down again, undid the top button and with both hands, lifted it over his head. Then he lay on top of Grace and she felt the weight of him over her.

Wilfred used his left leg to push open her legs. He brushed her hair from her face, put his arms under her and held her tightly. Grace bent her knees and lifted up her legs. How did she know how to do this, she wondered.

She thought she could do this without it hurting. She had licked her fingers earlier and dragged her fingers between her legs to moisten herself. And if it hurt she would bite her lips, she would close her eyes, she would think of the bees in their hive, think of each precise step of their dances. If it hurt or rubbed harshly she would think of her bees.

This was easier than with . . . she wouldn't think about it. She felt a blunt nub along her upper thigh, pushing blindly into her. Wilfred pressed his forehead into her forehead and took his weight on to his arms, hunching his shoulders. That hard-soft nub kept pushing into the flesh at the very top of her leg, searching blindly for what it wanted. Grace could feel it moving nearer and nearer to where it wanted to go, where it needed to be for the marriage to be consummated. Only an inch . . . less than an inch, and the way forward would be smooth and easy. Oh . . .

'No! No . . . ' Wilfred climbed off Grace, threw himself back on to the bed, legs apart, arms above his head. His face was covered in sweat. Grace saw the dark hair on his chest and stomach and his thick, muscular legs spread out on the sheet.

'No, Grace. I want it — God help me, I want it. But I won't want it in the morning, when I'm spent and empty.'

Grace looked at him. His body still wanted it: here, now, regardless, with her. That's what men's bodies wanted. Bodies didn't care about consequences.

'You are . . . you are lovely,' he continued, breathing deeply and wiping the sweat from his brow, 'and I was sweet on you in your yellow dress. Wanted to know, Grace, how you got out of it. Imagined you taking off your dress at the picnic, imagined where the buttons were. Wanted you there, on that blanket, naked, wanted to be inside you.' He breathed out audibly. 'But it was only for a moment. And that was the moment I proposed.' He rubbed his chest back and forth with his hand.

'I wanted to love you, but it was only for a moment, not a lifetime.' He brushed his hair from his face and brought the sides of his pyjama trousers together, covering himself. 'Grace, you are beautiful, you are good. And your brother has ruined your life.' He was lying spread-eagled in the middle of the bed; Grace was on her side at the edge, her hands across her breasts, her feet pulled up.

'I could take Madoc and I could hold him against a wall and I could . . . I could break his body, Grace, for what he's done to you.'

The room fell silent. The air was muggy with the sweat and smell of their bodies. They lay there, abandoned. Grace looked at the brown wallpaper. Eventually she spoke.

'Is there someone else?' she asked.

'Yes.'

12

The Notes

It had been so simple. Grace had stood there in her gabardine macintosh, despite the weather being too close for a coat of any description, because she felt protected and hidden in it. Wilfred once again had his sombre suit on. It was his funeral suit, his wedding suit and now his annulment suit. It was a suit for every occasion.

Grace and Wilfred were standing facing the magistrate who was wearing a wiry grey wig. Grace wanted to sit, her feet ached, but it wasn't allowed. The magistrate had enquired if the marriage was consummated. It was so intimate a question in so formal a setting. Wilfred said it wasn't. The magistrate asked Grace the same question. She shook her head.

'Speak,' he commanded.

'No,' she said. Grace thought back to Wilfred, naked, his white skin highlighted by the black hair on his body, lying in Madoc's bed, wrestling with himself. She had tried.

So there was just one more question left unanswered. Grace wondered if the magistrate would ask it. *Why was the marriage unconsummated?* And then there was the fact of her almost obvious pregnancy, which she hoped her coat hid.

'Is there a reason why this marriage is not

248

consummated?' the magistrate asked. Grace watched the dust floating in the air; sunlight was coming through the windows. Outside she could hear the bustle of market day. She trusted Wilfred would speak first.

'It was not possible to consummate the marriage,' Wilfred said to the bar in front of him; he was unable to look the magistrate in the eyes.

'And Mrs Price . . . ' the magistrate began. 'Why do you say the marriage is not consummated?'

Grace had decided that she would say — if questioned — exactly what Wilfred had said.

'It was not possible to consummate it,' she repeated.

'And the child you are carrying? Is that your husband's?'

Grace watched the dust move slowly and elegantly in the air. The courthouse was dirty, though she knew it was cleaned regularly. Mrs John Morgan from Water Street swept and polished it every Tuesday, but she imagined the room would always be airless, dusty and dark. The dust was like the shame of the accused — it was always present and could never be washed away.

'Mrs Price, is the child your husband's child? Answer the question.'

'No.' She heard her father's feet shuffle in the gallery behind her; it had to be her father's feet, he was the only other person in the courthouse.

Once she had said it, Grace knew she must leave Narberth — leave now. There could be no going back. Her tan leather suitcase was open and empty and waiting for her in the attic. She hadn't said to anyone that she was leaving, hadn't told her parents, but it was a tacit agreement; it was understood that there could be no place for her now in this small, very tightly bound, ancient corner of the world.

★   ★   ★

Knickers, stockings, suspender belt, brassière. She ran quickly through a list of undergarments. She grabbed a brassière and some knickers from a drawer. Her stockings were drying on the clothes airer hanging from the kitchen ceiling. She wouldn't go and get them — her mother was in the kitchen and she didn't want to see her. She had the stockings she was wearing. One pair would do, she'd wash and dry them each night. A skirt? Two skirts? Three skirts? How many skirts would she need? She unhooked a couple of skirts from the back of the door where they were kept. Grace folded them quickly and not very neatly, then put them in the suitcase. Really she should use tissue paper. She looked at the clock. There wasn't time to put tissue between the folds of her skirts.

Two blouses. One jumper. No, two jumpers. The round-necked one she'd knitted for herself. Her white nightdress. Her spare shoes. She lifted up the clothes and put the shoes underneath them at the bottom of the case. That was everything. No, of course not. Handkerchiefs, toothbrush, hairbrush. And why was she taking these clothes? Soon they wouldn't even fit her.

But she'd need clothes. Her purse, her savings book. What else? She wanted to take something from her life, this life. Her yellow dress. She pulled it from the hanger and pressed her face to it and felt as if she was holding herself. Her yellow dress had held all her hopes in it though now the silk was infused with the aroma of mothballs. Grace folded it, put it in the suitcase on top of her white nightie, and smoothed it flat. She would leave the navy scarf from her nana. That was all. That was enough. There was nothing else to take. Apart from the small framed photo on her dressing-table of her mother and father.

Suddenly tired, Grace sat on the bed, bewildered, facing the brown wall. She had stayed inside the house since she had been married to Wilfred, only venturing into the garden because she was too ashamed to step out and meet people, be greeted, congratulated, spoken to and talked about. She knew she was talked about — talked about almightily — but she didn't want to walk around town to see it, to know it and to have her shame proved to her. She had left 32 High Street for her wedding, for the annulment, and now she would leave the house to leave. She had not asked her parents for advice or her father for direction. She didn't know where she would go or who would have her — if, indeed, anyone would have her.

There was the train out of Narberth at eleven minutes past two. It went to Carmarthen. At Carmarthen she could change and go to Swansea. At Swansea there was a train to

Liverpool and also a train to London. Liverpool, she knew, had homes for fallen girls, for all the Irish women who were also escaping their lives. Then there was London, about which she knew almost nothing. Maybe London would accept a Welsh girl who was divorced, pregnant and alone. She could rent a room, she could work as a waitress and she could pretend to be married and wear her wedding ring, or pretend to be widowed. She didn't know. The train journey, if she went to London, took eleven hours and that would be long enough to concoct a story and to plan a life.

Grace knew that her mother and father would allow her to go downstairs and out of the front door, and that her mother's love, in particular, was not strong enough for her to beg her daughter to stay, whatever the circumstances. Her mother would let her go. She would ask for no forwarding address, she would ask for no telegram. She would simply let her go. From her father, Grace was hoping for more.

★   ★   ★

When Wilfred strode into the attic, Grace was kneeling on the floor trying to force shut her tan leather suitcase. He saw her suitcase — it looked too small, as if it could hardly contain all Grace would need for a new life somewhere else. He looked at her softly, kindly, and felt like a man defeated. Wilfred had what he wanted — his freedom from her — but he didn't want his own way at the cost of breaking Grace, just as he imagined Grace had not wanted their marriage at the cost of breaking him. He held his hand open, palm up in a gesture of renunciation.

Wilfred knew she was going, not for a few months to return soft and warm and forgiven with a small child, but that she was leaving and would perhaps never return because Narberth wouldn't find a place for a woman like Grace. Narberth was full of people who would only include a woman who became a mother in the Christian way and, God knew, Grace wasn't having a child in an acceptable way.

What can I give her? Wilfred asked himself. I must give her something to take for her journey. It was less than an hour until the Carmarthen train.

'Wait! Wait here,' he stated.

Wilfred bounded down the attic stairs noisily, out of the Reeces' front door, and ran straight along the High Street and Water Street then Market Street and into his house. Once in his bedroom, he shoved the iron bedstead aside with a screech, dropped down on to his knees, then used his penknife to lever up the unvarnished plank, the third from the back wall, the one with the gnarled knot of wood in it.

There in a bag with a tie string was the other half of their life savings. He opened it and there was the earthy, greasy smell of money. He had saved assiduously and there was a considerable amount: he knew exactly how much was there. He must keep some in case business became slow or — God forbid — another undertaker set up in Narberth; some for the outlay for the wallpaper shop; and some in case his da became unwell. He must look after his da . . . He looked at the pile of notes in his hand . . . but he must also be generous. He took all the money, folded it in half, putting it in his jacket pocket, dropped the dusty floorboard back into place, yanked the bed back against the wall and ran through Narberth to Grace's house.

In the attic, Grace was still sitting on the side of the bed waiting for Wilfred: she stood when he came in.

I'll do this with no fuss, Wilfred thought. He put his hand into the inside pocket of his jacket and took out the roughly folded wad. Grace looked at the money without expression. She didn't know how much was there — a lot, enough to start a new life. Wilfred held out the notes to Grace, gesturing for her to take it. She reached out timidly and accepted his parting gift. Then he pulled her to him and held her by the shoulders. He kissed her on the forehead.

'God be with you, Grace,' he said gently, and he walked out of the door.

★ ★ ★

Wilfred strode down the bramble-lined lane, stretching his legs and hoping to clear his clouded head. He needed a drink. His mouth was dry as sandpaper: a pint of Oakhill Stout at the Conduit public house would do a treat.

Wilfred set off down the lane feeling shocked. Grace was leaving. He shouldn't have been surprised: what choice did she have? She had

254

been pale this morning when Wilfred saw her sitting on the end of the bed, her hands underneath her, her legs swinging slightly. She still looked girlish. Wilfred could see in her smooth, gentle face that it wasn't long ago that Grace was a girl. He recalled his only memory of Grace from his childhood when he had known her by sight but never played with her. Wilfred had been crouching while searching for catchy-poles in the boggy water on the town moor when he noticed a lithe Grace turning cartwheel after cartwheel, one-handed as well as two-handed, her hands confidently slapping on the mud, her legs swinging over her head, spinning like the spokes of a wheel. On and on she had gone; standing up, twirling over, hand over hand across the grass. She was free then.

He looked around him. Narberth was so vividly green in spring and summer, with the castle prominent on the hill, the keep jutting elegantly into the sky. Narberth was enchanting. Seven generations of his family came from this town and there was no reason to think the next seven generations wouldn't also live and die here. But Narberth was not entirely the place he had thought it was. How many people over the years had stood alone and plaintive on the station platform leaving for they knew not where because the people of Narberth had banished them by making it impossible for them to stay?

He swung open the five-bar gate by St Andrew's and traipsed into the cow field. He and his family had stayed. Was it only those with well-ordered, fortunate lives who remained, while the unlucky and blighted were cut off and cast away like a rotting limb? But the memory of them stayed, always aching. Wilfred knew he was right to give Grace something like a hundred pounds — he didn't know exactly how much he had taken from his savings — there hadn't been time to count. For all he knew, Grace might purchase a mink fur coat and big diamonds. But that was unlikely; she seemed far too pained to be jubilant and celebratory.

Wilfred headed across the field, stepping over the odd hummock of grass. Should he tell his da what he'd done with around half of their life savings? But his da wouldn't ask, and if he found out he would understand; his da had spent too long with the dead to care overly much for money. Wilfred had been hoping to buy the portable wireless and take it to the cottage in the cove. That wouldn't be possible now. He would have to gradually build up his savings again and that would take several years at least. Unless there was an epidemic. But Wilfred didn't think there would ever be an epidemic again, what with medicine being so advanced and modern these days.

Wilfred loosened his tie and stood for a moment. Soon everyone would know the marriage was annulled and there would be many unanswered questions. Who was the man? Where had she gone? Would she come back? But Wilfred no longer cared about the gossip; it wasn't important any more. Gossip went on for ever. As Mr Auden said, 'There is always a great deal of interest in a door behind which something is happening' — but gossip belonged in the realms of a small and uncompassionate world, and Wilfred had seen that the world was larger and more multiple than could ever be described and explained by tittle-tattle.

Wilfred arrived at the far gate, his shoes rimmed with squelchy mud, and began the short walk down Water Street. Grace would have to find lodgings, pay the rent and, once the baby was born, she'd have to work — perhaps sewing or washing. Anyway, he thought to himself, he would never need a portable wireless the way Grace would need the rent.

★   ★   ★

Once he was inside the Conduit public house and resting on an upright chair in the parlour drinking a glass of stout, Wilfred was still thinking about Grace. When she was sitting on the edge of the bed this morning, Wilfred had seen the echo of that little girl she had once been. Her young face with her pregnancy was incongruous. Wilfred knew that if she went out of the house, people would notice her youth then her belly, and look at her surreptitiously out of the corner of their eye. He sipped his beer then placed the cool glass tankard on his leg. He'd given her the money; she'd taken it, her head down. She was broken — Wilfred saw it plainly as they parted, before he walked out of the door — and now she was abandoned. He didn't doubt that the world would be harsh with her, and he hoped she would be able to endure the life awaiting her. She was innocent and she was suffering.

'What you doing here, Wilfred?'

'Hello, Da! I could ask the same of you.'

'Oakhill Stout you got there, boy?' his da asked, removing his hat and putting it on the chair.

'Aye — anything's better than the parsnip wine,' Wilfred replied.

His da sat down slowly on a rickety chair against the wall.

'Pint of stout, Mrs Evans, please,' he called. 'Hell of a rush you were in earlier going up to your bedroom, Wilfred. You must have met yourself coming back. What was you up to?'

'Oh, nothing much, nothing much,' Wilfred replied in a low voice. He paused then he said, 'She's leaving, Da, just like that.'

'Do you know where?'

'No I don't know. Because, well . . . I's went to the courthouse and it . . . ' Wilfred wiped some froth from around his mouth.

'Did it go as you wanted it to, son?'

'Yes.' Wilfred took a mouthful of beer.

'There's good, then.'

'Yes, Da.'

'Sad, mind. Nice girl. You can't always be running away, Wilfred. Sometimes you's have to stay, whatever happens.' He drank some stout. 'I's stayed with your mam.'

'But you loved my mam.'

'Aye,' he nodded gently, 'but sometimes I didn't always want to stay.' His da was talking in that way again, revealing himself and his

258

wisdom, speaking frankly as if Wilfred was not the child he had brought up, but another equal and separate adult with his own life.

'You didn't want to stay, Da?'

'No. I was a young man once. I wanted everything and wouldn't tolerate anything.' His da looked around the bare, plain room. 'It never is the way you want it to be, Wilfred. It is always different, especially with women. Women are cleverer than men; they run circles around us, outwit us without us even noticing, but there's nothing much in life for a man if he doesn't have a wife. A man has to have someone to *be* for. A man without a wife is like a dishevelled and wandering beast who doesn't know where to rest on the earth.'

'Right, then, gentlemen — Welsh cakes,' announced Mrs Annie Evans, breezing into the parlour. 'Can't have you starving to death on my premises, can I?' she said, pushing her spectacles up her nose. 'Eat up, now.'

'They smell wonderful, Mrs Evans,' said Wilfred.

'Wilfred, you's look like you've seen a ghost. Do you want me's to heat some parsley pie on the range for you?'

'Thank you,' said Wilfred. 'I would appreciate that. That would be very kind.'

★　★　★

Grace looked down at the pile of money in her hand. It was still warm from being in Wilfred's pocket. She opened her suitcase with a click and

259

put the money in the case's cloth pocket. She shut the lid and looked at her wristwatch. She would wear her watch all the time from now on, she decided. She would no longer hear the grandfather clock in her father's surgery chime every quarter of an hour, or the bell in the Narberth clock-tower. Yes, she would take her wristwatch with her; it would mark the time for her now.

Her mother and father were waiting for her to come downstairs, sitting at the kitchen table, cups of cold tea in front of them. Grace stood in the doorway for a moment or two, holding her suitcase in front of her with two hands. If ever there was a time for any of us to say something to each other, then this is it, Grace thought to herself. They knew now it wasn't Wilfred. Her mother must assume that Grace, with a cheapness that was shocking, had gone easily and giggly with some cad in a dark alley after a dance and let him have his way with her. Her mother was too brittle to ask who it was, although the secret of who the scoundrel was who had done that with her equally sluttish daughter would shame and obsess Mrs Reece for the rest of her life. Her father wouldn't ask because that would upset her mother, and her father's first loyalty was to his wife. Grace knew their silence protected their sanity and their social standing.

Her mother got up and started laying the table for lunch in a cold businesslike way, taking the Willow Pattern plates from the Welsh dresser where they were displayed. They were a broken family now, too broken. The secret between them was better unspoken: she doubted her mother — or even her father — could survive the truth. This would be her parting gift to them, whatever they thought of her, and she suspected they judged her very harshly; she would allow them their illusions about their son, allow them these lies about their family and their children, even if it meant that she, Grace, would be blamed, hated and outcast. She would leave kindly. She would allow them their innocence.

Grace watched her mother sit down abruptly, and viciously pick at the hangnails of skin from her fingers and dab the blood away with her lips. If this was marriage and family life, Grace thought, she didn't want it.

Her parents were innocent in a town that pretended innocence and only allowed for innocence. Grace knew too much now to stay in the quiet and beautiful place in the west of Wales at the end of the world. She must go where other people who knew about a wider world lived, where there was a different commerce of knowledge. She put her hand to her pearl necklace and held it tightly.

Her mother was ferociously biting the skin around her nails again, and Grace could see that if her mother felt any sympathy towards her, it was well hidden behind accusation and self-pity. Her mother had not even made her a tin of sandwiches or filled a glass bottle with water. Her father, though, might offer to drive her to the station. Grace knew that her parents would not, under any circumstances, want her to be seen leaving the house with her suitcase — because that would be talked about. It would be more discreet if her father drove her to the station. That way, while the whole of Narberth would know why Grace had left, no one would have actually seen her leave, and there would be slightly — but only slightly — less for them to talk about.

Suddenly her mother stood up, her chair scraping sharply on the tiles, and in a flash of rage slapped Grace hard around the face. Grace's head flew back, jolted, her breath caught in her throat. Her hands flailed outwards, the suitcase falling. All the blood raced into the centre of her body. Her mother collapsed back into her chair and started sobbing hysterically. Dazed, Grace picked up her suitcase, her hands shaking, and walked to the front door.

'Grace,' her father said soberly, following her, 'the car.' She turned and followed him and they went out of the back door to the Morris Minor, which was parked waiting in the lane.

As they drove, Grace looked out of the window at the billowing verges and the tall trees in full leaf lining the road. It was raining clean, fresh rain — Welsh rain that made the grass so green and the trees so verdant. She wondered when she would see such greenness again.

Her father wound down the window and put his arm out to indicate he was turning left. Grace looked at the public house, the school, the row of houses, all so familiar to her for the whole of her life, and was unable to believe she would see them again.

When they turned into Station Road, Grace knew that her father would not wait with her for the train to come. She would have to stand on the platform on her own. She, and not her father, would lift her case on to the train. She put her hand on the silver door handle to let herself out of the car. It was cool and smooth in her hand. She had nothing and everything to say. But she had chosen nothing.

All he need say, Grace realized, her eyes filling, *all* my father need say is, 'Stay.' That's all. And my heart will break and I will stay. But in those few seconds while Grace's hand rested on the door handle, with her small suitcase on her lap, her father stared straight ahead, looking, Grace thought, like a broken king. Eventually he took an airmail envelope — like the one he used to write to Madoc — from his raincoat pocket and held it out to her, not meeting her eyes.

'Goodbye, Father,' she said.

★　★　★

The train bellowed and puffed languorously around the corner; Grace heard it before she saw it. It stopped with a powerful jolt. The train was a couple of feet above the platform so she pulled herself up on to the train and into an empty carriage. She sat next to the grimy window, facing backwards, hugging her suitcase. Then the train started up with a great hiss and chugged off. The small platform behind her was empty: there was no one to see her off.

'Any tickets from Narberth?' the conductor

called jollily as he trundled down the corridor looking into the carriages. The train turned the corner and entered the cutting between the hills. I am leaving Narberth, Grace told herself. I — and my child — am leaving. She looked inside the envelope her father had given her. Money. He must have taken it from his safe box without her mother knowing. Her father was kinder than her mother, cared more, was capable of caring more, though he had not asked her to stay, had not loved her more than he chastized her. Instead he had let her go, vulnerable and alone and frightened, into a world that was bigger — but surely not harsher — than Narberth.

Wherever I live, Grace thought, it will be better than it was in my own family.

She noticed that in the envelope, behind several £5 notes, there was a piece of paper. The paper had been pulled roughly from a prescription notepad. It was folded but not precisely, as was her father's usual way. She opened it; it was her father's handwriting, not his normal careful cursive script — it was written hurriedly — nor was it in his customary Kandahar ink. It was done with a pencil, but a pencil pressed hard and firmly into the paper. On it there was written only one word. *Write.*

13

A for Avocado

There was a loud clatter and the sound of something breaking. Flora and her mam looked at each other — Flora stopped mid-stitch. They went outside into the dying light and there in the driveway was the cause — a broken roof tile, cracked unevenly down the middle.

'Oh dear,' said her mam, 'where did that come from?' They both looked up at the roof and saw the empty square where the tile had dislodged and fallen.

'I didn't know it was loose,' Mrs Edwards said.

'We'll have to replace it as soon as we can.' Flora walked forward and picked up the two parts of the tile, the dark green moss tumbling from it. The tile needed to be replaced otherwise the roof would leak. Flora stood there gazing at the tile in her hand. The same thought was occurring to both her and her mam. What were they going to do?

'That's above my bedroom, isn't it?' said Flora.

'Yes, it is,' agreed her mother. 'At least it's not raining right now.'

Flora held the pieces of the tile in her hands. She slotted them together; it was a neat crack, the pieces fitted back together well.

'We need a new tile,' her mam stated.

They stood there, a wood pigeon cooing, the light quickly fading to dusk. Neither of them knew the way forward. Possibly if they waited long enough, Flora's father would stride out of the house, ask what was going on, what that almighty din was. He would see the tile, nod, pick it up, one leg lifting up as he bent down as was his characteristic way, say, 'Well, well, well.' He'd saunter to the outhouse then return in a minute or two carrying the ladder under his arm, trying to make it look as if he wasn't struggling. Then a replacement tile would be nailed down and the roof sealed. Her father would be proud of himself, beaming with a sense of satisfaction from a job well done. He would talk about it over dinner. It would be the main topic of conversation. Flora and her mam waited. But her father wasn't going to come. He was never going to walk out of the house again. He was never going to fix a roof tile again. Mrs Melbourne Edwards wiped her eyes modestly.

'Well, something will turn up,' Flora said, though she didn't know what. She didn't feel able to climb the ladder up on to the roof and wouldn't know how to nail the tile back. And anyway the tile was broken. It was dawning on her that the things her father had done they now had to do. They had to look after the house now and it hadn't been mentioned yet but they would have to have money coming in. They had savings, but those wouldn't last for ever. Perhaps they would sell the forge, or let the apprentice take it on. Flora and her mam would need more money. They were two women alone in the world without a man. They would need a man. To mend the roof tile. To bolt the door at nightfall. To sleep in the house at night. Even to open the lids on the jars when they stuck. Her father always huffed and strained theatrically until the jars popped open. Before, jammed jar lids had been a delight to her father so he could show his prowess. Now screw lids and jam-jars would be a problem. There would be things to do: in the autumn the guttering was cleared, in the winter the logs were chopped, and Flora wasn't confident that she or her mam would be able to do them.

Back inside, the tile lay on an old cloth on the dining-table, the two broken halves placed next to each other, a gap between them.

'Well, there's a cawl for dinner and it will be ready in a bit. It's on the range,' her mam said levelly.

Flora was grateful for some normality, for some routine. She liked cawl and had grown up eating it. It warmed her and soothed her and was known.

'And there's water for a bath afterwards.'

Of course, it was Sunday.

* * *

Flora sat in the tin bath, wiping her back with a flannel. The fire in the hearth next to the bath was glowing and warm. She rubbed more coal-tar soap on the flannel and washed her arms, moving the flannel along her forearms and to her wrists.

Her mother came into the sitting room and took a stool and sat down by the bath.

'Can I talk with you?' she said.

'Yes, Mam.' Flora pulled up her knees and rested her head on them.

'The undertaker, Mr Wilfred Price, seems thoughtful and gentlemanly.' Her mother looked down. 'I was wrong to refuse you going for tea with him.'

Flora swished around the water in the bath, listening.

'Would you like to go to the Staunton House Refreshment Rooms in Narberth with him?'

Flora looked at her bare feet.

'He's very handsome,' her mam continued, pouring more water into the bath.

'He is.'

'Send him a postcard, tell him you'd like to meet and that your mother approves.'

Flora Myffanwy searched for the bar of soap in the water.

'Perhaps take some of your photographs to show him and tell him about yourself.' Her mother warmed her hands on the fire. 'He tried hard to make a good impression when he came here with the invoice. He is surely in want of a wife.'

Flora smiled wistfully.

'I was happily married for thirty years. I want that for you, too. He seems kind. Kindness is important,' her mother added.

'I think he is kind. But I don't think he quite knows who he is yet.'

'That may be as it is, but give him time and he surely will know.'

'Yes . . . ' Flora Myffanwy replied, considering the wisdom of her mother's words. 'But he lives in a town.'

'He does.'

'And . . . ' but then Flora couldn't think of anything else to add.

Her mam pulled her shawl around her. 'It would be a different love from the one you had with Albert.' Flora washed her hands with the bar of soap, listening. 'Do you think you could find it in yourself to love again?' her mother asked gently.

'I still feel raw, still think of Albert. I could hide away for ever . . . '

Flora looked down at her suntanned arms. 'Albert was very beautiful — it was as if he was golden.'

'Yes,' her mother said, not disagreeing. Flora hugged her knees.

'But Albert has been dead six years now. You can't marry a ghost.'

'Feel as if I've been trying to.'

Her mam bent and kissed her forehead, then, putting the towel on the rail near the fire to warm it for Flora, she left, saying, 'You have to go on without him.'

Should she marry, Flora wondered, washing the soap from her arms. It would help. There would be money and protection. There might one day be children, more family and other people to love. Women were expected to marry, even the plain and the ugly and the coarse, even Suffragettes. Women married men. And she had always wanted to get married, expected it would happen. Another life was unimaginable. But then another husband — one who wasn't Albert — had been equally unimaginable. Though she had learned that just because something was unimaginable didn't mean it wouldn't happen. She began washing her stomach and her thighs, dunking the flannel in the water. She believed Wilfred and what he had told her. He was honest. She believed he had been forced into marriage. But the thought of him with another woman, even if he didn't want or love that woman, still hurt.

She bent over, filled the green wash jug with water and poured it over her hair, the water streaming down the thick, long strands and on to her legs. How could she love a man who was married?

Flora poured a pearly disk of shampoo into the palm of her hand and rubbed it between her fingers then through her hair. She wiped her eyes with the flannel and looked at the broken tile on the kitchen table, broken like her family, with a crack where the light came in. She washed her hair and some water droplets splashed on to the fire and hissed. The coals flashed and gave more light. She filled the wash jug with water and poured it over her head so that long rivulets of soapy water fell from the waves of brown hair dangling down in front of her.

So much had happened so quickly. There had been those quiet, empty years after Albert passed on when the world felt pointless and aimless. And then one day that spring there had been Wilfred, and it was as if in the silence of her life there had been a sound filling the quiet space around her, like a stringed instrument, like a violin being tuned before it was played.

Maybe she could have married Wilfred, but Wilfred was already married. And she would never have an affair: she was too dignified for that. She slipped down in the bath, lay back and dunked her head down until her face was completely under the water.

★   ★   ★

Wilfred, slightly woozy from the beer, brushed the dust from his bedside table. He hadn't dusted his bedroom since, well, last year and now big dust balls were falling lightly to the floor. He knew he was supposed to dust every room in the house and polish the very few ornaments they had at least once a week, that's what his Auntie Blodwen said — with emphasis — each time she visited. Last time she'd come, she'd pointedly wiped the kitchen chair with her handkerchief to get rid of a lump of dried mashed potato before sitting down.

Wilfred took his red dictionary from the table. He'd read nearly all of the *A* section — adamantine, Andaman Islands, alloy, audacious, augment, auspicious, avaricious — until his brain was brimming with words beginning with *A*. He'd learned what an avocado was; he'd like to eat one of those.

Wilfred flopped down on his single bed, stared up at the ceiling and watched the cobwebs in the corner flutter up and down in the summer breeze. He shoved his hands in his trouser pockets, crossed his ankles and laid the dictionary on his stomach. He could keep on reading in an abecedarian manner until he had read the whole of the dictionary: Mr Hughes at 22 Plain Dealings Road had read every word of the dictionary and it had taken him five years. But everyone had the utmost respect for Mr Hughes. Sometimes these days Wilfred marvelled at some of the words he heard himself use, and he wondered if anyone ever noticed that every time he said a big word of vocabulary it began with *A*? Nor had anyone said to him yet, as he half-expected them to, 'Good God, Wilfred, man. What happened to you, then, swallowed the dictionary?' but if they did he could reply, 'Well, I've swallowed the *A*'s. That much is true.'

Some of the *A* words were very unusual: axilary, that was a big word for armpit, and he liked aurora which was a sheen of light in the sky. And azure; that meant blue.

If he used these words he would be able to say some clever things — all, of course, beginning with the letter *A* — and yet . . . He sat up, took the dictionary and flicked through its marble-edged pages. It was heavy because it had a lot of words in it, many words that a man around town — a purveyor of superior funerals — might need. He opened it randomly at *F*.

Fiddle: *a stringed instrument played with a bow, esp. a violin.*

Fidelity: *faithful devotion, esp. in marriage.*

What was the final word, he wondered, turning to the last page.

Zeno: *a philosopher who had an unanswerable paradox.*

What use was that, Wilfred thought, if he were to read the whole of the dictionary and the very last entry was about some poor chap who had a problem that he didn't know the answer to? He had bought this dictionary from Laugharne Books because he wanted answers! But he was no longer that innocent young man he had been at the beginning of the spring when he'd gone to Laugharne Books. There had been so many things this spring and summer that he'd wanted to say, and which his dictionary hadn't been able to tell him. Wilfred had thought wrongly, very wrongly, that everything he needed to know would be inside that three-shilling, cloth-bound, bloody red dictionary from Laugharne Books. Bloody Laugharne Books! Bloody antiquarian bookshops! That's what happened if you went to Carmarthenshire to do your shopping!

He closed the book for the last time, smoothing the red covers, touching its bare blunted corners, and lost himself in his thoughts. Words went on for ever. And it was strange how the most important moments in life required one to speak, to say what one felt. What I need, he thought, is another kind of dictionary, one that tells me what to say when I don't know what to say. Wilfred wondered what words such a dictionary would have. Phrases such as 'I'm sorry,' 'Forgive me,' — even that most difficult of phrases, 'I was wrong.' It wouldn't be a very big dictionary, maybe even only one page with a list entitled, *Difficult Things to Say*. The words he really needed were the ones his heart spoke. 'I don't love you.' 'I made a mistake.' 'Please tell me the truth.' 'I love you.' 'I want you.' The words he had needed were so simple, any child could speak them. They were simple words to write and spell. Big words, clever words — all those words beginning with *A* — were rather grand, too grand really and unnecessary. When would he ever need the word *avocado* in Narberth?

Wilfred ran his hand through his hair. It was sufficient, more than enough, to speak plainly, to say what was in his heart. And that wasn't about long words with lots of syllables. It was about simple words. And courage. It wasn't the words he knew, it was the words he spoke that mattered. And it was about being honest.

★   ★   ★

Awake in the depth of the night, Flora decided go outside, take some air. She pulled on her cotton dressing-gown, found her shoes and went and sat on the dewy lawn. There was clover and camomile among the roughly scythed grass, the moon was getting fuller and there were many stars. She felt doubt creeping over her, like a thick, damp blanket. With Albert there had been certainty. And also with Wilfred — until now. She was used to knowing herself with clarity: this is where she was from, this is whom she loved, and this is what she wanted. She didn't like doubt, didn't like the effort it took.

She carefully picked a daisy, which was closed

against the night, its petals folded tightly and protectively around its yellow centre. She ripped away one pink-tinged petal. *He loves me*, then another, *he loves me not*, then another, *I love him, I love him not*. She would let the daisy decide, trust the wisdom of the flower and the force of nature which pushed it out of the earth. Sometimes there was a way forward and sometimes there wasn't. She didn't know the way now. She would let nature tell her.

'Flora?' her mother called, lifting up a sash window and looking out. 'What are you doing?'

'Just thinking about things.'

'Come inside, cariad, it's damp out there.'

'I will now in a minute.' Flora heard the swish of the window closing.

Would she love Wilfred? Would he love her? And love Grace? How? Why? One couldn't force love. Love was like the plants that came out of the earth, like the flowers and the trees. It could be for a season, like the daisy, or it could last longer than a lifetime, like the trees, like the regal beech with the rope swing on which she, her mam and no doubt her grandmother, had played, lying on their tummies on the driftwood seat and kicking themselves backwards and forwards. The tree must have watched generations of her family live and grow and die.

Flora put her hand on the grass. Love came out of the earth like a will-o'-the-wisp that danced away in the breeze, or, if it stayed, it grew roots and reached up to the sky and spread its leaves. One could attempt to garden, sow seed, bed cuttings and bend over the earth and call the plants to grow, but nature itself was the gardener.

Flora would not push or force Wilfred, nor tempt him; Wilfred must come of his own accord and she would or would not accept him, although she could not imagine how his situation could change so that she could accept him. She would do nothing but wait and see what, if anything, could grow in such compromised ground.

★   ★   ★

Wilfred was standing in front of the counter, deliberating in his head over the right words: *the arrangement of an audience . . . It would be an auspicious occasion if one . . .* and beginning to feel muddled. He could use a verse from a poem, but it was best to be careful with poetry. Flora might mistakenly think he had written the poem himself, or maybe she wouldn't understand the lines because poetry was often so unclear. Goodness knows what poetry meant, half the time. That poem about every hair of the head being numbered sounded as if every single hair had a number on it, which didn't make sense at all. The plain words of his own choosing would surely be better. He straightened his tie. Plain words, he told himself, then dictated aloud.

'*Saturday. Wilfred.*'

'*Saturday, stop, Wilfred, stop,*' Willie the postmaster repeated.

But Flora might not want to see him again. It was so difficult to form the question because he feared her answer. And if she said no? He blew his nose into his handkerchief with a great trumpet. Then Wilfred straightened his cuffs.

Perhaps *Saturday, Wilfred* was a bit too plain, he thought, watching Willie type. It was very curt. And unromantic. Maybe this straight talking could go too far, he realized with a flush. Then again, it wasn't so much what he said as whether Flora would understand, and he thought she would. Flora would know that he meant the cottage — their cottage — and that he wanted to meet her there. If he'd been really plain speaking, said exactly what he'd meant, he would have told the postmaster to type:

Dearest comma Flora stop please meet me in our cottage comma the one I think of as ours comma in the cove comma this Saturday at one o'clock because I want to be with you stop, love comma, Wilfred, stop. Mind, that would have cost a bob or two. And he would have been most embarrassed saying all that to the postmaster — it was enough to make a chap blush.

'That'll be the standard price,' Willie stated, adding, 'do you's want the addressee to receive it on a greetings telegram? A new style's just come in; it's got some fancy drawings of leaves on it and a gold border. Very nice it is and all.'

'No, no,' responded Wilfred. 'A plain GPO telegram is sufficient.'

Willie began looking in a drawer under the counter.

'Yes. A plain telegram will do the job just as well — more ways of killing a cat than stuffing the bugger with cream,' said Willie. 'Nice and

277

cosy in here, isn't it? That's the new central heating system for you. Worth the sixty pounds.'

'Yes, central heating,' Wilfred replied absent-mindedly.

'Busy day tomorrow,' Willie added with a proud sigh. 'I'm giving telephone instructions lessons in Narberth Intermediate School.'

'Oh,' said Wilfred, still preoccupied. The important thing was that Flora understood the message. 'A plain telegram will do nicely,' he repeated.

He hadn't known what certainty was until he met Flora. He remembered back to when he was last with her. He had told her everything. It had been as if a dam within him had broken and a deluge released. Would Flora love him after all that truth: brutal, hopeless truth? Would she? Would she still love him? For Flora, hearing what he said must have been like walking barefoot on broken glass, each harsh fact like a new fragment of glass for her bare-soled foot to stand on. Each revelation would be cutting into her, hurting her, making her bleed somewhere inside, somewhere tender. And she had lost her camera in the sea. And she wouldn't kiss him when they said goodbye. So Wilfred sent the telegram, clear that he had used the right words, but knowing that Flora probably wouldn't come.

★   ★   ★

On Saturday Wilfred entered the cottage at the cove with great trepidation. Flora wasn't there. So he began waiting, dearly hoping she would

278

come. His heart was racing, though each moment seemed an eternity. He knew he would wait all afternoon, all night, that within himself he would wait days, weeks, years, a lifetime — as long as it took for this woman to come to him.

He had been waiting almost three hours, and was upstairs sitting on the floorboards, peering out through the moth-strewn window at the sea and the soaring gulls when he heard the door jolt open. He jumped up and walked straight across the landing to the top of the stairs, almost not daring to look. There was Flora in a cream linen dress, looking up at him, holding a wicker basket in her hand. Wilfred closed his eyes and felt himself reel with relief. She had come.

He didn't know what to say. He had thought about what he would say to her — if she came — thought about it in the barber's, in Mrs Evans's public house at the Conduit and all of the preceding days, yet no words — not the right words — had come to him.

'Come,' she said, turning and walking out of the door. Wilfred bounded down the stairs, took his hat from the three-legged chair and followed Flora, who was now heading down towards the sea. When they reached the cliff path Wilfred could see that the cove was empty. It was nearly always empty and he didn't understand why, not really. No one, it seemed, apart from him and Flora — at first separately and now together — came here. The sea and the sky were still and beautiful, and there was the immense curve of Welsh wilderness and beauty. Wilfred was grateful that the day-trippers visited

Saundersfoot instead to eat Sidoli ice cream or to Tenby to eat a Knickerbocker Glory at Fecci's, and marvel at the orange lifeboat on top of its timber ramp. The world left the cove for Wilfred and Flora.

He felt excitement race through him. Wilfred knew that when he was an old man, like his da, and he looked back, it would be these months, these weeks, these days, these moments that he would remember most. This was the time of his life, the most exciting and charged his life would ever be. He couldn't imagine there would be anything in the whole of his life to match these moments and these feelings, he was certain of it.

He continued to follow Flora down the hill. It was her beauty, her shoulders, her straight back, the slight swing of her hips, but most of all it was her dignity that drew him in. This woman, who had both humility and dignity. He knew, too, it was her full breasts and long waist as well, and the outline of her thigh against the linen of the dress she wore. That was what made him desire her strongly; it distracted him and made him ache, almost powerfully sometimes, with his need to be with her. Her beauty attracted him, but it was her humility and dignity that made him love her.

When they reached the top of the boulders, she stopped.

'Here,' she said, and gestured. The blackberry bushes were laden, the fruit untouched. Many of the berries were no longer red, hard and sharp, but large, lush and almost perse. Flora was already reaching forward, picking them and placing them in her basket. The blackberries did not resist but came willingly from their branches. Wilfred looked around him. He didn't know where to start, there were hundreds, thousands, of blackberries — a glut. He began picking one at a time and placing them in the palm of his hand, and when his hands were full he went to Flora and placed them in her basket.

They worked calmly, side by side. Flora would be making jam, he thought, for the winter. And blackberry and apple crumble. This woman, the woman by him, was intelligent; she had known, Wilfred realized, that there was so much feeling between them that a simple, natural task would help them navigate themselves through the sea of emotion. She was making them both calm, despite the near drowning and Wilfred's marriage.

As Wilfred picked the fruit, he moved nearer to Flora until he was standing next to her. She was taking the waist-high ones while he pulled the berries that were growing higher up on the bramble, the ones beyond Flora's reach.

It was very warm now; the sun was beaming in a cloudless sky. They had been eating berries as they went along, the most succulent ones they had found at the perfect moment, as ripe and as perfect as they would ever be, only a night away from spoiling. Their fingers were stained magenta and Flora's lips, Wilfred saw, were also stained. It looked like she was wearing lipstick.

We are working together, Wilfred thought. We are side by side. He felt himself very alive — the preciousness of it enervated him. Flora's basket was filling up. Wilfred wondered at the abundance of fruit, the sheer endlessness of berries, more than they could ever pick; even if they picked all day from the green bushes they could never take all the fruit that nature offered them.

The silence between them deepened and became more charged. I will speak now, Wilfred thought. I will speak now.

'It was annulled.'

Flora stopped mid-gesture; she was poised to pick a berry.

'The marriage,' he added.

Flora stopped, her hands by her side, her basket hanging loosely by her leg. She looked straight ahead of her at the thorns, the leaves and berries. She felt the enormity of what Wilfred had said and the opportunity now open to them. She felt as wide and free as the cove around them. Annulled!

After a moment she asked, still looking straight ahead, 'Unconsummated?'

'Yes,' Wilfred said.

They could have turned to each other, chattered excitedly, asked questions, jumped up and down, grasped each other and hugged. Instead, Flora sat down on the grass, collapsed almost, her legs to her side, her hand going to the earth for support. Her basket knocked against the path and rocked. Wilfred understood: a world had fallen around her — the life where she loved Wilfred but he was married, that painful, over-illuminated sphere with its relentless truth of unfulfilled love from which she

— and he — had thought there would be no escape ever, had cracked apart, its order broken and a world had passed away. Many things were different now.

Wilfred sat down beside her; he waited until she seemed more composed, then took her hand.

This time it was Wilfred who led the way back to the cottage. The shade of the leaves protected them somewhat from the sun. Inside, he took one of the plates and put some of the fruit on it, opened the water bottle and gave the plate and the bottle to Flora. Wilfred felt calm and certain. They sat down together and ate the berries they had picked. He reached out and touched her forearm, and said, 'You lost your camera in the sea.'

She nodded.

'I'm sorry. I would like to replace it for you.'

'Yes, thank you,' and her eyes lit up. He took her hand.

'There is something I would like to ask you,' he said.

Acknowledgements

Thank you to Sandra Newman, Helen Fox, Blake Morrison, Stuart Proffitt, Panos Karnezis, Peter Ayton, Kate Mays, Nicky Forsyth, Johnnie Moore, Philippa Perry, Julie and Colin, Austin Price, Christina Hopkinson, Rachel Watson and Neil Shashoua.

My warmest thanks to Peter Straus, Jenny Hewson, James Gurbutt and Sam Evans for their professionalism, advice and sense of fun. I owe particular thanks to Gwyn Thrussell and friends for their suggestions and guidance. I would also like to thank Isabel Clementine Evans.

We do hope that you have enjoyed reading this large print book.

Did you know that all of our titles are available for purchase?

We publish a wide range of high quality large print books including:
Romances, Mysteries, Classics
General Fiction
Non Fiction and Westerns

Special interest titles available in large print are:
The Little Oxford Dictionary
Music Book
Song Book
Hymn Book
Service Book

Also available from us courtesy of Oxford University Press:
Young Readers' Dictionary
(large print edition)
Young Readers' Thesaurus
(large print edition)

For further information or a free brochure, please contact us at:
Ulverscroft Large Print Books Ltd.,
The Green, Bradgate Road, Anstey,
Leicester, LE7 7FU, England.
Tel: (00 44) 0116 236 4325
Fax: (00 44) 0116 234 0205

A LAND MORE KIND THAN HOME

Wiley Cash

One Sunday, nine-year-old Jess Hall watches in horror as his autistic brother is smothered during a healing service in the mountains of North Carolina. The unimaginable violence that follows must be untangled by a local sheriff with his own tragic past.